KILLER OF MINE

OF MINE SERIES
BOOK 1

ALEXIS GRACE

Copyright © 2024 Alexis Grace

All rights reserved.

No part of this book may be reproduced in any form or by any electronic or mechanical means, including information storage and retrieval systems, without written permission from the author, except for use of brief quotations in a book review.

This is a work of fiction. Any names, characters, places, brands, media, and incidents are either the products of the author's imagination or are used fictitiously. Any resemblance to actual people, places, or events is purely coincidental.

Cover Design by Ali at Dirty Girl Designs

For my parents.
For loving me forever and supporting me always.
Even though I won't let you read this book.

TRIGGER WARNINGS

Although this is not quite a dark romance it's also not the lightest. Triggers include torture, child abuse (reference and flashbacks), kidnapping, drugging (not by the love interests), murder, mutilated dead bodies, explicit sex scenes with BDSM elements (including spanking, anal, group sex and bondage). Please only read if you feel comfortable doing so.

1

FREYA

There's a mutilated body on the screen. You'd think given my history it would be easier for me to get used to, but if anything, it hits me worse than my fellow officers. Dizziness swims in my head. I forget sometimes that it's important to breathe.

The scent of too many different colognes overwhelms me as I scan the lecture theater, taking in the dozens of other officers here and double checking the exits. I'm sitting at the back, so no-one is behind me and the set of double doors at the top of the seating are just to my left. I could get out of here in under five seconds if I needed to. The thought calms me a little.

I close my eyes and focus on the sounds of pens scratching and the rich, commanding voice of the Special Agent giving the presentation. We're in Quantico at the FBI Academy, but his presence fills the room like he's on a Broadway stage.

"Madison Briggs is assumed to be Arthur Maxwell's seventh victim."

'I'm Maddie. What's your name, sweetheart?'

Her voice was trembling when she asked me that, her lip swollen and cut.

I grind the tip of my pen into my notebook and open my eyes, forcing myself to focus on the lecture and not get sucked in by the memories. The body still dominates the screen, empty eyes staring out at me. A wave of nausea swirls in my stomach. I force a shallow breath through my nose and shift my attention to the man on stage.

He's tall, Asian, and too damn beautiful to be hunting killers. He strides across the stage. Everything about him is controlled, even the way his hair is neatly coiffed, black silk against khaki-toned skin.

He introduced himself as Agent Park, but everyone here already knew who he was. The All-Star of the Serial Crimes Unit or SCU is somewhat of a legend to rookie detectives. He leads a team of three other guys which, frankly, I think is sexist, but there's no denying they are good at their jobs. Right now, he's teaching us about one of the few known serial killers they're yet to catch.

The Cross-Cut Killer, so named because of the crosses cut into his victims' chests.

Agent Park points his laser at the series of small, delicate crosses, like kisses in blood. There are fourteen of them on Maddie. The crosses are about the size of a child's fist and fall in two neat, vertical lines, seven on each side of her chest.

"One of the most unusual things about Maxwell's MO is that the number of crosses on his victims vary. His earlier victims didn't have any at all. Madison Briggs is the first." He guides the red dot along the darker, crimson lines. "If you look closely, you'll see the cuts are shallow and slightly jagged at the edges which suggests Maxwell was somewhat hesitant."

"Or that someone else made the cuts." The words are out of my mouth before I can think better of it and Agent Park's stony eyes scan the audience.

I gulp when they land on me. *Nice job, Sherlock.* Drawing attention to myself is the last thing I should be doing.

"What's your name?" he asks.

Unfortunately, I'm unable to travel back in time and tell myself to shut up, so I give him what he wants. "Detective Danvers, Sir."

His gaze stays locked on my face, and I find myself adding, "Freya." The word falls softly from my lips. I try so hard to keep my personal life separate from my professional one but something about Agent Park demands I give him all of me. Maybe that's what makes him such a good hunter.

"What makes you say that, Detective?"

My heart kicks at my ribs. I can't exactly say because I know who made those cuts. My fist tightens around my pen as I search for an explanation.

Always make people feel like they're the ones in control. It will make it all the more tempting when they realize, they're not.

"It's just, you told us earlier that it was only a person's first few kills that were hesitant. The Cross-Cut killer had been slicing throats for years before the crosses started. It doesn't make sense for him to be hesitant with a knife. Does it?"

Agent Park inclines his head. "You're not incorrect but we've profiled Maxwell as needing a high level of control. He wouldn't be capable of working with anyone."

I swallow. *Just nod your head and let him carry on, Freya.*

I've already drawn too much attention to myself. I know I should shut up, but Maddie's lifeless face still stares out at me. She deserved so much better than that. She deserves for her killer to be caught.

I shift my attention back to Agent Park. "Not even someone he saw as an apprentice?"

His jaw twitches. "An astute observation but in this case, it's unlikely." He tilts his head. "Though there have been cases of serial killers taking on protégés, inevitably the protégé will need to break free from their teacher's control. The crosses were a consistent feature of Maxwell's kills for eleven years. It would be nigh on impossible to keep another killer under your control for that length of time."

He's right. I may not be an expert, but I've done my fair share of research into serial killers. A partnership like the one I suggested could never last so long.

Not unless the protégé was a child.

2

RIVER

Freya Danvers doesn't speak another word for the rest of my lecture. I'm not used to someone so brazenly interrupting me. I continue through the slides on autopilot, but my gaze keeps coming back to her. The way her ginger hair tumbles in front of her face as she makes her notes. The way she flinches ever so slightly when the slide shows yet another victim. The way she refuses to make eye contact with me. I wait till the rest of the attendees are gathering their belongings, then call out to her. "Detective Danvers. A moment, if you will."

She looks up from her bag and meets my gaze.

I raise my eyebrows a touch and wait at the bottom of the lecture theater as Freya makes her way down the stairs. The woman who only moments ago was speaking up in the middle of my lecture seems timid now, her feet unsure as she fidgets in front of me.

"You've studied the Maxwell case before," I state.

She shrugs, her hand gripping the strap of the bag hooked over her shoulder. "A little. We did it my second year at the Academy."

I want to question her. To keep her here until I figure out what it is about Freya that has my profiler sense on high alert. Before I can think of an excuse to delay her exit though, a young woman calls her name from the doors.

"Sorry," Freya says, "I have to go. My shift starts soon. Thank you for the lecture, Agent Park." She spins on her heel and is up and out of the auditorium faster than a suspect fleeing the scene. I know how to read people. The last thing Freya wanted to do was talk to me. The question is why? I don't like not having answers and her comments from earlier bite at my heels as I leave the stage.

"Find out everything you can about Freya Danvers," I snap the order at Oz.

He stands up from where he was leaning against the wall and blinks at me as I walk past, but I'm already on my phone. "Dr Knightly. I have a theory and I need you to tell me whether or not it's likely."

"Hello to you too, River." Sarcasm colors Dr K's smooth voice. "I can fit you in tomorrow afternoon."

"Today."

The line goes silent. My Oxfords clack against the Academy's hard wood floor. Oz is already tapping at his phone as he follows. The Quantico representative who organized for me to give my talk today is chatting with a colleague and I don't have time for pleasantries. I bypass her and the security in the front of the building. I walk through the sliding doors and head towards the black SUV out front.

Dr Knightly's voice sharpens. "Agent Park-"

"It's the Cross-Cut Killer," I say.

A rush of air carries down the line. The grey sky

darkens through the tinted windows as I get in the SUV and a few spots of rain hit the windscreen.

"You're already on your way, aren't you?"

My answer is to put the phone on speaker and turn on the engine.

Dr Knightly sighs. "Fine. But you can talk to me while I dissect."

That's fine by me. After five years chasing the worst killers in the States my ability to detach myself from a situation has developed to an unhealthy degree. It allows me to get the job done though, and that's all that matters.

I'm checking my mirrors when the passenger door opens and Oz slides in.

"Don't wait for me or anything," he grumbles, shrugging out of his suit jacket without taking his eyes off his phone.

I indicate and pull out into the road. "What have you got on Danvers?" The name feels wrong on my lips. I don't want to call her Danvers, it seems too impersonal, too generic when this woman is anything but. Calling her Freya would be unprofessional though. In this line of work, you form walls, certain lines you don't cross in order to stay sane. I keep things professional. Always.

Oz taps at his phone. "Not much."

I do a double take, glancing across at him as I speed down the road. His brow is knitted, his ginger hair mussed up by the drizzle outside. Oz is the best hacker this side of the Atlantic, give him internet access and he'll know your entire life story in minutes. "'Not much' as in nothing of interest?" I ask, hoping he's merely being selective with what he shares. He does that at times, for a hacker Oz has a bizarrely healthy respect for privacy.

"'Not much' as in she's practically non-existent."

My grip around the steering wheel tightens but I'm not altogether unsurprised. I follow my instincts for a reason and Freya Danvers, with her fiery gold curls and cream white freckled skin, sparked every last one of them.

Oz scowls at his phone before slipping it into his pocket. "I need my laptop. All I've got so far is that she graduated from the Police Academy third top of her class and was promoted to detective a year ago, aged twenty-two.

"Young."

Oz shrugs. "You were twenty-two when you made detective."

"I am the anomaly."

Oz's lip quirks as he eyes the death grip I have on the wheel. "Apparently, so is she."

I force myself to loosen my fingers. Profiling isn't a skill any of us can switch off and I don't need Oz analyzing my response to Freya. For some reason this woman provokes more emotions in me than I've felt in years and emotions do nothing but cloud judgement. I need to shut it down. "I'll drop you off at The Lair before going to the morgue."

The Lair is what we call the SCU offices. The nickname was our teammate Jude's invention because, in his words, our crime case boards filled with images of dead bodies are better suited to villains than the good guys. It's foolish and unprofessional but if I don't indulge Jude from time to time, he would do more sulking than work.

"You going to talk to Dr Knightly?" Oz watches me carefully. "Do you think Danvers might be right?"

My jaw ticks and I turn on the windscreen wipers,

pushing away the increasing rain. "If she is, whoever did Madison Briggs' autopsy is getting fired."

3

FREYA

I need a new obsession. I don't have much of a reference but I'm pretty sure most twenty-three-year old's don't spend their time researching serial killers.

Footsteps approach my desk and I flip shut the file I've been analyzing. It's not my official case. If I got caught working on it my captain wouldn't be happy and she is one scary woman.

It's just my partner, Luke, though and I lean back into my chair, doing a quick scan of the precinct. I don't like how wrapped up I get in my work; anyone could have snuck up on me. A few of my fellow detectives sit at their desks, clicking away at their computers. Others lounge on the sofas in the break area, the hiss of the coffee machine filtering through the open door. Once I'm sure everyone is going about their business as normal, I turn my attention to Luke. He's got soft blue eyes and mussed up, surfer boy hair. He may have left California years ago, but California hasn't left him.

The corner of his lip ticks up as he hands me a coffee and leans against my desk. "So did you fangirl?"

I glower at him over the lid of the coffee cup, but the look is ruined by my chagrined smile. "I was 100% professional." I had to be. Even if I am in awe of Agent Park and his team, I can't afford to fall under the scrutiny of the SCU.

"It was good though?"

I take a sip of the coffee, savoring the caramel kick. "Yeah."

Luke taps his fingers against the brown paper folder I spend far too much time reading. "I hate to break up your serial killer hunting, but the far from glamorous world of domestics is calling us."

I'd been partners with Luke for less than two months when he caught on to my extra-curricular activities. I passed it off as a true-crime obsession and having ambitions to be a profiler, but the slip up served as a reminder not to get too close to anyone. I like Luke and part of me wants to tell him the truth, but I broke laws to get where I am, and I can't give up my position as detective. It's the best chance I have to catch The Cross-Cut Killer.

Right now, though, my side gig will have to wait. I grab the file and lock it away in my drawer.

Luke chucks me the car keys and I snatch them out of the air as I walk past him. Normally, we take it in turns to drive but I have the wheel for the whole week because Luke lost a bet. He always thinks he's going to be better at picking up men than he is. I smirk to myself, remembering the forlorn look on his face when the mountain man left with the chef. If the sun-kissed, blond Adonis was looking for more than just a one-night stand, I might feel bad for him, but Luke isn't one for settling down.

I, on the other hand, dream of it. The idea of having someone to lean on, someone always in my corner, someone to look after me, seems so perfect it's unreachable. It's a fairy tale so far away from anything I've ever had in life, and I can't see it happening anytime soon. Relationships are built on honesty. How can I fall in love with someone when I can't even tell them my real name?

Luke fills me in on the details of the case as I drive. "Neighbors heard shouting, a ruckus next door and called it in. Apparently, the beat cops radioed for back up when they arrived to find a woman in hysterics over her missing sister."

I bite the inside of my cheek and force my expression to stay neutral. I hate cases with siblings.

The directions take us to a row of cookie cutter houses with vibrant green grass and freshly painted doors. It's not the usual type of place for domestics, not because they don't happen in neighborhoods like this but because when they do, they tend to stay under the radar. The whole case isn't your usual domestic though, or Luke and I wouldn't be here.

I put the car in park, and we head up the drive to a sweet, pink hued house. Sobs reach me before we're even through the front door.

I glance at Luke, panic fluttering in my chest. He rolls his eyes but takes the lead and goes ahead to calm the woman down. We both know he's better at the emotional stuff than me. I hang back, checking in with the Uniforms that got here first. It's not that I don't empathize, it's that I feel everything too much. I can't handle the intensity without internalizing the emotion myself. So, I shut it out. Maybe a little too much given the number of times I've been called an emotionless bitch.

I walk around the living room, letting Luke calm our witness as I take in the wooden blinds that are drawn shut even though it's day. The cream walls are decorated with photos. Groups of friends. Smiling faces in graduation shots or dressed up for a hen night. Not for the first time, I find myself longing for the experiences I missed out on. I never graduated from high school. Never got the chance to go to college. I don't think I've even ever spent the night just hanging out with friends.

The sobs behind me quieten as Luke works his magic. I turn my back on the photos and face the woman. She's got blonde, wavy hair that flows past the shoulders of her cardigan and blends in with the golden-haired dog in her arms. Her face is blotchy and damp and her eyes look like someone's taken sandpaper to them, but she manages to calm herself enough for us to question her. She tells us her name is Elsie. Her words are still shaky, but she answers as best she can.

"I was supposed to meet her here for lunch. I know it's not been twenty-four hours, but she didn't call yesterday, and Rocco's bowl was completely empty when I arrived." The woman runs her hand through the little terrier's fur. He's trembling, which is a dead giveaway that something isn't right.

"Is it unusual for her to not call?"

"We're twins. Identical. We haven't gone a single day of our lives without talking to each other. Until now." Even though Luke was the one to ask the question, Elsie looks at me as she answers. Like she feels I'll understand better than him. Maybe I do. "Please, you have to find her."

I hold her gaze, refusing to break away from the pain I see there. I may have ulterior motives for becoming a cop, but I honestly do love my job. The chance to help people like Elsie is a lifeline that keeps me grounded, that makes me feel like I can do something, *anything*, good in this world.

"We'll find her," I promise. It's a stupid thing to say and I sense Luke giving me the side eye. You should never promise a victim anything, but I'm determined to find Elsie's twin. I know I shouldn't get emotionally invested but I already know I'm not going to be able to let this case go.

Once we've looked around the house, we say goodbye to Elsie and head back to the car.

"Agent Park would disapprove," Luke says as he slides into the passenger seat. "Other than your serial killer obsession, I don't think I've ever seen you break protocol." He's teasing but his comment hits the mark. I always play by the book. A therapist would probably tell me I'm overcompensating for the things I've done, the things my father made me do. The therapist would probably be right.

But is it really much of a surprise that the daughter of a serial killer would spend her whole life trying to be good?

4
ELI

I beat River to the morgue. I'm not usually so punctual. My grams says I work on ranch time. Even though we moved to the suburbs after my dad lost himself to the alcohol, I've still got cowboy blood. It drives River up the fucking wall. I smirk, loving nothing more than winding him up.

He called five minutes ago telling me to get my ass down here, but I was only round the corner, so I flirt a little with Dr Knightly while we wait. It's somewhat of a challenge flirting with someone when they're wrist deep in a corpse's torso but she humors me, a rosy tint blooming beneath her ebony skin.

"You're incorrigible, Eli. You know where I stand on this."

I lean against the counter opposite the wall of cold drawers filled with bodies. It probably says something about me that the morgue is one of my happy places, but Dr K's made it her own with biology posters above the sinks and a model skeleton who's always frozen mid-wave. I spin my Stetson round the tip of my finger. "I know, I know. 'More than one night will blur the lines,' so you say."

Dr Eva Knightly is strict about keeping things professional. It seems to be a running theme in my line of work, which is hard for the wilder side of me to get on board with.

Eva eases the dead guy's liver into a silver dish. "Go find your adrenaline kick elsewhere, Cowboy."

I stretch my neck till it cracks, relieving the never-ending tension that's buried itself there ever since I got high at seventeen and crashed my bike. River saved my life that night and I've not touched drugs since but Eva's right, I do still search for adrenaline highs.

I put my hat on and place a hand on her shoulder, stopping her from diving back into the body. "You know you were more than that to me, right?"

Her brown eyes soften and that's one of the reasons I actually want her to agree to go out with me. She sees more than just the broody cowboy chasing highs. "I do," she says, "but I'm not changing my mind."

I shrug it off, paste a smile on and tuck my thumbs through my belt hoops. "Fair enough, Doc. But if you ever want anyone to do that thing with their fingers, you know where to find me."

She blushes again and shoots me a scolding gaze. I grin, the thrill of it filling the hollowness in my chest.

The air shifts and River enters. He's got his doom and gloom look on but it's the way Dr K tenses that has me standing up straight. "What's going on?"

River doesn't answer. He just spreads a folder out on the clean autopsy table and points to a picture.

I move to take a look, but River shakes his head and that's all it takes for me to connect the dots. River was giving a lecture on Arthur Maxwell this morning. The pity in his eyes tells me the photo in that folder is not one I want to see. My hands clench into fists and I hang back as Dr K goes over to inspect the photo.

"I need you to tell me whether these cuts could have been made by someone other than Arthur Maxwell."

It's rare for Dr K to show a reaction but her eyebrows inch upwards. "You don't think Maxwell killed her?"

River shakes his head, a few strands of his neatly styled hair coming loose. He doesn't fix them which is how I know he's shaken. "Maxwell killed her, I have no doubt about that, what I want to know is if someone else could have made the crosses. The cuts, they're thinner, more jagged."

Dr K takes off her gloves and picks up a magnifying glass. River and I wait in silence. I don't know the full story here, but I get the feeling Dr K's answer could change everything.

After a long minute of comparing the images – a minute I spend convincing myself not to lose my fucking mind - Eva straightens up. "There does seem to be a hesitation to the crosses that isn't present in the cut to the throat. It's hard to say for sure without being able to examine the body, it could just be that he was more delicate with the crosses, taking more time, but..." she looks up at River. "Yes, it's possible. My gut tells me it's more than possible."

River runs a hand over his face. "Shit."

I notice my own hand is shaking and I tuck it in the pocket of my jeans to hide the tremors.

River picks up the folder. "I'm going to send you the files for each of his victims. I need you tell me when these cuts stopped looking like they were made by an amateur."

Dr K nods. "Sure thing." She lets out a puff of air. "The Cross-Cut Killer having a partner. That changes things."

"More like a protégé," I say. There's no way Maxwell would work with someone. He'd have to be the one in charge. Even the idea of a protégé feels far-fetched. "What made you question the cuts?"

River meets my eyes across the room. "Not what. Who."

The rush I get when something unexpected manages to break through the numbness hits me. I don't think I've ever seen that look in River's eyes before. It's similar to the one he gets when we're closing in on a killer but this time it has a heat to it. Whoever this person is, I'd bet my last paycheck they're a woman. One that seems to have done the impossible and wriggled her way under River's iron-clad armor.

A smirk tugs at my lips. "Is she a red-head?"

The stern set of River's face warns me I'll pay for that, but before he can respond both our emergency pagers go off and River's phone rings.

I silence the 911 message and listen as River takes the call. "Ma'am?"

His brows draw together at whatever our unit chief, Director Syed says. "Do we have an ID yet?" River's gaze drops to the photos on the silver autopsy table and sweat gathers on the back of my neck. This isn't just any murder. "Yes Ma'am. Eli and I will meet Jude at the scene. I'll get Oz to track down any possible connection between everybody at the Academy and Arthur Maxwell. I don't believe this was a coincidence." River presses his fist into the table. "He knew I was giving a talk on him and he's rubbing it in our faces."

I close my eyes and try to slow my racing heart. It's impossible not to get a kick of adrenaline at times like these but this isn't the sort of rush I like. Betting, flirting, they make me feel alive. Right now, I just feel nauseous.

I jolt as a soft hand lands on my shoulder and my eyes flick open.

"You'll get him Eli, just hang in there," Eva's voice is quiet, like she knows it isn't something I want the world to hear.

I force the feelings down, flash a smile and tip my hat at her. "Of course we will, Dr K, we've got the best coroner in the states on our side."

I keep the grin on my face as we leave but from the way River eyes me, I think it looks more manic than breezy.

I want to rage at the whole mother-fucking world. Instead, I put up all my walls and steel myself for seeing the Cross-Cut Killer's latest victim.

5

FREYA

I hate dead-ends. They make me feel useless. What point is all the effort I put into getting my GED, training every day and all the hours over time I worked to become detective, if I can't help? By the time we finish canvasing the neighbors and stopping by Camilla, Elsie's sister's, regular hangouts, our shift is almost over. She seems to have just disappeared without a trace.

I hold the door to the station open for Luke and we head back to our desks. The low-level buzz in the bullpen is a little louder than usual. Everyone's talking in hushed voices and a cloud of tension hangs over my shoulders. Luke must sense it too because he throws a ball of paper onto Sofia's desk. "Yo, Ruiz, what's got everyone all hyped up?"

"Get your trash off my desk, Harrison." Sofia Ruiz is about as hardcore as detectives get, but she has a soft spot for Luke and her words lose their heat when she spins in her chair, the whisper of a smirk on her tan face. She picks up the ball of paper and throws it back at him.

"Word going round is that the Cross-Cut Killer's claimed another victim."

My spine goes rigid. "Arthur Maxwell? Are they sure?"

Luke gives me the side eye and I force my shoulders to relax. *He's not here*, I say to myself. *You're okay*.

"I thought the working theory was that he retired after his daughter died?" Luke asks.

The hairs on my neck prick. The urge to flee is growing by the second.

"Well, maybe she's come back to life because it's definitely him. O'Connor found the body." Ruiz nods towards the uniformed rookie sitting outside the captain's office before spinning back to face her computer.

O'Connor's face is sickly pale.

It's all about being in control. If you're in control, you have all the power.

My hands shake. I move them behind my back and lean against the edge of my desk. "Who's on the case?"

"Gone straight to the FBI," Ruiz says without turning around. "If Maxwell thinks he can hunt in the FBI's own backyard he's got another think coming."

Right, of course. For a moment I'd hoped the case was still unassigned, but a rookie detective like me has no chance of being given such a high-profile case. If I want to know what's happening, I'll have to continue with my off the books investigating. I swallow, trying to keep my breathing steady. Looking at paper files is one thing, but this is real now. He's killing again.

Luke grabs his jacket off his chair and catches my panicked eyes. "Come on, I'll give you a lift home."

I nod and follow him out.

The drive back to my place is quiet. I'm busy processing the fact that my father has killed again, in the very state I'm living in, and Luke appears to be busy analyzing me.

When I reach for the door to get out, he finally speaks up. "Freya, you need to leave this alone. The FBI will figure it out. I know there's more to why you're obsessed with Maxwell, but if you go anywhere near this case, you won't just get off with a slap on the wrist."

I turn back and meet his eyes. "I'm not going to do anything, Luke."

Luke purses his lips. Squints at me a little. "I like you. I like having you as my partner. Don't do anything stupid."

The corner of my lip quirks upwards but I drop my eyes before answering. "I wouldn't dare."

I climb the steps to my house and unlock the door. I lift my foot, careful to step over the sensor I have in place at the bottom of the doorway because I know how easy it is to pick a lock. I flick the light switch on and debate the merits of just turning it off again, so I don't have to look at my living room.

It's not awful, it's just kind of empty. I got a sofa off Craig's List when I first moved in, and I keep meaning to finish furnishing but the closest I've got is a flat-packed bookshelf that's still in its packaging. Turns out interior decorating is not my strong suit and every time I try to do something about it, I get distracted by the murder board hidden behind the horrendous NSYNC poster on the back wall.

I try to do what Luke said. I honestly do. I make up some Pot Noodles in my tiny, linoleum coated kitchen but eating them just makes me feel sick. Images of Maxwell's victims flip through my brain like a rolodex. I dump the noodles in the sink and grip the metal edges. I shouldn't go. I really shouldn't. But nothing about my house makes me want to stay. I grab my jacket off the hook by the door and turn my back on this place that's supposed to feel like home.

I hurry down the steps and click the button on the remote to open the garage. The door whines as it lifts open. I duck under as soon as it's high enough and head over to my motorbike. He's a beauty, a Harley Davidson Sportster and yes, he's a he because personally, I like riding men.

I hook my leg over the seat and pat the midnight black surface as it purrs to life. "All right Joey, let's go do something stupid."

I overheard where the body was found before we left the station and I slow Joey down as we near Quantico Municipal Park. It's just starting to get dark, and the clouds hang above the Potomac. A warm autumnal breeze rolls over from the water, playing with my hair as I take my helmet off and stow it under the bike's seat.

A little way down the park, blue lights flash against the grass, and I head towards the cordoned off area. I show my badge to one of the officers and hold my breath, but he barely glances at it before lifting the yellow tape for me. I shake my head. It frustrates me how many police officers don't do their jobs properly and I want to pull him up on it but right now his carelessness is working in my favor.

I avoid looking at any of the people milling around and slip inside the white marquee, the type they erect around a body to protect it from the elements. I strike lucky and find it empty. The only other person inside isn't breathing. I hesitate before looking down. It's been six years since I saw one of my father's victims and I'm not sure I'm ready to see another.

I take a deep breath. The kill must be fairly recent because there's not much of a smell. I'm already a mess inside, I can feel a meltdown building but I'm holding myself together with clenched fists. When I finally look down at the body my grasp stutters and I stumble to my knees.

Her face is bruised, the gash on her neck a horrifying red. Her blonde hair is stained from the blood, but there's no mistaking who she is. The woman lying dead in front of me is the spitting image of Elsie.

"Camilla." Her name falls from my lips, and I reach a hand out, stopping short of touching the body. I know what happened to Elsie's twin now. My father killed her.

6

FREYA

I don't know whether it's because I'm distracted by the situation or whether he's just that good, but I don't notice the man approach. I jump up when he speaks, my already edgy heart racing.

"There are fourteen people here. Six Uniforms, four techs, a crime scene photographer, and three special agents, myself included. You are not on that list, so why exactly are you standing next to that body?"

"Her name's Camilla."

The newcomer tilts his head to the side, making his loose afro of curls bounce. "Right now, I'm more interested in your name."

I reach into my pocket. The change is subtle, but I see him tense. The lines of his strong jaw sharpen and his eyes narrow. The tent rustles and Special Agent Park, from the lecture, walks in.

"Just getting my ID," I say and show them my badge. "Detective Freya Danvers. We met earlier." I nod to where Camilla lies lifeless on the grass. "This woman is my missing person case."

Special Agent Park takes my ID. He inspects it for a moment before putting it in his back pocket and looking down at me. "Your missing person case is now the FBI's homicide and you're going to need to come with me, Detective Danvers."

I push my tongue into my cheek but manage to refrain from saying anything I shouldn't. At least with Camilla as the victim I have a valid reason for turning up here. I can tell from the glower on Agent Park's face that I'm in enough trouble as it is.

He steps back to let me pass and I feel entirely too much like a scolded child.

"Go talk to the Uniforms. I want to know how hell she got in here," he says to the other special agent, who I'm pretty sure is Jude Elroy. Agent Elroy is a certified genius. He has legend status for being recruited by the FBI before he even left school. I'm pretty sure he can figure it out, but I decide to save them both some time.

"The officer with the slicked back hair and gym rat muscles," I say, and Agent Park locks his gaze on me. I tilt my chin. "The one that looks like he should be starring in a porno. He glanced at my badge and let me in."

He shoots a look at Elroy who nods.

Shit. I think I just got Gym Rat fired.

Agent Park circles his hand around my upper arm and guides me away from the tent. He has no right to touch me but I'm too busy focusing on the heat spreading from his hand to call him on it. There is nothing particularly sensual about the way he's holding me, but every one of my nerves jump to life. Normally, I shy away from casual touch. I've experienced too much pain to be okay with strangers putting their hands on me unless I'm in control of the situation but something about Agent Park is different. I think this might be the worst possible moment for my libido to kick in. I should want to get away from him but instead his firm, steady grip has me feeling safe.

My heart sinks a little when he lets go.

"You called her Camilla."

I nod. The dread I get whenever I have to tell a loved one the last thing they want to hear curls like a snake in my stomach. "Camilla Banks. My partner and I were called to a disturbance this afternoon. We found her sister Elsie mid-breakdown because her twin was missing."

"And you tracked her here?"

My tongue darts out over my bottom lip.

Agent Parks' gaze drops to my mouth.

It would be stupid to lie to a profiler. "No. I heard about the murder in the station, and I had a hunch." My hunch wasn't that Camilla was the victim, but he doesn't need to know that.

Agent Park hums. "Either you have very good instincts or you're not telling me everything. Which is it?"

I don't know what prompts me to say what I do next, clearly today is the day for doing stupid things but something about Agent Park's strait-laced demeanor makes me want to play with fire. "Can't it be both?"

Dark eyes pierce into me. I hold his stare, both of us caught in a tangible net of tension. It's not till a new voice speaks that I snap out of it.

"Oh shit, she really is a red-head."

I whip around.

"Eli," Agent Park warns.

I press my lips together to try and hide my amusement. Eli looks like he just stepped off a ranch, cowboy hat and all, but instead of a plaid shirt he's got a crisp white suit shirt tucked into a pair of black skinny jeans. The whole look is like cowboy meets GQ.

"Howdy," I say, before I can stop myself.

Eli stares at me for a long moment, then the corner of his lip pulls up and he chuckles.

The sound reverberates down my spine and my core tightens. Who the hell put an aphrodisiac in the air tonight? Apparently, FBI profiler is my type.

"It would seem our murder victim is Detective Danver's missing persons case," Agent Park says.

Eli whistles and closes the distance between us. "That is one very pretty coincidence." He hooks a finger around one of my curls and I bat his arm away.

Agent Park pushes him back with a hand on the chest. "If you want to be here, on the scene, you need to pull yourself together."

Eli's eyes shutter and he tips his hat towards me before stepping back.

I turn back to Agent Park and steel my spine. "I want to be involved in the case."

He's going to say 'no', I can sense it, but before he gets a chance Eli pipes up.

"It might not be a bad idea. She was right about the cuts."

Agent Park glares at Eli but Eli just tilts his head, his eyes squinting like he's trying to figure me out. "What made you think they were done by a different person?"

It comes as no surprise I was right, but I can't exactly tell Eli how I knew what I did. I shrug.

Agent Park grunts. "Let me guess, another hunch?"

I shove my hands in the pockets of my jacket. "Something like that."

A few meters away Jude ducks out of the tent.

I stare at the white canvas, thinking of the woman inside. "Do you know when time of death was yet? Or why he targeted her?"

"I thought you were the one with all the answers?"

I look back at Agent Park, he raises a single eyebrow, and it should be condescending. It *is* condescending, but it's also kind of hot. "Is it just me or do you not like anyone who knows more than you?"

Jude covers a laugh as he joins us. "If it were the latter, he wouldn't be able to stand me."

"Who says I can?" Agent Park quips.

Jude brings a hand to his chest like he's mortally wounded.

"Aren't geniuses supposed to be modest?" I ask him.

"Aren't detectives supposed to follow the rules?"

I open my mouth but have nothing to say.

Jude grins and sticks his tongue out at me.

Agent Park sighs. "Why does he insist on behaving like an eight-year-old?"

Eli shrugs. "You coddle him."

I know how to deal with eight-year-olds though. I slip my hair tie off my wrist and ping it at Jude.

"Oh good, there's two of them," Agent Park says, his voice drier than sawdust.

The way they talk with each other is fascinating. They seem more like brothers than partners and their familiarity tugs at me. I want that. But so long as my father goes free, I'll never have it.

I won't risk getting close to people when there's a chance he'll tear them away from me.

"Technically, this was my case first," I say, trying to get back to the matter at hand. "I've already interviewed her sister, done the preliminary work."

"All of which we'll need to do again anyway," Eli says.

Jude twirls my hairband round his finger. "I say we keep her."

"Keep me? I'm not a dog."

Eli eyes me up and down. "True, you're more like a kitten. All ginger and feisty."

I gape at him. "Do either of you have a professional bone in your body?"

Eli smirks. "Sure, I've got a bone. Do you want to taste it?"

Before I can respond to that atrocity Jude whacks Eli on the shoulder and Agent Park's phone rings.

He puts it to his ear and tells the boys to behave before walking away.

I watch him go, a sinking feeling settling in my gut. I lost myself bickering with Jude. Our back and forth made me forget what happened tonight, what I was risking by coming here. I'd thought it was worth it but the way Agent Park's shoulders tense before his sharp eyes land on me, makes me think I've just made a huge mistake.

7

RIVER

Freya Danvers is a liar. I look at the woman in question. A moment ago she was holding her own with the men I call my brothers, now she's watching me like she's ready to flee. That will not be happening.

"You still there, River?" Oz speaks down the phone.

"What do you mean she's not who she says she is?" I ask through gritted teeth.

"I haven't unearthed her real identity yet, but Freya Danvers is an 86-year-old-woman who, according to her grandson, died six years ago."

I clench my phone so hard I'm surprised it doesn't crack. "You're telling me she enrolled in the Police Academy under a false identity, and nobody realized?"

Oz sighs. "This is next level shit, River. Even I almost missed it. I only dug so deep because I know better than to ignore one of your gut feelings."

I close my eyes, taking a moment to stay focused. Controlled. "I need a name, Oz."

"I know, I'll get you one, it's just going to take a bit of time."

I end the call and make my way back over to the woman whose name is not Freya.

She takes a step back as I approach, and I nod to Eli and Jude. Jude shoots me a questioning look but they both position themselves so that *Freya* has nowhere to go. Even so, her eyes dart over my shoulder like she thinks she might be able to escape me.

"Don't," I warn as I close in on her. "You won't get far."

Her chest rises under that leather jacket of hers, her breaths coming a little too heavy. "What's going on?"

I reach for my cuffs and keep my face blank. I barely know this woman, the fact she lied to me shouldn't feel as much of a betrayal as it does. "Turn around."

Her voice shakes. "Why?" She steps back into Eli, but he just spins her around, his hands on her waist. Her palms land against his chest and I reach up, circling a slender wrist and bringing it behind her back. I lock the metal bracelet around it before reaching for her other wrist and securing the cuffs. She doesn't fight me, but I can tell she wants to. Her body's rigid from holding herself back.

"I'm arresting you on suspicion of criminal impersonation and perjury." I recite her the Miranda rights, focusing on the words and not how good she looks in cuffs. A traitorous part of my brain wishes I was doing this under different circumstances. Like one where she was naked in my bedroom.

Christ. I need to get over this little obsession. My relationships in the past have had their issues, but lusting after a criminal is beneath me.

I force myself to let go of her arms and hand her over to Jude. Eli probably already has a nickname for the little she-devil, but Jude I can trust. He may be a goofball, but he doesn't play the field. Jude is a relationship kind of guy.

"Take her to The Lair," I say.

"Really?" Jude quirks a brow.

I nod. Normally, we set up base at whatever precinct has jurisdiction on the murder and take the suspects there. But Freya or whatever her name is, isn't directly connected to this case and taking her back to her own station would be a bad idea. Loyalty runs deep in the police force. I'm not going to risk any of her fellow officers helping her slip away.

Freya Danvers is mine.

8

JUDE

I love mysteries and Freya might be my new favorite one. Most things come easy to me, a side effect of having an IQ of 163, but people are complex. I guess that's why I became a profiler. My fingers tap a restless beat on my thigh as we sit in the back of the car. Freya's quiet on the way to The Lair. Eli drives, his eyes on the road while mine are busy watching Freya. She's shut down. The fiery spark and jaw-dropping confidence she had on the scene has been replaced with anxiety. She's hiding it well, but I can tell she's scared, it's simmering just below the surface of those subtle green eyes of hers. The puzzle is figuring out what she's scared of. Us? Or what we might find?

She catches me watching her and holds my gaze for a moment. I'm fascinated by her eyes. They're like a vibrant emerald coated with a thin cloud. Even her eyes are in hiding.

I don't know what Oz told River on the phone but when I left The Lair, Oz was deep down an internet rabbit hole. Whoever the woman sitting across from me is, I get the sense I'm not the only one fascinated by her.

Eli pulls into the underground carpark. It only took us fifteen minutes and forty-eight seconds to get here which means Eli broke the speed limit. He's not supposed to do that, but we have a deal where I don't tell unless it's unsafe and he helps me with my paperwork.

I hop out to open the back door. Freya tenses as I lean over to release her seatbelt. I adjust my actions, careful not to touch her more than necessary. I move slowly so she knows to expect it when I wrap my hand around her upper arm to help her from the car. Part of the mystery clicks into place.

The SUV bleeps as Eli locks it and I guide Freya after him towards the elevator.

"So, you want to fill us in?" I ask her, mostly to break the silence. My ADHD is pretty well controlled these days, but I still hate the absence of sound. People think I'm extroverted, and I sort of am but mostly I'm hyper because I need the stimulation.

Freya doesn't say anything.

"I have a feeling you're more in the know right now than I am which, if you knew me, you'd know is not a common occurrence," I press.

It's not till the elevator doors close and we're on our way up that she responds. "Don't I get a lawyer?"

I cock my head, analyzing the tone of her voice. "Do you need one?"

The cuffs clink behind Freya's back as she shifts to face me. "Even just questioning that is a form of refusing me my basic right to a defense."

Eli snorts. I shoot him a look. He's leaning against the

elevator wall, his legs crossed, and his Stetson pulled down over his face. Anyone would think he was bored but this nonchalance attitude is Eli's way of coping. I move one of the stones in my left pocket to my right, a small reminder to tell River Eli's struggling. I have a lot of information in my brain but at times it feels like a sieve. The stones were River's idea. Later, when I find one in my right pocket it will help me remember whatever it is I need to do.

The elevator pings and Eli strides past us into the office, tipping his hat to Freya as he goes. "Don't worry, Kitten, you'll get your lawyer."

I forget to warn her when I take her arm this time and she jolts. I don't comment on it, but I loosen my grip till I feel her relax. It shouldn't bother me. If River is right, which he is 87% of the time, this woman is a criminal. But I'm exhibiting clear signs of attraction and a part of me really hopes River is wrong.

I take Freya to one of the interrogation rooms and adjust her cuffs, so she's chained to the metal table in front of the chair. I want to get her to talk but it's clear from her face she's not ready to.

"I'll have someone bring you some water," I say before heading to the door.

"Jude," she calls after me.

I stop and turn back around. I should tell her it's Agent Elroy, but I've always hated the formalities of the FBI and I find I like the sound of my name on her tongue. "Yes?"

"If you're as smart as they say you are, why haven't you caught him yet? Why haven't you caught the Cross-Cut Killer?"

My jaw tenses. I wasn't expecting that, and her words

hit me right in the solar plexus. From the vulnerability on her face, I don't think she meant it as an insult, but Arthur Maxwell is a sore spot for my team and the question she just asked is the one I ask myself every single day.

I swallow past the rock in my throat and leave the room, locking the door behind me.

9

———

FREYA

My heart is beating too fast. I've been in countless rooms like this. One way mirror. Metal table. Chairs nailed to the floor. It's cold. Isolating. I worked so hard to become a detective, studying for months to catch up on schoolwork after my unconventional childhood. I'm not supposed to be the one in cuffs.

I squeeze my eyes shut and breathe in through rounded lips. I need to pull myself together and make a decision. I press my forehead to the table. The icy metal shivers through me as I work the hair grip out from where it's hidden under my curls. I sit back up and turn the thin bit of metal over in my fingers.

I could stay and hope they don't figure out who I am. Luke would find me a good lawyer and I could try and worm my way out of this mess, but the arrest was too specific. Even if they don't find my real identity, they know I'm not Freya Danvers. I lied to the police. I'll lose my job, probably face jail time.

I want to work with Jude and his team. I could help them, but I can't explain how without telling them who I am and that would involve confessing to falsifying my identity.

I close my eyes. I can talk myself round in circles, but it will only be so long before they're back and I really don't have a choice.

I sigh and get to work picking the lock on the cuffs.

I can't go to prison. I have a promise to keep.

10

OZ

I adjust my glasses and lean in towards the computer. To be honest, I feel more at home in front of a screen than I do in the real world, but I've been trailing through the internet, adjusting the algorithm, and narrowing the search parameters for hours now. I'm running off energy drinks and the high of the chase as reality fades into the background. A thump vibrates my desk, dragging me back to my office.

"Feet off." I push Eli's cowboy boots till his chair spins and his feet hit the floor. He's left a mark on the glass, but I don't have time to clean it right now. Information skims across my screens and I scan it rapidly, tapping at the keys to make sure nothing slips by.

Eli knows better than to mess with my workspace but, to be fair, I'm more irritable than usual right now. The search for Freya's true identity is frustrating me to no end. This woman doesn't exist. I'm trying to connect her to who she was before she took on a dead woman's identity, but I keep coming up with a whole load of nothing. Normally, I would relish in a challenge like this, but

River's impatience is bleeding through my office. I want to meet whoever hid Freya so well. She won't have done it herself; I don't get tech vibes off her. The person who did this is next level and I wonder what it would be like to go up against them in a hackathon. They're good, sure, but I'll find out who Freya really is, it's just a matter of time.

The door opens and Jude walks in, his face drawn in a scowl. "Do we know who she is yet?"

Eli chucks an M&M into his mouth. "I say we just call her Kitten."

River confiscates Eli's candy. "Whoever she is, she's off limits." He turns to Jude. "Did she say anything to you?"

"No. Nothing."

My computer finishes its search and I stop listening to their conversation. The results flash on the screen and I lean closer, scanning the photos the facial recognition software has pulled up until I find a decent match. It's a school photo, she's a tiny spot in a sea of faces. Someone tried to bury the picture and they'd done a seriously good job. If I hadn't been looking this hard, I never would have found it. She looks younger in the photo, maybe only sixteen and her hair is brown not ginger but her green eyes suggest the brown is a dye-job. I zoom in on the names listed along the bottom of the photo, counting as I go until I find the one that belongs to our mystery woman.

"Holy cannoli." My mouse stills, the cursor hovering in place. "And bingo was his name-o," I mutter.

It's a testament to how much we're all invested in this case that no one calls me up on the dreadful catchphrase. I choose a different one each time to drive Eli mad, but he doesn't take the bait.

"You found her?" he asks. *Oh, I've found her alright.*

River plants his hands on my desk and looks at the screen. "Who is she?"

I point at the name on the bottom of the photo. "Angelica Maxwell."

Eli jerks up out of his chair. "As in Arthur Maxwell's daughter?"

"I thought she was dead?" Jude says.

River stares at the photo of her. "She's supposed to be." He pushes away from the desk and runs a hand through his hair. "Oz, get me everything you can on the car accident she was in. I want the crash report, autopsy, the name of every single person who worked that case."

"On it." I spin back to my computer, but I hear the vulnerability in Eli's voice as he faces River.

"I don't think I can do this," he says.

My heart squeezes for Eli. I can't imagine what he's feeling right now.

River doesn't show him any pity though. He just pulls back his shoulders and heads for the door. "Yes, you can. Let's go."

11

RIVER

She's gone. I stare at the unlocked cuffs on the table. I should have put guards on her. I knew what I was going to find the second I turned into the corridor and saw the door was ajar, but a lightning strike of shock shoots through me. Despite my instincts warning me about her, I still managed to underestimate the tiny woman. It's unacceptable.

Angelica Maxwell. I don't like the name; Freya suits her better.

I shake my head. I barely know the little con-artist and already I'm attached. I should be trying to keep a professional distance, but I know, the second she's back in my custody, I won't be letting her out of my sight.

I stride back to Oz's den, Eli and Jude on my heels.

"Back so soon?" Oz asks.

Jude runs a hand through his curls. "I screwed up."

Oz frowns and pushes back from his desk.

"Pull up the security cameras for the interrogation rooms and the building perimeter," I order.

Realization dawns and Oz does as I asked.

Eli is a dark shadow behind me as we watch Freya – *Angelica* – pick the lock like she's done it a thousand times before. She glances up at the camera, something like regret flashing across her face before she slips from the room.

"Like father, like daughter," Eli mutters.

A feeling deep inside me rebels against his statement. "She hasn't killed anyone yet."

He shakes his head, his lip curling up. "That we know of."

I put the building on lockdown the second I realized she was gone, but we were too late. Oz tracks her out of the building and manages to hack into the neighboring security cameras, but we lose her at the end of the street.

I straighten up. "I want officers at her house and her precinct." I doubt she'll be there but it's protocol.

"She managed to fake her death, steal an identity and become a detective," Oz says, voicing what we're all thinking. "We might have already lost her for good."

The door slams shut as Jude walks out. I sigh. Part of leading this team is dealing with everyone's emotional baggage and we have more than most. I tug down the sleeves of my suit jacket and follow Jude into the corridor.

He's leaning against the gray wall, staring at the ceiling, his fingers playing with the stones in his pocket.

"This isn't your fault," I tell him.

"I should have stayed with her or placed an officer on the door."

"She was cuffed and locked in. Jude, we didn't know who she was or what she was capable of."

"You would have known. You'd have had some sort of instinct."

I hold back another sigh. Jude has a habit of comparing himself to others. He comes from a wealthy family and is a certified genius, but his parents see his ADHD as a weakness. They refused to even send him for an assessment and every time he struggled or made a mistake, they compared him to his brother. If I ever meet his mother, we'll be having words.

I step in close and grasp the side of his neck. "If I was going to have an instinct, I would have had one and told you to stay with her. I didn't. Some things are just out of our control."

Jude finally looks at me, a smirk playing at his lips. "Says the control freak."

My lip twitches. We both know he's right. "I don't need you to be like me, Jude. Or Eli, or Oz. I need you to be you. So, stop moping and use that genius brain of yours to profile our little escape artist. Where would she go?"

Jude nods and closes his eyes. His eyelids flicker as he sifts through his thoughts like Oz searches the internet. After a minute, his eyes snap open. "She's a detective," he states. "Why do that? Why fake her death and become a police officer? It's risky. She had a fresh start, she could have disappeared and lived a normal, happy life."

I cock my head. "You think she's trying to catch her father?"

"I don't know, but you don't make detective at twenty-two if it's just a job to you." Jude's eyes lock on mine. "I know where she is."

12

FREYA

I'm used to being on the run. In some ways it's been my default state since I was seventeen and I know that the last thing I should be doing is returning to the scene of the crime. But here I am.

The crime scene teams have cleared out of Quantico Park and the moonlight bounces off the river. Two Uniforms stand guard outside the tent, their chatter drifting over to where I'm hidden behind a tree. They look familiar and I smile when I realize they're both from my station.

I hook my camera strap over my neck. Thankfully, my bike was still parked here so I'd managed to grab the camera from under the seat along with one of my knives. I hate knives and I hate that once again dear old dad's put me in a position where I might need one. But I'm good with them and since River and his team confiscated my gun, I'd rather be armed than vulnerable.

I stroll out from behind the tree, the dampening grass soft under foot. The cops stop chatting as I approach. "Danvers?" One of them asks, his brow furrowed.

If Agent Park's team have already gotten word out that I'm a fraud, then this could end badly, but with any luck they still think I am safely locked away in their cozy little interrogation room.

"Hey boys," I say, "The photographer from earlier messed up, forgot to get shots after the body was removed. Agent Park sent me down here to take some photos while it's all still fresh."

"You working with the FBI?" The one who recognized me asks. Jacobs, I think.

Don't just tell the lie, tell the truth in the lie.

"Yeah, the vic is my missing person."

The other cop, Patrick, grimaces. "Never good when they end up that way." Luke and I worked with Patrick a few months back on an assault case. He's a good guy, sensitive. Guilt curdles in my stomach, but I push it down.

Patrick pulls back the tent flap. "You go on in Freya, get what you need to catch this son of a bitch."

I give him a smile and duck inside the tent. The material falls back into place behind me and I try to calm my racing heart. I might actually get away with this. Sure, my whole life is upturned, and I'll have to go on the run but as long as I have my freedom, I can do what needs to be done.

I lift the camera and snap some photos, gathering as much evidence as I can. The body's been removed, but a pool of blood sinks into the grass under the glare of the fluorescent lights. It doesn't really matter that I can't get photos of the body itself, the image of Camilla lying naked is still imprinted on my mind. The gash across her neck. The thin crosses cut into her chest. Twenty-three of them. One for every year I've lived.

I crouch down to take a photo of the blood. The scent of iron hits the back of my throat and my body seizes, a flashback pulling at my skin. I let the camera hang around my neck and press my cold hands to my cheeks. I haven't had a flashback in so long, I can't have one now. As far as I am aware my father hasn't killed a single person since I faked my death. He has an unprecedented amount of control and restraint for a serial killer, and I have a feeling killing Camilla wasn't a slip up. It was a message. He knows I'm alive.

I'm so busy trying to keep the panic at bay that it takes me a moment to realize I'm no longer alone in the tent.

My eyes snag on a pair of shiny black loafers and I dig my teeth into my lip. I follow his long legs up till I'm looking at Agent Park's scowl. I swallow and shift my gaze to the person next to him. I've not seen him before. He's ginger like me, his ruffled hair a couple of shades darker and his skin a freckled cream. He looks at me through a pair of wire framed glasses, disbelief flashing in his eyes. This must be the final member of Agent Park's team. Oscar 'Oz' Reynolds, the tech guru.

"Well darn," he curses, "You just lost me a bet."

I stare at him. My brain is still a little stuck on how unfair it is for every single one of Agent Park's team to look like a model. Dressed in chinos and a knitted jumper, the whole geek chic is really working for Oz. "What?" I say, when his words register.

"I told Jude you're way too smart to return to the scene of the crime. He said emotions make people stupid."

Well, given my almost-panic attack meant I didn't see these two sneak up on me, I could hardly argue with that. I run a hand over my hair.

Agent Park is still glaring at me.

"What happens now?" I ask.

Agent Park steps forward. "Now, *Angelica*, you come with us."

I tense but it's no good, hearing that name again pushes me over the edge and I can't stop the panic from rising. My vision blurs and I fall into a flashback.

"Slowly Angelica, nice and slow. If you go too fast, it hurts less."

My little hand trembles as I hold the knife, blood welling at its silver tip. I try to pull away, but my dad covers my hand in his and digs deeper.

"Please," she cries, "please stop."

"Please, please stop. Please, please stop," the words spill into the air, and I realize I'm the one saying them. I rock back and forth, hugging my knees until Agent Park appears in front of me.

He slips his hand around the nape of my neck and uses the other to cradle my cheek. "Look at me."

I stare at the grass.

"Freya, look at me," he orders.

I blink and our gazes collide.

"You're safe. No one is going to hurt you."

I wet my lips and study the specks of color in his eyes, hazel against a deep brown.

His hand squeezes my neck. "I won't let anyone hurt you."

This man is about to lock me up and throw away the key. I shouldn't believe a word he says. But something about River Park settles around me like a security blanket and I feel safer than I ever have before.

13

FREYA

They don't take me back to the interrogation room. Instead, I find myself in Agent Park's office, sitting in front of his mahogany desk. Bookshelves line the wall behind him, and paperwork is stacked in neat piles on the desk. I'd feel like a kid in trouble with the headmaster if it wasn't for the fact I'm cuffed to the chair.

I've already scoped the place for escape routes but unless he's hiding some secret door in one of the many bookshelves, the only exit is the door we came through. Said door leads back into an open plan desk area, sort of like the bullpen at my precinct but fancier, with glass desks and sleek computers. A large window to my left looks out over the city night lights, but I don't like my chances of surviving a five-story fall. That's if I even managed to get the cuffs off and make it to the window before Agent Park stops me.

He's sitting on the other side of the desk, slowly spinning the knife he found when he searched me. His disapproval is heavy on my shoulders, but I'm too busy trying not to remember how it felt to have his hands on me. He was professional to a T, but my skin tingled all the same. It was the first time in a long time that I've been touched, and I know he felt it too because tension still fizzles in the air between us. I move my wrist up and around, testing my range of motion.

Neither of us says a thing until the door opens, and Jude comes bounding in. "Found one," he says, holding a hairbrush up.

I quirk a brow. "Are we forgoing jail time and heading straight for corporal punishment?"

Jude chokes on a laugh.

River scowls.

I'm not normally so brazen, but the downward spiral my life is heading on has me acting reckless.

Jude coughs as he walks up behind me and settles a hand on my shoulder. "It's for your hair. Apparently, you live in a teen tv show and hair grips double as lock picks."

"Ah."

His fingers land on my ponytail. "May I?"

"There aren't any more in there." I lock eyes with Agent Park. "You found the only one I had in my pocket."

His eyes drop to the jeans hugging my legs before moving back up to my eyes. "You'll forgive me if I don't take your word for it."

I shrug. Of course, they're not going to believe me. That shouldn't sting as much as it does.

Jude eases the hair tie off. His fingers thread through my hair and my eyes flutter shut as his nails send the best kind of shiver down my spine. My father used to brush my hair, but it never felt like this. I'd sit with my back straight, my hands clenching the underside of the chair because I could never let my guard down with my dad.

Sitting in the FBI offices is the last place I should feel relaxed, but Jude has magic fingers and I sink back into the seat.

I don't realize Agent Park has moved until the door clicks shut behind him. I blink my eyes open.

Jude must have finished checking for hair grips by now, but he keeps running the brush through my hair. I'm too desperate for his touch to ask him to stop.

"Eli thinks you're helping your father. Keeping him one step ahead of us every time we get too close."

You will be my perfect weapon.

I force myself not to react. "Eli's the one with the cowboy hat, right?"

I hear the smile in his voice. "Don't tell him I told you, but he's got the boots too."

I trace a knot in the wood on the arm of the chair and the cuffs rattle. "And what do *you* think?"

Jude's hand stills, then he splits my hair into sections and begins to braid it. "I think you were the one to leak Arthur Maxwell's identity to the police after you faked your death."

I don't say anything. Nine hours ago, I was waking up to a normal day as a detective for the 23rd precinct. I was excited to go to a training lecture by a profiler I, as Luke puts it, like to fan-girl over. Since then, I've been arrested, escaped custody, had a panic attack in front of said profiler and been re-arrested. And now I need to decide how much I tell Jude.

He finishes the braid and uses my hair tie to secure it. "Angelica –"

"Don't." I pull away from him as far as the cuffs will allow. With just one word the calm his touch created abandons me entirely. "Don't call me that."

Jude holds up his hands. "Okay. Freya it is." He raises an eyebrow. "Though it feels kind of weird to be calling you the name of a dead woman. How about I call you Angel?"

I sigh and lean back against the chair. I guess that answers how they figured out I wasn't who I said I was. There's no getting out of this. They know I'm Arthur Maxwell's daughter. All I can do now is damage control. I want to catch my father, I really do, but I can't do that from inside a prison cell.

Jude rounds the chair. He leans against the desk, his head cocked as he watches me. I see the moment that genius brain of his realizes I'm ready to talk.

He shakes his head, a smile playing at his lips. "You want to make a deal."

"I'll tell you what I know on two conditions. No jail time and I want in on the investigation."

Air whistles out of Jude's rounded lips. "No jail time I can do but River's not going to let someone whose intentions are... unclear so close to an active investigation."

"I was raised by the man you're trying to catch. I know him better than anyone. As far as my intentions go, your theory is nearer to the mark than Eli's." I lean forward. "Besides, I'm a wild card, wouldn't you rather keep me close?"

Jude's eyes flare and an entirely inappropriate image of me pressed up against his body flashes into my mind. My cheeks heat and I look away.

Jude gets out his phone and makes a call. "She just confirmed her identity," he says. A second later River comes back in. He places some papers on the desk in front of me. It's an immunity agreement.

"You already had this prepared." I tip back my head. I

hate that they made me think I was facing prison time when this was their plan all along.

River sits down on the opposite side of the desk and meets my eyes. "It seemed the most likely outcome. After your little escapee act earlier, I do have a condition of my own though." He opens a drawer and pulls out a tracking anklet. "You get a five-mile radius. Do we have a deal?"

I eye the thick black plastic anklet. It's sleek, like everything at the FBI, but it's still takes away your freedom. It's going to make what I need to do tricky, but five miles is lot better than a 3x4 cell.

I look back at River. "Deal."

He smiles, but there's nothing gentle about it.

I read the agreement, which basically says I need to tell them anything I know that could aid the investigation. They've agreed to keeping me up to date with the case so long as I'm an asset but if they discover I've held something back the agreement is void and I'll be thrown in prison. This is where it gets a little tricky. There are some things I can't tell them, but this is my best shot at catching my father. I guess I'll just have to make sure they never find out what I'm hiding.

I sign on the dotted line.

Agent Park or River, I don't know what to call him anymore, stands up and crouches down beside my chair. He lifts my foot and places it on his knee. His fingers brush against my leg as he rolls my pants up and I have to force my breath to stay even. The click of the tracking anklet locking shut fills the room.

River takes off the cuffs holding me to the chair and tugs on my hands till I'm standing in front of him. He looks down at my shiny new piece of jewelry. "If you don't turn up when I call you or you step one foot outside of your radius, we'll be on you in minutes. Understood?"

I nod.

"Use your words, Freya."

I bristle at his tone but I'm not exactly in a position to argue right now. "I understand."

"Good." River's eyes drop to where Jude left the hairbrush on the desk then flick back up to me. "And Freya," he says quietly, "if I were going to spank you, I wouldn't use a hairbrush. I'd use my bare hand. And the imprint would mark your pretty pale skin for hours."

I suck in a breath. His words set me on fire and freeze me at the same time. River leaves the room but I stand there like a statue, trying to get over the shock. I know what I said earlier was inappropriate, but I never expected him to respond like that. I don't know whether I'm more surprised by his words or the way my body reacted to them. Because right now my panties are wet and having River's hands on me sounds like a far better idea than it should.

Jude coughs and I jump. I'd forgotten he was still here.

"Well, I guess that answers that question," he says cheerily. Then he takes my hand and pulls me towards the door. "I wonder what the rules are for fraternizing with an asset because if River's going to go there, I am most definitely throwing my hat in the ring." Jude looks over at me and grins. "Metaphorically of course, Eli's the only one with an actual hat."

I stare at him, my mouth hanging open.

He winks. "What do you say Angel, want to go on a date?"

14

FREYA

Jude's idea of a date ends up being an interrogation with not just him but the entirety of River's team. I'd only just got home after signing the immunity agreement when my phone rang, Jude's name flashing up on screen. At some point, after they'd confiscated my belongings, one of them had programmed all of their numbers into my phone. Despite his order, if River had been the one calling, I'd have been tempted to ignore it, but the memory of Jude's gentle fingers in my hair had me picking up. I like Jude—he's goofy, in a way the others aren't. Case in point, he'd set his ringtone as Taylor Swift's 'Love Story', so I'd answered, and he'd lured me to his house the next day with the promise of Chinese food.

His place is different to mine. It's not that it's messy, because it's not. The books under the coffee table sit in neat piles and the kitchen is tidy apart from a couple of mugs on the draining board. Maybe it's the warm yellow light from the lamps in the corner of the room or the fact that the books have clearly been read from the creases in the spine, but the house feels lived in. Comfortable.

Against all odds I find myself relaxing but we only have the living room to ourselves for about ten minutes before River, Eli and Oz arrive.

Oz blinks at us through his glasses, taking in the spread of Chinese boxes on the coffee table and the way I'm sitting cross-legged on the couch next to Jude. "Well, this is cozy."

Eli tears off his cowboy hat and stares at me. "No."

"Eli–" Jude takes his legs off the table.

"No," Eli snaps again. I don't know what happened to the flirty version of Eli from the crime scene, but this Eli is looking at me like he would rather kill me than kiss me. "I don't want her in this house. Our house." Eli turns to River. "Get her out of here," he says, before storming from the room.

River sighs and pins Jude with an exasperated look. "I told you to arrange a meet-up, not invite her to our house for a damn date."

I swallow the mouthful of spring roll I'd stopped chewing when everyone arrived. "So, you guys all live here together?"

Oz sits in the chair opposite the couch and grabs a prawn cracker. "Just makes life easier what with the hours we work and everything." Oz quirks a brow at me, as if daring me to judge but I think about my house and how lonely I've been for the past six years. The life of a cop is not an easy one and it doesn't lend itself to having a family. "That's kind of nice actually," I say.

Oz cocks his head and considers me. "Yeah, it is."

River still stands just inside the door, like he can't decide what to do about this situation.

Jude looks up at him. "She's got immunity Riv, we can't treat her like a criminal."

River runs a hand over his face and sighs. "I'll go get Elijah."

An hour later, mostly empty Chinese containers are scattered across the coffee table and four, far too attractive, faces are looking my way. Jude is still next to me, and Oz takes the armchair to my left. River sits with one leg crossed over the other in the armchair at the head of the room and Eli leans against the wall by the TV. I have no idea what his problem is, but he'd refused to sit, eat, or do anything other than glower at me.

I wipe my fingers on a piece of screwed up kitchen roll and shift further back on the soft leather couch. "So," I say, looking at the four people who want to stop Arthur Maxwell almost as much as I do and realizing I can't put this off any longer. "What do you want to know?"

River leans forward in his chair and links his fingers together. "Let's start with why and how you faked your death."

15

RIVER

Freya tenses. Part of me regrets ruining the peace she found over dinner, but we've got a killer to catch and as team leader it falls on me to get answers. So I keep a stony gaze set on Freya. Ever since she had a panic attack when I said her actual name, I refuse to call her Angelica. Even in my head. It never felt right anyway. Freya is fiery. Stubborn. But there's a softness to her underneath it all, one she's had to bury away to survive. Angelica feels like a stranger, but I can see her remembering who she used to be. The light flickers out of her eyes and she grows distant.

"It wasn't planned. The accident was real. I took my dad's car. I wasn't supposed to but... I'd made a friend. She said her name was Hannah, but I don't think it was her real name. She was living on the streets. I tried looking for her family afterwards, but I never figured out who she was let alone how she ended up homeless." Freya tucks her legs in tighter and the delicate lines of her neck tense as she swallows. "I was never very good at making friends. It was hard to when –" She cuts herself off.

"When what?" I press, keeping my tone detached.

Freya meets my gaze and smirks. "Serial killer dad and all that."

I narrow my eyes. That smirk is hiding something, but I let it go for now.

Jude reaches out to tuck a curl behind Freya's ear. My narrowed gaze shifts to him but Freya carries on.

"Hannah liked to chase highs. Not with drugs, just with life. She'd never driven before and she convinced me to bring my dad's car one afternoon, to let her drive." Freya runs her fingers along the scar behind her right ear. I've been wondering how she got it since I first noticed it when I searched her. "We crashed on a back road by the cliffs. Hannah was dead on impact. I'd seen enough dead bodies to know that straight away. And I don't know..." Freya shrugs, a faraway look in her eyes. "I guess I saw my chance."

Eli scoffs, disgust dragging at his face. I get where he's coming from but right now, I want to punch him because Freya shuts down even more. Her words come without a trace of emotion, like she's reciting a shopping list.

"I got the gas can out of the trunk and doused the car, used a lighter to set it all on fire with Hannah inside. She was about the same height and size as me, but I needed her to be unrecognizable. My dad's phone was in the car. I used it to call a contact of his, a coroner."

"Name," I say, latching onto the first piece of actionable information Freya has shared. One of the reasons we've struggled to catch Maxwell is because we can never connect him to anyone else. We know he must have had help over the years, but we've never found out who.

"Chris Mackelvy."

I look to Oz but before he can get his phone out Freya

adds, "he's dead. Two weeks after I blackmailed him into identifying Hannah's body as mine."

Oz taps away for a second then nods at me to confirm what she's saying.

"A kid at school who made fake IDs got me something to use till I could find someone professional."

"Criminal, you mean," Eli snaps. "There's no such thing as a professional forger."

Freya pulls her sleeves down over her palms and eyes him. "Right, sure. Well anyway, I found someone good, and they got me set up with a new identity as Freya Danvers."

Oz tilts his head to the side. "They're who buried any trace of Angelica Maxwell, too aren't they?"

"My dad was a private man so there wasn't much to bury, but yes. They've kept me safe."

Jude nudges her with his toe. "How did you afford that?"

Freya softens a bit when she turns to face him and a flash of jealousy streaks through me. Somehow, in just over a day Jude has managed to connect with her. I shouldn't care, but I do. I want her to look at me like that.

"I was a seventeen-year-old girl clearly on the run from something. I think they took pity on me."

"I'm going to need their name," I say.

Freya shakes her head. "They have nothing to do with my father. I found them on my own."

I sit forward, leaning my elbows on my thighs. "That's not how this works. I ask, you tell. You don't get to pick and choose, darling."

Freya's jaw hardens. "The agreement says I need to tell you anything I know that could aid the investigation. My father has never had any contact with the forger, knowing their identity will not help you catch him."

Eli pushes off the wall. "This is bullshit. She should be in an interrogation room not our fucking living room." He points at me. "I told you this wasn't going to work. We can't trust her."

His outburst has Freya flinching but before I have a chance to respond, Freya pins Eli with a ferocious look. "I want to catch my father. You can trust that. I will do everything I can to help you put him behind bars, but I will not give up the person who saved my life."

Her defiance hangs in the air for a moment. Eli's waiting for me to put an end to this but I'm not going to. Whether we can trust her or not, we'll get more out of Freya when she's calm and relaxed than if she were locked up again. I know why Eli's hurting and it kills me to make him do this, but I have to think about the end goal. Right now, working with Freya is the best chance we have of catching Maxwell.

Jude reaches out to Freya again. He takes her hand in his, rubbing circles on her wrist with his thumb.

She tenses at first but then settles back into the cushions.

"You never answered the first part of the question," he says, "why did you run?"

Freya shrugs. "Because if I didn't, he would have made me kill his next victim."

16

FREYA

A lethal silence sucks the air out of the room. I don't think anyone's surprised. I asked for immunity for a reason after all, but Eli's glare is thunderous. To be honest, I prefer that to the pity twisting Jude's face.

I draw in a breath and block out their reactions. I knew the second I signed the agreement I'd have to talk about this shit but apparently that doesn't make it any easier. I'm self-aware enough to know that I probably look like a robot right now but inside I'm trembling.

"Had you previously killed any of his victims?"

My nails dig into the couch. I was expecting the question, but River's words still tighten like a noose around my neck. I swallow against the pressure and make sure my next word comes out loud and clear. "No."

"Have you killed *anyone*?"

I'm still sitting cross-legged and Jude's palm curls around my socked foot. I jolt a little, but his touch grounds me. "No."

Eli asks the next question, glaring at me over crossed

arms. "Were you in any way involved in the murders of Maxwell's victims?"

And there it is. The question I've been dreading. The one I never wanted to have to answer out loud. I can feel a flashback clawing at my mind, but I lift my head and meet Eli's accusing gaze.

Never show them you're scared.

Eli's hands tighten into fists, his knuckles whitening.

Oz shifts in his seat and keeps one eye on Eli. Until this moment, I didn't think Eli would actually hurt me, but the way Oz positions himself, as if he's ready to intercept at any moment, has me second guessing myself. I force the answer out anyway. One simple word. "Yes."

Jude swears under his breath.

I turn just in time to see River put the dots together. "Your question, at my lecture. How did you know Maxwell wasn't the one to make the crosses?"

He knows the answer already, but I say it anyway. If we're going to work together, there are certain things they need to know, and this is one of them. "I knew," I say. "Because I'm the one who made them."

River just nods but Jude's hand leaves my foot, and my toes go cold.

Eli slams his fist into the wall, and I jump, scrambling back on the couch. He takes a step towards me, but Oz shoots up and blocks his way.

"Take a breath, man."

Eli's eyes bleed darkness and I think he's going to plough right through Oz to get to me but instead he spins on his heel and storms from the room.

I watch him go, trying to calm the adrenaline his reaction sent flooding through me. I'm not mad at him. Out of the four of them he's the only one treating me the way I deserve to be treated. I may not have killed anyone, but I hurt them, I tortured them. It didn't matter that my father made me do it, if I'd been stronger, I would have refused, no matter the consequences. Flashes of wide eyes and blood on pale skin flick through my mind. Tears dripping down faces, screams as sharp as the knife I held.

"I think perhaps we could all do with a break." Oz's soft voice brings me back to the present.

River nods.

I avoid looking any of them in the eye as I stand up. "I'm going to the bathroom." I pause at the hallway when I realize, I don't know where I'm going. I close my eyes.

"Second door on your right," Oz says gently.

I don't trust myself to speak yet, so I carry on without saying anything.

Their bathroom matches the rest of the house, sleek and modern with a black marble counter and a shining white sink. I guess being an FBI agent pays an awful lot better than a detective. Somehow, I don't think I'm going to be getting a cut. For years I've dreamed of being a profiler. Now this case is the closest I'll ever get. I may have gotten my phone back yesterday, but River kept my gun and badge. When this is over, chances are I won't even have a job, let alone a shot at working for the FBI.

I turn the faucet on cold and splash water on my face. My hands tremble as I grip the edge of the sink. I watch the water drip down my pale cheeks in the mirror. I'm always fair-skinned but right now I'm just a shade off ghost. There's only one other person in the world who I've told what I confessed to River and his team. Carmen. The forger who got me a new ID, did more than give me a fresh start. She took me in for a year until I turned eighteen and was old enough to apply for the police force. She also gave me all the skills I'd need to get through the Academy and make detective so quickly. River can ask all he wants but I'll never turn her in.

My phone buzzes in my pocket. I take it out to find a text from Luke asking how the hell I managed to get on the case with the FBI and can I get him in on it too. River didn't want to blow my cover, so we agreed to let everyone believe I'm consulting in my capacity as a detective, not a murderer's daughter. I guess word has spread. I text Luke back saying he's out of luck, but I'll buy him a beer to make up for it.

I need to leave the bathroom before someone comes looking for me, but I hesitate, opening up the contacts app. One call to Carmen and she'd get me out of here without a trace. I could start over again, somewhere new.

Of course, there's my new piece of jewelry to consider. The black tracker collars my ankle, a constant reminder that in River's mind I'm a criminal. Carmen could probably figure out a way to disable it, but River isn't wrong. I am a criminal. I may not have killed anyone, but I stood by as my father did. Over, and over again. I want to be mad at Eli for making me feel like shit, but I can't be, because he's right. I don't deserve to be free and if I have any chance of clearing my conscience, I need to stop my father. I need to keep my promise.

I tuck my phone into my pocket and dry off my face, then I put my poker face back on and leave the bathroom.

17
―
ELI

*F*uck. This shit is harder than I thought it would be. I don't think I can work with her. Hearing what she said, what she's done...

I link my hands together behind my head and drop my chin to my chest, stretching out my aching neck. I need to talk to River.

I pull myself together enough to come out of my room, but the second I open my door I see *her*. She freezes, like she can feel my eyes on her, but she doesn't look up. After a second, she finishes closing the bathroom door and turns to walk down the corridor back to the others.

"Scared to be alone with me?" My normally jokey tone comes out mocking.

Freya stops walking, her long ginger waves flicking over her shoulder as she twists to look at me. "Should I be?"

Her calmness pisses me off. She acts like the things she's done don't matter. The lies she's told, the people she's hurt. I want to fucking shake her, shout at her, show her that there are consequences to her actions. *Should she be scared?*

I take a step forward, my hands clenching by my sides. "Maybe."

Instead of running to the living room, Freya walks towards me and tilts her head back to meet my gaze.

"Do you treat all your assets like this or is it personal?"

Her words hit a little too close to the bone. I don't remember deciding to move but the next thing I know I have Freya pressed up against the wall, my hand around her throat. My heart kicks against my ribs. I breathe in, the sweet strawberry scent of Freya's shampoo teasing my senses. My cock hardens inside my jeans. Before Oz discovered her true identity, I'd already been making plans to get Freya in my bed. She'd have purred like a kitten as I played with her, running my tongue along her pussy, sucking at her clit, and pulling away just before she came.

Instead, I've got her pinned against a wall.

I'm not normally like this. Horny, sure, but not violent, not angry. I'm never myself when it comes to Arthur Maxwell though because Freya was right - it's personal.

My hand flexes, squeezing her slender neck. Each breath she takes presses against my palm. I'm not cutting off her air, but she doesn't scream. In fact, she squirms a little and when I lean in close, towering over her, her pupils dilate. Apparently, I'm not the only one turned on by this.

"Well, you're full of surprises now, aren't you?"

Her voice comes out raspy. "What are you talking about?"

I edge closer and push my leg between her thighs. A choked moan slips from her throat. "Are you wet for me, Kitten?"

She presses her lips together and sets her gaze on the wall behind my shoulder.

"Not human enough to feel bad for carving up women's chests but human enough to get turned on by being collared."

Freya's eyes flash and her hands snap up to grab my wrist. "Who said I don't feel bad?"

It's the most emotion I've seen her show and it's enough to make me second guess myself for a moment. That's all she needs to break my hold. She moves lightning fast till she's out of arms reach, her chest rising and falling with heavy breaths.

"Never touch me again," she says.

I curl my lips in disgust. "Don't worry Kitten, I'd rather stick my dick in a beehive than fuck a murderer like you."

Her cheeks flush. "Screw you Elijah, I haven't killed anybody."

I step forward. She raises her hand to slap me, but I catch her wrist and tug her in close. "You don't get to call me that." The only person who's ever called me Elijah was my mother.

Freya's eyes burn. "Then don't call me a murderer."

I shrug, still holding onto her wrist. "If the name fits."

Freya shrieks and tries to wrench her arm from my grip. When I don't let go, she stomps on my foot. She's too small for it to hurt much but I release her so she'll calm down. Only, letting her go doesn't help. She claws at me.

She's a detective, she must know how to fight, but it's like she's in a frenzy. I try to grab her arms to get her to stop, but every time I touch her, she shrieks again and lashes out, her nails scratching at my skin.

Footsteps pound against the wooden floor as River, Jude, and Oz run into the corridor.

"What the hell is going on?" River demands as Jude narrows his eyes on me.

"What did you do?" he asks.

"Nothing," I say, tilting my head back so Freya can't reach my face. "Will someone do something about this?"

River and Oz drag Freya off me. She doesn't calm down till she's pinned against the wall again and River's snapping cuffs around her wrist. It's not till she's stopped thrashing about that I see the tears streaming down her face.

"Fuck." I run my hand over my jaw and stalk back into my room. I should apologize but half of me feels like she deserved what I did, what I said. The other half knows the way I just behaved was despicable and I've earned the sock to the face River's parting glare promised.

18

JUDE

I glower at Eli's back as he walks away. The dopamine hit from the adrenaline rush slows my brain down enough that I don't make any rash decisions.

I don't know what Eli did, but I have no doubt it's his fault Freya's upset. I'm a little surprised I'm so protective of her after such a short amount of time but unlike River I'm not one to suppress my emotions.

According to my parents that's just one of my many weaknesses, being ruled by my feelings. They don't rule me though, I just feel them more strongly than most and I'm not egotistical enough to try and ignore them. If I'm feeling something, there's a reason and listening to that always works better than burying it. Right now, I'm feeling like I want to whisk Freya away and make sure she never has reason to cry like this again.

I stride over to River and draw Freya to my side. "I've got her," I say, "you go deal with Eli."

River's jaw sharpens, his dark eyes lingering on Freya for a moment before he gives a brisk nod.

He heads towards Eli's room, and I put my arm

around Freya's shoulders. "Come on, Angel." The tears have stopped falling but she's almost catatonic as I walk her to my room on the other side of the corridor.

"I guess I'll just wait here then," Oz calls as we leave him in the hall. I glance over my shoulder and smirk at the dry look on his face.

He focuses on Freya. "You all right going with him?"

She blinks but something inside of me loosens when she gives a small nod and leans into my touch. The youthful part of me, the side most people frown at, feels like a superhero.

My room is a bit of a mess. The bed's unmade. Sheets of music lay scattered by my guitar and every surface is littered with fidget toys and a variety of things I've taken out and forgotten to put away. Eventually the clutter will get to the point that I can't stand it anymore and I'll start a big clear out that I'll abandon halfway through till Oz quietly turns up to help.

I know it's the ADHD, but a blush heats my cheeks as I usher Freya inside. I snatch the clothes off the chair in the corner and sit her down. "Sorry about the mess," I mutter, but I needn't have worried. Freya's eyes are glazed over. She's not paying attention to the state of my room. "Hey," I say, raising my hand to dry her cheeks with the soft edge of my hoodie. "Come back to me, Angel."

Freya blinks a few more times before her eyes focus on me and she lets out a shuddering breath.

"There you go." I rest my hands on her knees, rubbing soft circles against her jeans. Her hands are still cuffed behind her, but she leans back into the armchair, little tremors running through her body.

"What happened?" she asks.

"You, uh, got a little violent with Eli. Not that I blame

you, I've wanted to claw his eyes out a time or two before."

She squeezes her eyes shut. "He called me a murderer." Her words are so soft I don't think she meant for me to hear them. My hands tighten on her legs, and I have to force myself not to storm out of here and finish what Freya started. She needs me here right now. "Eli has his own issues, Angel. He shouldn't have said that."

"I hurt people."

"Hey, look at me." I grip her shoulders and sit her up straight. "You were raised by a serial killer. You were just as much his victim as they were."

She shakes her head but I'm not having it.

I curl my hand around the back of her neck and sink my fingers into her hair, holding her still. "Did you choose to cut those women, or did he make you?"

Freya wets her lips and I'm momentarily distracted before I draw my gaze back to her eyes. "Answer the question, Angel."

"He made me. It started when I was seven. One cross for every year I'd been alive, like some sort of twisted birthday candles."

Jesus Christ. My childhood was far from perfect, but I can't even begin to imagine the trauma Freya's been through. It's a miracle she's sitting here in front of me.

I kneel between her legs and cradle her face in my hands. "You are not to blame. Say it, Freya. It's not your fault."

Freya's throat bobs and another tear falls down her cheek. "It's not my fault."

I say it again, just to make sure she really hears it. "It's not your fault."

We sit there for a long moment, her letting the words

sink in and me getting distracted by little details. Freckles scatter across the bridge of her nose, but one is further out than the others, just to the edge of her left eye. A single tear catches on her lashes and when I go to brush it away with my thumb Freya sucks in a sharp breath. I'm worried I've scared her, but her gaze drops to my lips, heat blooming behind her emerald eyes.

I should back away, she's vulnerable right now but then she opens her mouth. "Hey Jude, are you going to kiss me or what?"

I curl my hand back around her neck and pull her towards me. My lips press against hers, just a whisper at first then harder, hungrier. I pause for a second, checking to see if she pulls away but she leans into me, opening her mouth and asking for more.

I comply, diving in and tangling my tongue with hers. Gone is the scared little girl from a moment ago, Freya meets me stroke for stroke. I twine my fingers through her hair, positioning her just how I want her.

She tries to press her legs together but I'm in the way.

I pull back from the kiss and trail my hands down her thighs to her knees.

"Undo the cuffs," she pants.

I run my hands back up her legs, sweeping my thumbs out teasingly close to where her thighs meet her core.

She shudders. "Jude, please."

"I don't know, Angel. Normally, the cuffs are more River's thing but there's something about seeing you this way, spread out before me like a feast." I press my hand to her chest. Her eyes flare as I gently push her back until she's resting against the chair. I brush my knuckles over her breast and her nipple pebbles hard enough I can see it through her top.

My cock swells but I barely even notice it, I'm too busy watching the way her mouth falls open and her back arches. I bring my hands back down and she gasps as I tug on her waist, sliding her hips to the edge of the chair. I lean down and press my lips to the soft skin of her stomach where her shirt has ridden up. My fingers pause at the button of her jeans. "Say 'red' if you want me to stop, okay?"

She moans.

I run my tongue along her skin. "Freya," I ask again, "what do you say if you want me to stop?" I pull back till I get her answer.

"Red," she says, her breaths choppy.

"Good girl." I undo the button and draw down the zip before hooking my fingers around the tops of her jeans and panties. I tap her back with two fingers. "Hips up, Angel."

She does as I say, and I pull her pants down, baring her to me. My mouth waters at the sight. Fine ginger curls, damp with her arousal frame the prettiest shade of pink I've ever seen.

Freya squirms under my scrutiny and I reach under her shirt to pinch her nipple. "Stay still," I scold.

"Son of a –"

I squeeze a little harder. "What was that?"

Freya glowers down at me but she doesn't finish her sentence.

"That's it, you just sit back and let me play." I run a knuckle along her slit, reveling in the wetness I find there. "Is this all for me, Angel, or did fighting with Eli turn you on?" She stills beneath me, and I curse myself for bringing up Eli's name but when I look up a deep blush colors her skin all the way down to her collarbones. *Interesting.* I press the pad of my thumb against her clit and a soft moan slips from her lips. "It's all right, you don't have to answer, it's better for my ego if I assume all of this is for me."

I dip my head and drag my tongue from the bottom of her pussy to her clit.

Freya moans louder and bucks beneath me. "Jude," she whines.

I hook my arms under her legs and lift her core towards my face. "I told you," I murmur, grazing my teeth against her clit, "to stay still."

With her hands cuffed behind her back and me holding her hips in the air, Freya doesn't have much of a choice but to do as she's told. I'm starting to see why River likes the cuffs so much. I dive back in, devouring Freya's pussy like it's my favorite dessert, sweet and creamy against my tongue.

I hold her still as she squirms and whimpers while I fuck her with my mouth. I can feel her getting close, so I let go of her leg and slide one, then two fingers into her tight pussy, curling them till I find the spot that makes her scream.

"Jude, please. I need, I–"

I know what she needs. I move my fingers faster and suck hard on her clit till Freya throws back her head, her pussy clenching around my fingers as she comes apart in my arms.

I drink her up, my cock throbbing in my pants.

My phone buzzes in my pocket but I ignore it. I press a kiss to Freya's stomach as she comes down from her high. "Back in a sec," I whisper.

Her eyes flutter in acknowledgment.

I duck into my ensuite and run a washcloth under warm water. When I come back to clean her up, she's still catching her breath, splayed across the chair with loose limbs and a dazed look in her eyes. I smile to myself and drop to my knees again.

I'm just pulling her panties back up when someone pounds on my door.

"Get your ass out of there, Jude and bring Freya," River calls, "They've found another body."

19

FREYA

I do not have the headspace right now to see a dead body.

All the tension Jude managed to melt away with that talented tongue of his has come back with a vengeance. I need time to process, to go home and maybe call Luke so I can talk to someone about what the hell I'm feeling.

I've had sex before but what happened with Jude was different. It was more than just a release, and I can't get it out of my head. The way his hands held me steady, the soft brush of his afro against my thighs, how he took charge while still making utterly sure I was okay the whole time.

He catches my eye in the rear-view mirror and I look away. There's too much depth to his gaze. If I let myself, I could get lost inside of Jude, but I need to be stronger than that. I'm not one of the team. I'm an asset to them and if Eli has anything to say about it, I won't even be that for long.

I rest my head back against the seat. If thinking about Jude is complicated, thinking about Eli might just break me. I hate that he called me a murderer. I hate that part of me thinks he's right. I hate that I have never been more turned on than I was with his hand around my neck.

He and Oz took a separate car so at least I don't have to deal with being in an enclosed space with him.

It's almost eight in the evening when we arrive, the darkening sky lit by street lamps. I brace myself for another verbal attack from Eli but when we get out of the cars, he ignores me. I, in turn, ignore Jude.

I can feel Jude's eyes on me, but I need to create some distance between us or I'll never be able to focus. I'm a detective. They may have taken my badge, but I still have all the training and it's my job to get justice for the person whose life was so brutally ended.

River parked up in a military housing neighborhood and we follow him across the road towards a kids' playground. Blue and red police lights flash off the shiny surface of a plastic slide and what looks like a pirate ship. *God, I hope the body wasn't found by a kid.*

My steps falter for a moment and Oz comes up beside me. I don't know where I stand with him yet. He seems to be the quietest of the group and he doesn't say anything even now, just waits beside me and falls into step when I start walking again. "So, are you Team Jude or Team Eli?" I ask.

Oz shrugs, his brown leather jacket rustling in the quiet night. "Consider me neutral ground for now."

I tap my fingers against my leg and nod. I can work with neutral.

"I do have one question though."

I glance across at him. "Shoot."

"Why didn't you ever go to the police?"

It sounds like a simple question but it's really not, and

as a profiler he must know that. I wonder whether he wants an answer or whether he's just trying to get a read on me.

A Uniform walks past us and I drop my voice before replying. "Growing up, my father had me convinced I was just as guilty as him. When it came down to it, I was too scared to go to the police." I look up to gauge his reaction, but his face is blank, so I carry on. "A month after I faked my death, I made an anonymous call to 911 and gave them his name. I told them I used to walk my dog past his house, and I'd seen him with one of the victims. You were part of the team that raided the place, so you know he was long gone by then."

Oz sighs and runs a hand through his russet hair. "We never managed to trace who made that call."

I chew the inside of my cheek, debating how much to tell him but they already knew of Carmen's existence, even if they didn't know her name. "That's why I waited. I know I should have called sooner but I needed to make sure I wouldn't be found. When I was doing my police training, I realized the chances of me being prosecuted for what I'd done, what Maxwell made me do as a child, were practically non-existent. But by then I'd broken about a dozen other laws. I always planned on stopping him. I was just going to do it as Freya Danvers, not Angelica Maxwell." It's the truth but not all of it and I wonder whether Oz can tell.

He nods but, unlike with most people, I can't read what he's thinking. We've reached the edge of the play area now, where the grass turns to wood chips. I stop before going any further and turn to face Oz. "I've made a lot of mistakes but believe me when I say finding my father has always been my top priority."

Oz's gaze is steady but when he looks over my head to the park behind me his throat bobs. "Looks like he might have found you first."

A chill runs through me at his words. I already know I don't want to see what Oz is looking at but like too often in my life when it comes to dead bodies, I don't have a choice.

I breathe in the cool night air to steady myself, but the tang of iron makes me feel sick. If things were different, I would have run far away from all this after I faked my death. Gone to some small town and opened a bakery, lived in a cottage by the sea. It's a dream that shatters into pieces every time I remember why I didn't do just that. Why I couldn't. I shake free the broken image from my mind and turn to face reality.

The kill is different this time. My father always left the bodies where they'd be found but he never displayed them quite like this.

Half the fun, Angelica, is what comes after.

The woman is sitting on the swing, her arms drawn up and tied around the metal chains. Her head is tilted back like she's praying to the sky but the deep gash across her throat means it's far too late for prayers. There's no blood on the wood chips so she can't have been killed here. She's completely naked and as my body carries me closer, my eyes drop to her chest.

I'm vaguely aware of Oz following me. Of River, Jude and Eli watching as I approach. I pay them no attention. I can't. The only thing I can focus on is what's carved into the woman's chest. There's just one cross this time. A large X cutting through the letters of my name. Not Angelica. Freya. Oz was right. My father's found me.

I turn away from the body and leg it to the trash can

at the edge of the playground. I grasp the cool metal edges and throw up the contents of my stomach. I stay there for a moment with my head in the trash can, taking shallow breaths as sweat chills my burning skin. When I'm relatively sure I won't hurl again I straighten up to find Eli has wandered over. I freeze.

"Would've thought you'd be used to seeing dead bodies by now," he quips. He could be referencing the fact that I'm a detective, but I know he's not. He's talking about the twenty-four bodies I'd seen before I even left school.

I glare at him. "Screw you, Elijah. Next time I'll throw up in your precious cowboy hat."

He scowls as I stalk past him and reaches up to take his Stetson off, cradling it to his chest.

I hide my smirk and stomp away, letting him think I've gone off in a huff. When I'm sure no-one is looking, I slide the folded piece of paper I'd found, wedged under the rim of the trash can, into my pocket. I had needed to throw up, but I'd also needed to check the trash can without anyone noticing. It wasn't a coincidence this body was left in a park. That was where we always left our notes.

20

RIVER

I take in the scene around me. The lab techs are marking up all the evidence. There's about twenty people on the scene and I cast my eyes over each and every one of them, double checking everyone here is who they say they are. I'm being overly anal about it all, but I've been on high alert ever since Freya managed to slip into my last crime scene. Twice.

My brain has a virtual map of the area, cataloguing where everyone is and what they're doing.

Jude's over by the ambulance, talking to the man who found the body. Thankfully, it was too late for children to be out playing. The man was cutting through the park on his run and is now wrapped in a shock blanket.

Oz is getting the lowdown from the cops on the scene and Eli is still scowling at Freya. I had to stop myself from going after her when she took off. My hands itched to hold her hair back as she bent over the trash can. I've always had that instinct to care, even when I was five and my mother spent her nights throwing up in the toilet. '*My little protector'* she'd say, *'always looking after me.'* She was so proud. It wasn't until I was a teenager that naive little me finally twigged he shouldn't have to look after his alcoholic mother.

Whenever I'm around Freya I'm filled with that nagging urge to care. To protect her. I can't do that though, not for her, and especially not at a crime scene. Freya's wellbeing is not my responsibility. Eli's, on the other hand, is.

I try to shield him as best I can from the Maxwell case but if I keep him out of the loop too much he pushes back. I understand his need to be involved but it's a fine line between allowing him that control and stopping him from getting obsessed. For years, Maxwell was all he cared about. When he started with the drugs it got really bad and I will never forget finding him on the side of the road, his limbs bent at odd angles. Oz, Jude, and I worked hard to pull him out of his own head, to give him a life worth living and I dislike that bringing Freya in is risking that. It's my job to think about the bigger picture though and what Eli wants, more than anything, is to see Maxwell behind bars.

A new set of headlights flood the park. A moment later, Dr Knightly climbs out of the black Mercedes and heads over to the body, kit in hand. I call Eli over to join us. Being near Eva will be good for him. On the surface Eli likes most everyone, but he has very few friendships. Eva seems to have gotten past those walls of his though.

She brushes a hand against his arm when he approaches. His shoulders relax a little, but he doesn't flirt with her like he normally does. He just flashes her a small smile then glances back at Freya.

Curiosity sparks in Eva's eyes, but I give a subtle

shake of my head. I trust Eva, but Freya's identity is need to know.

Eva puts her case on the ground a good distance away from the body and snaps on a pair of gloves.

I watch her as she works, each step calm and methodical. People are inclined to think coroners are cold hearted but they're just very good at compartmentalizing. It's a trait Eva and I share. Or at least we used to, but no matter how hard I try to tuck thoughts of Freya away in a locked box, the little escape artist always manages to get out.

She walks up to us, like my thoughts drew her back to me. Her breathing is calm, and she's got a bit more color in her cheeks now, but her hand trembles as she brushes a loose curl back from her face.

She catches me staring.

I pull my gaze away from her and back to the victim. I have a case to solve. I refuse to let Freya distract me.

"Initial impressions?" I ask as Eva straightens up.

"Rigor Mortis is just starting to set in so you're looking at about two hours since time of death." Eva points at the wood chip covered ground. "She wasn't killed here, obviously. No blood. The laceration across her throat looks like it was made in one continuous movement. The edges are clean which means the blade was sharp. I'm guessing it will match Maxwell's other victims, but I'll need to take her back to the lab to be sure. We can get a better idea of both the victim's and the killer's positioning by looking at the angle of the wound too."

I nod, taking in the woman's body. Her eyes stare in shock at the sky, her mouth open on a scream. Eva moves the torch over her face, the light shining on the still-wet drops of blood in the woman's hair. It's ginger, the same color as Freya's. I make note of the similarities between the woman dead on the swing and the one standing next to me. Given the name carved into the victim's flesh it's likely not a coincidence. I blink away the image of Freya bound to the swing, her throat cut open. *Compartmentalize.*

"What do you make of the presentation?"

"He's escalating," Eli says.

Eva nods. "It's different to usual that's for sure but the basics remain the same. I can see some rope burn under the edges of the rope which suggests she was tied up before being killed. I'd say the cuts on her chest were probably made pre-mortem too. There doesn't appear to be any sign of hesitation this time, but I'll take a closer look at the morgue. There's not much more I can do until then."

"Thank you, Dr Knightly."

She rolls her eyes at my formality. "You're welcome, Agent Park."

Eva goes to talk to one of the crime scene techs and I turn back to the body. If Freya used to be the one making the cuts on the chest, logic dictates they'll have been done by Maxwell this time.

Eli speaks up again. "He's displaying her. Sending a message."

It's pretty clear who that message is for.

"Did your dad ever take you to the park?" I ask.

Freya's still staring at the body. She jolts a little at my question. "No. I used to go by myself, on the way back from school. I'd stop and sit on the swings and wish my-" She cuts herself off. "And wish I had someone to play with."

I nod, not letting her see that I noticed her slip up. Freya's not telling me everything, but I'm a patient man.

Eva returns to gather her belongings and on the other side of the park Jude leaves the witness and heads back over to us. "I've got an ID. Once Kyle over there calmed down, he recognized the victim. Posy Winters. He said she just moved in with her husband one street over. They're a military family. Husband's on tour. Next of kin are her parents who live out of state."

"All right. Jude, Eli, follow up on next of kin. See if we can reach her husband too. Get him home. I'll send Oz out to her house to look for any tech, and Uniforms scouting the area to see if we can find the abduction point. Eva, let me know when you've finished your autopsy."

Eva looks up from packing away her kit and gives me a nod. "It'll get to it as soon as I can."

"I'll walk you to your car," Eli says, bending down to pick up Eva's kit.

She shakes her head but her lips twitch with laughter. "Such the southern gentlemen."

"Hush now you." Eli slings an arm over her shoulder as they walk. I'm glad he's feeling better.

I turn to Freya to tell her I have more questions but when I look down, she's staring at Eli and Eva. Her eyes narrow in on Eli's hand at Eva's back as he guides her into the car. *What the hell happened in that hallway?*

I'd restrained from scolding Eli because he looked guilty enough already, but he refused to tell me what had been said. Or done. I run my eyes over Freya's stubborn face. Somehow, I don't think I'll have any more luck with her.

"Come on," I say, snapping her out of it. "You and I are going back to The Lair. Time to answer more questions."

Freya raises her eyebrows. "The Lair?"

I sigh. "Ask Jude."

Freya glances at Jude but quickly looks away, a blush blooming under her freckled skin.

Apparently, I need to have a word with my team about boundaries.

21

FREYA

River is driving me insane. I have never met a man so relentless and single-minded.

"I don't know, maybe." I squeeze my eyes shut and pinch the bridge of my nose.

"I need you to be more specific, Freya," River demands. "Now where-"

"I swear to god River, if you ask me one more question, I cannot be held responsible for my actions."

River looks up from his notebook where he's been recording everything I've told him over the past three hours. Yes. *Three hours*. A single, dark brow raises. "I thought you wanted to catch your father."

I draw in a deep breath and concentrate on not stabbing one of his perfectly sharpened pencils through his eye. "I do. But I'm no good to you if I'm not thinking straight." I slouch down in the wooden chair in River's office. The seat is cushioned but, even so, my butt went numb about an hour ago. At least I'm not cuffed to it this time.

I stare at him across the mahogany desk. "I'm tired

and hungry and I've told you pretty much my entire life story, three times over." River had wanted to know everything. From the schools I'd gone to, to the gritty details of my father's kills. How he chose which women to take, how he kidnapped them, where he kept them, were they awake or drugged, did I talk to them. The questions went on and on and each one dug at my brain like a scalpel cutting out the mold. In some ways it's freeing to finally tell someone the nightmares that haunted my childhood, but it's definitely not easy.

I also haven't had a chance to look at the note I took from the park yet and the thin slip of paper feels like a razor blade in my pocket.

I sit on my hands, so River won't see them tremble.

He tucks his notebook into his desk drawer. "Alright, we'll stop for now. I'll order us some food.

I shake my head, needing to get out of here. "No, it's fine. I'll grab something at home."

River's hand freezes halfway towards his phone. "Right, of course." He clears his throat and runs a hand through his jet-black hair. It somehow stays neat even after he's messed with it. "Oz brought your bike over from the house earlier. It's in the garage."

My eyes widen briefly in surprise. "Tell him thanks for me."

"You've got his number."

I'd forgotten they'd programmed their numbers into my phone. Even Eli's. "I guess I can tell him myself then."

River nods. For a second there he almost softened. When he offered to order us some food like we were friends, not agent and asset. He's all business again now though. "Good. I'll call you in the morning and we can pick up where we left off."

I grimace. "Can't wait."

River stands and leans forward, planting his hands on the desk so he looms over me. "Watch the attitude. You have the freedom to come and go at the moment, Freya, but I'm trusting you to behave yourself." His eyes drop to the tracker on my right ankle. "That five-mile radius can be decreased. Do you understand?"

The threat crawls up my back but I push myself to standing, my smile dripping with sweetness. "Yes, Sir."

River's stoic mask breaks, heat flaring in his chocolate eyes at my words.

I smirk but he's not the only one affected. His eyes warm my back as I walk to the door, goosebumps prickling my skin and heat curling in my core. Yeah... I need to get away from these men.

I rev my bike and speed out of the garage. The visor on my helmet and my leather jacket protect me from the cold, but I still feel the wind whipping over me. It's like I'm flying.

Normally, a ride on my bike would be enough to settle my mind but today has left me frazzled to the extreme. I can't bring myself to go home yet. After I read the note, I don't want to be alone with my thoughts.

I take a sharp right and head to Mozzy's. It's the bar Luke and I hit when we want to avoid the overcrowded cop bar. I wedge my helmet under my arm as I walk inside and message Luke to see if he's up for a drink.

He sends a message back with the eggplant emoji and a question mark.

I roll my eyes but scan the stone brick walled room for the sort of guys Luke likes. Mozzy's is a queer friendly spot so there's a good chance at least half of them are into guys. The place is fairly busy tonight with groups of people spread out on the old brown sofas over by the LGBTQ+ flag on the back wall. An old-fashioned duke box pumps out songs from the nineties and the owners dog snores away on his bed next to it. I type out my response: 'Plenty here but most look out of your league.'

I make my way to the bar and slip onto a tall black stool, raising a hand to Josh, the bartender, when he nods at me. My phone buzzes and I grin at the photo of Luke giving me the finger. He's on his way.

My mind flicks back to the note in my pocket and my smile slips away. I need to stop putting it off and just read the damn thing. I take the slip of paper out but before I can bring myself to unfold it Josh appears.

He wipes down the bar in front of me and swings the towel over his shoulder. "You look stressed."

I screw the note up and shove it back in my pocket. I scowl at Josh. "Why aren't you as nice to me as you are your other customers?"

He shrugs. "None of my other customers throw drinks in my face."

"That was one time, and I was aiming for Luke!" I was a few drinks in at the time and my co-ordination left something to be desired.

Josh chuckles. "He coming down this evening?" He keeps the question casual, but I see him tense as he waits for the answer.

I nod.

Josh forces a smile, his hand tightening around the towel. "Great. You want your usual?"

I hesitate, wishing I could give him what he wants. He and Luke would be perfect together. I know Luke likes him but every time the topic comes up, he brushes it off. He doesn't do committed relationships and Josh isn't interested in anything less. Not when it comes to Luke.

I shake my head. "I'll just take a cider. I'm on my bike tonight."

Josh turns away to get my drink and I spin on my stool, leaning back against the bar and scanning the room. I can't get drunk, but I've got a decent track record for picking up guys here if I'm in the mood. I could do with losing track of reality for a while.

There's a group of firemen playing pool. I recognize a few of them from work. The police and the fire station have a love/hate relationship, but the high levels of animosity make for good chemistry.

Rocky, a guy I've slept with before, catches my eye and lifts his glass to me. He raises his brows in question, but I sigh and shake my head. As much as I want to lose myself for a few hours, I can't get Jude off my mind. Or River, or Oz or even goddamn Eli. I don't know where I stand with any of them. It's not like we're in a relationship. If I went and slept with Rocky I wouldn't be doing anything wrong but if I'm honest with myself, I don't want anyone else.

I spin back round and plant my head in my hands. *Great, not only have I been arrested by the FBI team I most admire, I'm now lusting after all four of them.*

"Well, that answers my first question."

I look up as Luke drags out the stool next to me and takes a seat. "What?"

"I was about to ask how you were doing but I'm going to go ahead and guess not so great."

"Wow," I say dryly, "you should be a detective."

Luke laughs.

Josh reappears and flips two coasters onto the bar before putting down my cider. He turns to Luke, another glass still in hand. "I took a gamble and brought you a beer."

"Blue Moon?"

"Of course." Josh hands Luke the glass, their fingers brushing a little before Luke pulls away and clears his throat.

"Thanks, bud." He shifts so he's facing me, effectively dismissing Josh and I want to kick him.

"That was rude," I say after Josh leaves.

Luke sighs and runs his thumb over the condensation on his glass. "I'll apologize to him later."

"Before or after you make him watch you leave with another man?"

"Jesus, Freya. You're brutal tonight."

Now it's my turn to sigh. "Sorry. Today has been a lot."

Luke nudges my knee with his, letting me know we're okay. "So, are you going to tell me why Captain called me in this morning and told me I'm partnerless for the foreseeable future?"

I pull back my shoulders and take a breath. The downside to hanging with Luke is that I can't tell him everything. Even if I wanted to come clean, the contract I signed requires me to keep my true identity a secret. "I'm consulting with the FBI," I say.

Luke's crystal blue eyes zone in on me. "Why do I get the sense there's more to it than that?"

The tracker anklet digs into my skin under my boot, like a tiny little collar. "Because you're good at your job. I can't tell you any more though."

"It's the Maxwell case, isn't it?"

I don't say anything, but that, in itself, is answer enough.

"Christ, Freya. Just... promise me you'll be careful."

I reach across the bar and give his hand a squeeze. "I promise."

Glass shatters and a roar goes up across the room. I tense, my shoulders curling in as I duck my head.

Luke's thumb runs back and forth over my hand, and I realize I've latched onto his fingers. "Hey, it's okay. Someone just knocked over a glass."

I force my fingers to unclench and look over my shoulder. The firefighters are jeering at one of their group as he grabs some paper towels and wipes up the mess. I must be more on edge than I thought. I'm not normally triggered by things like that anymore.

I flash Luke a smile. "Sorry, just feeling a little jumpy."

We go back to our drinks and Luke catches me up with what's happening at the precinct. I'm still rattled though. I've got that feeling you get when someone's watching you. When I turn around, I catch Rocky's eyes. I shake my head again and he shifts his attention to a curvy blonde, but the feeling doesn't go away.

22

FREYA

I try to distract myself by playing wingman to Luke.

A guy with dark brown skin and these cute nerdy glassy sits down at the bar and I wiggle my fingers to say hello. He introduces himself as Eoin and I tell the story of how Luke once rescued a kitten from a tree. It would be cliché and over the top if it weren't for the fact his pants caught on a branch on the way down and tore right off his body. I've got a photo of him holding the little ginger ball of fluff wearing only a shirt and his heart dotted underwear.

I turn the screen round to show Eoin and Luke tries to snatch the phone.

"Oh, come on, Freya. You've got to stop doing this."

I hold him back with a hand to his chest and he gives up, running his fingers through his surfer boy hair. I smile to myself when I catch Eoin watching the movement before looking back at the phone.

"Is this your go-to way of getting him a date then?" Eoin asks me.

I shrug. "Lucky for me, Luke provides enough content for more than one story."

Eoin grins. "I'd love to hear another."

"Or..." Luke says loudly, inserting himself between us and turning his back on me. "You could just talk to me."

Eoin presses his lips together. "I don't know, I feel like Freya will probably tell me all the good stuff."

Luke reaches out and runs his finger along the back of Eoin's hand. "Maybe, but there's very little chance *she's* going to go down on you later tonight."

Eoin blushes, pink blooming under his soft brown cheeks.

I lean back and take another sip of my drink.

They get chatting and Luke is good about including me, but they keep getting lost in each other and soon I'm stuck being the third wheel. I'd go and find my own guy to chat with but my mind circles back to Jude which then reminds me of the note in my pocket. I need to read it.

I stand up and tap Luke on the shoulder. "I'm just going to the restroom."

Luke nods and I weave my way through the bar, past the couples on tables and the fire fighters who are getting progressively louder with each round of drinks.

Rocky is now intertwined with the blonde, and she's falling for his romantic Italian act, hook, line and sinker as he presses kisses to her neck. He doesn't spare me a glance when I walk by, but I still feel like I'm being watched.

I duck into the restroom, go into one of the cubicles and lock the door. A toilet flushes in the stall next to me and footsteps clack across the tiled floor. The white noise of the tap running calms my nerves a little, but I wait till the other person leaves before I take out the note.

My hands shake. The paper is all crumpled now but when I flatten it out the writing is clear. Dark blue ink on a torn scrap of lined paper. It's like a note you'd get passed in class, but the words are written so hard I can feel the indent of the letters on the other side of the paper. The message sends a shiver down my spine.

Bad things happen when you break promises.

I tilt my head back and stare at the paneled ceiling until my breathing steadies. I think I'm going to be okay. I think I've managed to stay in the present but when I close my eyes images flick into my mind, and I'm sucked into a memory.

I watch her, another version of me, standing over the woman tied to the post. The thin silver knife gleams in her hand.

"Come on now Angelica, I'm not waiting all day. Make the cut." His deep voice is quiet but stern in the open barn. The woman holds herself still, her wide eyes watching, waiting. She's blonde, like they always are, with a kind face.

The little girl runs her thumb up and down the engraved hilt of the knife. Making people bleed is what she's been taught to do.

Deep down, I know this is wrong, but I'm not sure she does, not yet.

"I promised I wouldn't," she says.

I wince. Part of me is still back in the bathroom stall and I know what happens next. The man that raised her – us – me, grabs her ponytail and yanks back her head.

"Promised who?" he demands.

The little girl's eyes dart around but she doesn't say

who. She just repeats what she's been told. "I can't break my promise. Bad things happen when you break promises."

Her father snatches the knife from her hand and presses the blade against her t-shirt, his grasp on her hair keeping her close. "Whoever you made this promise to, bad things are going to happen if you don't break it." And with that he slashes the knife down, cutting from her chest to her hip.

I cry out and slide down the stall door to the cold floor, feeling the pain all over again in a burning line on my stomach. I try to focus on the cool tiles, to pull myself back to reality but I'm still caught in the past.

The little girl is crumpled on the ground now, curled in on herself. The man gets down on one knee and takes off his shirt. He presses the material against the wound to stop the bleeding and strokes her hair. "It's okay, sweetie, you're okay. I need you to make a promise to me now though, okay? I need you to promise daddy you'll always listen to him first, no one else, just daddy. Just me, sweetheart."

"I promise," I say as she cries the words and I finally come out of the flashback. The stall door rattles as my shoulders shake. Tears stream down my face. I let it out, knowing that now the crying has started it's best to get it out of my system when I'm alone, else I'll end up breaking down in front of River. Again.

After a few minutes the crying slows. I use some toilet roll to dry my eyes before leaving the stall and splashing water on my face. I brace my hands against the ceramic rim of the sink and look at myself in the mirror. My skin is all pale and blotchy, but my eyes are strong. A cool green. I am not broken. I am not a little girl anymore.

So many promises were made back then, but there's only one I intend to keep.

23

FREYA

When I get back to the bar, Luke and Eoin are leant in close, heads bent together as they talk in low voices.

Josh is at the other end of the bar, studiously ignoring them. My heart hurts for him. I can relate. Love isn't on the cards for me, no matter how much I may want it. There are times I've been tempted to try but I could never bring myself to start a relationship when I was hiding so much. A little voice in my head whispers that that isn't the case anymore. There are people who know who I really am now. Four of them. Four unfairly attractive FBI agents.

I shake the thought from my head and hop up onto my stool next to Luke.

He pauses his conversation with Eoin and turns to face me. "Hey, where'd you go?"

I frown at him. "Uh, to the restroom."

"I thought you came back already?"

"No." I draw out the word, confusion lacing my tone.

Luke shrugs. "Weird." He links his fingers with Eoin's

and smirks at their joined hands. "I guess maybe I was a bit distracted."

I snort and take a sip of my drink.

Eoin leans across Luke to talk to me. "Freya, would you mind terribly if I stole your friend for the rest of the night?"

Luke's hand drops to Eoin's thigh, making him blush again and Luke suppresses a smile while they wait for my answer.

"Sure, at least one of us should have some fun tonight."

Josh comes over once they're gone and clears away the glasses. "You want another drink?"

I shake my head. "I'm just going to finish this then I'll head out." I pick up the glass and down the rest of my cider. My life may have taken an unexpected turn, but I'm not depressed enough to sit here drinking alone.

The room spins a little as I hop off the stool, and I realize I've been up for almost eighteen hours. The cold night air wakes me up a bit when I step outside. I check my phone as I walk to my bike and find messages from all the guys except Eli.

Jude: You were quiet this evening. You over thinking?

Oz: Jude's trying to convince me to be on Team Jude...

River: Don't get drunk. And don't stay at the damn bar all night.

My eyes drop to my right ankle. Apparently, River's

been using my tracker to play babysitter. I tap out a message back to him.

Freya: Stalking is illegal you know.

His response is quick.

River: It's called controlling my assets.

Well, doesn't that just give me the warm and fuzzies.

Freya: Your asset is going home now, so you can chill your beans.

River: Chill my beans? How eloquent.

I don't like this. I don't like how casual and normal messaging him feels.

Freya: Leave me alone, River. Please.

He doesn't send a reply and I don't respond to Jude or Oz. I can't let myself get close to these guys.

I put my phone under the seat of my bike, so it doesn't dig in while I ride, then I slide my helmet on.

It's not far to my house but I'm only halfway there when my head spins again. I blink and the road ahead of me blurs. I use the back of my glove to wipe my visor, but it doesn't help. The bike swerves to the side and I yank down my hand to get it back on track.

Something's wrong.

I'm slowing down to pull over when lights from a vehicle behind me flood the road. The engine revs, the car getting too close for comfort. This isn't right, I should be worried, but I just feel numb. Like I've drunk too much or like -

I've been drugged.

Ice trails down my spine.

My drink. Luke said he thought I'd already come back from the restroom, but I hadn't. My brain flips in my skull, like your stomach when you drive over a hill. I need to pull over but I'm pretty sure the car is following me and if I stop now, I'll be defenseless. *Dammit, why did I have to put my phone under my seat? Think, Freya, think.*

I've got a bike that I won't be able to ride for much longer, I can't reach my phone and I don't have my gun. *Assets don't get weapons*, I think bitterly, *they get trackers*.

The tracker.

I only have a five-mile radius. If I go outside of it, River gets sent an alert. I try to picture the boundary map he sent me but my brain's all foggy. My house is straight ahead, and I know that's inside the limits. *Screw it.* I take a chance at the next turn and swerve left.

The car follows me.

Gravity tugs at my limbs and my breathing feels sluggish. I keep having to open my eyes again. I need to stop before I pass out and crash, but I don't think I'm over the boundary yet.

My boot slips from the foot peg and bounces off the tarmac. I try to pick it up, but I can't. I'm not going to last much longer. The road ahead of me is clear. I make a split-second decision and roll the throttle, accelerating as fast as I can, only easing off when my vision goes spotty. I misjudged though, I don't have time to fully stop before I lose control of the bike, my fingers slipping from the handles.

Metal screeches through the padding of my helmet and the world flips as I skid across the road. The impact shakes my bones, but I don't feel the pain. I roll across the tarmac before coming to a stop on my stomach. Cold air filters through my helmet and I realize the visor's smashed.

I can't move.

Hands touch my body and my stomach lurches. I'm on my back now. The stars, big white blurs in the sky. A figure leans over me. Ginger hair, like mine. I can't hear what they're saying.

Everything is muddled. I don't think I'm safe. I need them to leave. My eyes flutter closed but I manage to say one word. "Tracker."

The figure disappears. I'm trying to float away but something's tugging on my boot. After a second it lets me go and then nothing's holding on to me. I don't float though. I sink. Down into the darkness.

24

OZ

Jeez Louise. I lean back in my chair and sneak a look at my phone as Jude and Eli descend into another argument. Still no reply from Freya. I messaged her earlier this evening, before River came back in a huff and ordered a team meeting in the living room. It's been going on for over an hour now. An hour which I could have spent trying to track Maxwell.

We work well as a group, it's why we have such a high closure rate but adding Freya to the mix is like introducing a computer virus. The thing is viruses don't have to be bad. Sure, most people design them to do harm but there's nothing to say they can't be designed to do good, like an encryption virus that automatically attaches to files and protects your data.

The issue with any virus, even the hypothetically good ones, is that once they've been released, they're uncontrollable.

Freya is a wildcard. I wasn't lying earlier when I told her to consider me neutral ground. Part of me wonders if she might be good for us. We're all getting a little jaded, darkened by the things we deal with every day. Freya's sparking emotions we haven't felt in a long time.

On the other hand, if we can't get them under control, those emotions could wreck us.

Jude pushes himself up off the sofa and I zone back into the conversation.

He glares at Eli. "You are judging her based on her father's actions," he says. "You know that's not right; you know we don't do that." Jude's eyes flick to River whose jaw tightens. River's past goes unspoken most of the time, but Freya's not the only one to be born to a criminal. There's a reason he's a stickler for the rules.

"Enough," River snaps. "Sit down."

Jude does as he's told, and I tuck my phone away.

"Whether we can trust Freya or not doesn't matter right now. I called this meeting to talk about boundaries. Boundaries which have clearly already been crossed." He locks eyes with Jude which doesn't surprise me but when he turns to Eli my curiosity is peaked. *Interesting.* I wonder what's going on there.

"Freya is an asset," River continues, "any form of sexual relationship with her is highly inappropriate."

Jude lifts his chin. "In the eyes of the world she's just a detective consulting with us on a case. It's not against the rules to have a relationship with a colleague."

River pins him with a cool stare. "It is now. I am not having my team fall apart fighting over a woman."

Eli scoffs. "I want nothing to do with her. If Jude wants her, he can fucking have her."

Jude pulls a face. "You need to get over yourself. You like her just as much as I do, you're just too buried in your own grief to see it." He turns back to River. "And we don't need to fight over her. We've talked about this before, we all have."

Oh boy. I close my eyes and shake my head. I knew this was where Jude was going but I should have talked to him, told him to wait a bit longer before bringing it up.

"One girl for all of us, that's what we decided," he says. "We knew coming into this job that any serious relationship would be hard. Everyone ends up getting divorced or leaving their partners as fucking widows. Freya is ours. We share her. That way she never gets left alone."

Eli stands up. "For fuck's sake. No. Not her. Anyone but her. We all have to agree, remember? And I will never agree to this with her." He storms off. The coffee table shudders as Jude kicks it.

River runs his fingers through his hair. It's actually starting to look disheveled which means he's more stressed than he's letting on. "You've got to let this go, Jude. Nothing can happen anyway, not while she's working for us. Not when we don't know if we can trust her."

"I trust her," Jude says. "She needs us, River. Just like we all needed each other."

I tilt my head and consider him. Jude's utter conviction that Freya is the one for us does a lot to sway me to his side.

Every person on this team is like a brother to me, but Jude and I connect on a different level. We're just in sync, always have been.

The two of us have shared women before so it's not a huge step to imagine being in a relationship with Freya and the others. Plus, Jude's a literal genius, if he trusts Freya, I'm inclined to listen to him.

My phone pings at me even though it's on silent which is never a good sign. I take it out of my pocket and an alert pops up on the screen. *Crap balls.*

"Riv?" I grimace at him and hand over the phone.

He swears at the screen. "Fucking, infuriating woman." He glares at Jude. "If Freya's so trustworthy, why the hell is she trying to run?"

25

JUDE

I fiddle with the window button, opening and closing it again and again. I can't believe I read her so wrong. She's already tried to run from us once before, but like an idiot, I trusted her. We moved too fast. I *always* do things too fast. But I've never felt about anyone the way I feel about Freya, and I thought she felt it too.

She let me close, let me hold her. She came on my goddamn tongue.

I still can't get the taste of her out of my head. Her heady musk, like strawberries and cream.

I'm not like Eli, I don't do casual. I wanted Freya the moment I saw her in that tent but God, I might have just screwed up big time.

Eli takes a sharp turn. "Will you stop that?" he snaps at me. I snatch my hand away from the button and grip onto the door handle instead.

"Sorry." The need to fiddle switches to my leg and my knee bounces up and down.

"Update," River demands from the passenger seat. Next to me, Oz's eyes are glued to his phone.

"I don't like this," he says. "She hasn't moved for the last ten minutes, she's barely outside the boundary."

Hope flutters through my heart. "Maybe it was a mistake."

Eli grunts. "Or she's found a way to take the fucking tracker off."

I swallow. My mind spirals, imagining a hundred different outcomes and analyzing the probability of each one. I don't like the results.

Streetlights flash past as we speed through the suburbs, only slowing down when Oz announces we're a mile from her location.

I see her bike first. Or rather, pieces of it.

Ice trickles under my skin as I take in the carnage. Shards of carbon fiber. A snapped exhaust pipe. Red specks of a shattered break light. I follow the tire marks to where the bike itself lies on its side at the edge of a road. Like a metal corpse.

"Shit," Oz swears.

Panic claws at me. Oz never swears.

The indicator ticks as Eli signals to pull over and I'm opening the door before we've fully stopped.

I scramble round the hood of the car, my eyes darting desperately across the dark road.

"Freya!" I call.

Eli flicks the headlights on full and I catch a flash of golden hair further down the road. *No.*

I run towards the crumpled form, the tarmac digging through my jeans when I drop to my knees. "Freya."

She doesn't answer. She's lying on her back, out cold. Her helmet is still on but the visor's smashed and a trickle of blood runs down from a cut above her eye. "Shit. Shit, shit, shit." I'm first aid trained but my mind is spiraling right now, and I can't focus.

Oz appears at my side. He presses two fingers to her wrist and lowers his head to her chest. "She's breathing fine."

I catch my own breath and finally manage to get my brain working. We're trained to shake someone to try and get a response, but motorcycle accidents are high risk for spinal injuries.

Oz pinches the tip of one of her fingers instead, but she doesn't stir.

River joins us, his shadow falling across Freya's still body. "Paramedics are on the way, Eli's talking to them now. How is she?"

"Unconscious," Oz says, "but she's breathing, and her pulse is steady. She's got abrasions on the left side of her torso where her jacket's ridden up, a minor laceration above her eye and bruising to her right ankle. I can't tell if there are any other external injuries without moving her which I don't want to do until we can secure her neck and spine."

"Why isn't she waking up?" I ask.

Oz was pre-med at college and out of all of us he has the most medical training, but he just shakes his head. "I don't know."

I twine my fingers through Freya's, careful not to jostle her. "Come on, Angel, come back to me."

I hold her till the ambulance arrives, watching her closed eyes for any sign of movement. Oz uses his sweater to apply pressure to the wounds on her side. Eli keeps 911 updated and River paces back and forth.

I feel like there are threads connecting all of us to

Freya, pulled so taut right now that if they snap, the rebound will cut us to pieces.

The world goes quiet as we wait and the sirens, when they come, are deafening. River pulls me away from Freya so the paramedics can work, and I tug at my hair.

Eli stares at Freya as they slide a board under her back. His eyes narrow on her ankle. "Stupid woman."

I whirl on him. "What did you just say?"

Eli shakes his head, scorn dragging at his face.

"This wasn't her fault," I shout. "She got into an accident Eli, she wasn't running away."

He turns to face me. "Then why was she outside her boundary? Look at her ankle, it's like someone took a bloody hammer to the tracking device."

I put my hands to his chest and push him out of my personal space. "What? You think she did that to herself? Why would she run if she didn't manage to get the tracker off?"

Eli shrugs and steps back towards me. "Like I said. Stupid. Woman."

I clench my fist but River's hand on my shoulder tugs me back. "Enough. Now is not the time. We need to figure out what happened, and Jude is right, she's not stupid, she would have known we'd come after her."

"Maybe that was the point," Oz mutters.

My gaze snaps to him, jaw tight. I thought, of all people, he'd be on my side. On Freya's side.

Oz stares at the road, back the way we came. "What would you do if you were being chased and you couldn't call for help?"

I look where Oz is pointing, and the pieces click together. Tire marks bisect the road. A four wheeled vehicle, like someone pulled sideways and skidded to a stop.

"Someone else was here," River says.

I look around. Woods border each side of us, and the road ahead disappears into the darkness. No one flees from an accident unless they've caused it.

Maybe it's a coincidence. Maybe it was some drunk driver. But then who took off Freya's boot and tried to remove the tracking device? And where the hell are they now?

26

FREYA

I wake to find River glaring down at me. It's a look I've seen so often recently it's almost comforting.

The soft beeps of the monitor and the chemical clean smell tells me I'm in the hospital and just one look at River's face lets me know he's somehow going to blame this mess on me.

I close my eyes and wonder if I can get away with pretending to be asleep until he leaves.

"Nice try, darling." River's voice rumbles over me. The deep timbre soothes my headache which only irritates me more. I feel betrayed by my own body. We're not supposed to like him.

I give up my pretense at sleep and ease myself up till I'm propped against the pillows. I'm still a little woozy and my left side burns like a bitch. I can feel bandages wrapped around my middle and my ankle is heavy. I look around the room. The curtains are drawn across the window and brightly colored switches and wires interrupt the cream walls.

River's not my only visitor. Jude's sitting by my side to the left of the bed, Oz is on a chair in the corner of the room and Eli's leaning against the door, arms crossed. He should trademark the pose.

"Eyes on me, Freya," River orders.

I scowl at the demand but turn to face him. "What happened?" I ask.

"That's what we've been wondering." He holds up the tracker anklet between us. The surface is scuffed but it's still intact. It's just not where it should be.

"I didn't take it off," I swear. The tracker was still on my ankle when I passed out but if somehow it wasn't when they found me, they're not going to believe I wasn't the one to remove it.

Jude reaches out and squeezes my hand. "We know, Angel. We took it off once we got you to the hospital. Your ankle was pretty bruised, and the doctors wanted to wrap it."

I glance at my feet, hidden by the blanket, then look back at the battered tracker. "My ankle's bruised?" I ask, starting to put together what must have happened.

Eli scoffs. "I told you she would play dumb."

I stare at him.

It's really rather easy to kill someone, Angelica. Just a simple flick of a knife.

I push my father's words away. "Do you not have any ounce of empathy?" I ask. "I'm in a hospital bed after getting fucking chased and crashing my bike. Do you really think I planned that?"

"Just tell us what happened," River says.

I turn away from Eli and sort through the blurry mess of my memories. "I was at the bar, but you already knew that." I give River a pointed look.

"I put the tracker on you for a reason darling, it's not my fault if you thought I wouldn't use it."

I scowl at him.

"Your text said you were going home," River prompts me to continue.

I nod. "I was halfway back when I started feeling off. Dizzy. Confused. I was losing control of my bike."

Jude's hand tightens around mine. "Why didn't you pull over?"

"There was a car behind me. I figured I must have been drugged but I couldn't reach my phone and I didn't want to stop while I was being followed. It was stupid, but the only way I could think of to call for help was to cross the boundary and set the tracker alarm off. I didn't know whether I'd made it far enough or not."

My hand shakes a little as I think about what might have happened if I hadn't. I tuck it under the blanket before anyone sees.

"You made it," Oz speaks up from the corner. "We got the alert and came after you. We thought you were trying to run."

"The doctors are doing a tox screen," Eli says, an edge to his voice, like he's trying to catch me in a lie.

I meet his cold eyes. "Then I'll have proof I'm telling the truth."

"Who was following you?" River asks, breaking up mine and Eli's staring contest.

An image of the figure looming over me flashes through my mind. "I don't know," I say, which is technically true. My vision was too blurry to know for sure.

River's face gives nothing away, but I feel like he knows I'm withholding the truth.

Oz leans forward, resting his elbows on his knees and

clasping his hands together. He nods at the tracker River's still holding. "That thing probably saved your life. We found you unconscious on the road. If whoever was following you had managed to get the tracker off, they would have taken you with them."

My fingers grip the sheets. I know he's right. It's a cruel irony that the very thing that's taking away my freedom is what kept me alive.

"It's going back on," River says.

"I kind of figured."

He gets up and walks round to the end of the bed. He pulls the blanket out from over my feet and trails his fingers over the bandage on my right ankle before switching to my left.

I hold my breath as he lifts my leg up and clicks the tracker shut around my good ankle. His touch sends tingles running through my body. He holds my foot a moment longer than necessary before placing it gently back down.

I wet my lips.

River rests his hands against the plastic rail at the end of the hospital bed. "Give us a moment."

Eli and Oz share a look before leaving the room.

Jude squeezes my hand then gets up and follows them out, leaving me alone with River.

"Wanted me all to yourself, did you?" It's probably not the best time for jokes but I thought it might lighten the mood.

River moves his hand back to my good ankle and drags his thumb down the bare sole of my foot.

My core clenches.

"Oh, I'm not opposed to sharing," he says, "so long as I'm the one in charge."

I go still. I was not expecting him to play along. Now I have images of all four of them with their hands on me. My body tied up on the bed. River ordering Jude to fuck me harder.

He keeps running his thumb up and down my foot and it's taking everything in me not to squirm. Or beg him to touch me somewhere else.

"I know you're lying to me, Freya." His words are dark, threaded with warning.

My breathing shallows. "I don't know what you're talking about."

River's hand stops moving. He pulls it away from my body and I almost whimper at the loss of his touch. Does this count as a form of torture?

He slips his hand into his pocket and takes out a piece of paper. It's not till he reads the note that my blood runs cold and my arousal dies.

"Bad things happen when you break promises."

I push myself further up on the bed, ignoring the throbbing in my side. "Where did you get that?" I glance around the room, only now seeing my clothes folded over the back of Oz's chair. "You went through my stuff?" I accuse. "That's private."

River works his jaw and walks back round to the side of my bed. He places his hands on the blankets either side of my legs, trapping me, and leans over till his face is inches from mine. "You're a criminal, Freya, and you're lying to me. From this point on, you have no such thing as privacy."

I grit my teeth and breath through my nose, too angry to say any of the things I'm thinking. "I have an immunity agreement."

"One that requires you to tell the truth." River lifts a

hand and I flinch but all he does is tuck one of my curls back behind my ear. His face softens. "You could have died tonight. Talk to me. Tell me what is going on. Let me help."

I'm so grateful tonight ended the way it did, but it doesn't change anything. "Thank you for coming after me," I say instead.

"Who's the note from?"

I press my lips together.

"Who drugged you?"

When I don't answer River pushes up off the bed and runs his hand through his hair. "I can't protect you from a danger I'm not aware of."

When I was much younger, I used to dream of someone coming along to save me, but no one ever did, and I learnt to protect myself. What River is offering is tempting, but it would be selfish to take it.

River shakes his head and any softness disappears. He pins me with an unforgiving stare. "Fine. From this moment on, consider yourself under house arrest. You go nowhere without one of us by your side."

Panic floods my system and instinct has me pushing myself off the bed, eyes set on the door. My feet barely graze the floor before River's arm loops around my chest and pulls me back onto the bed. I grip his forearm with both hands, his muscles rock hard beneath my fingers. I glare up at him. "Why do you even care?"

"You are our best chance at catching Maxwell. You're no good to me dead."

We're so close, we're breathing in each other's air. He's proved his point, there's no way I'm getting out of this room, but he doesn't move away. I think about his gentle hands on my feet, about his whispered words that always catch me off guard. "Is that the only reason?" I ask.

River grits his teeth. A muscle in his jaw ticks. "Yes."

I tilt my head and reach up so I can whisper in his ear. "Now who's lying?"

27

FREYA

They let me out of the hospital later that day after my tox screen came back positive for GHB, a date rape drug.

I got the satisfaction of seeing Eli look at least a little remorseful before River took control of my discharge and escorted me to his car.

He's been quiet since our face off, no doubt brooding over the fact that I'm lying to him. But two can play at that game because I'm still pissed about the whole house arrest thing. Neither of us say a word in the car.

River's gaze is set on the road ahead as he drives, and I pass the time trying to figure out how I got drugged. It must have been when I went to the toilet. I could kick myself for being so stupid. We're supposed to be the ones chasing my dad but, right now, it feels like the other way around.

The car slows down and River turns onto the drive. I've not been paying attention, which is a credit to how distracted I am right now and a mistake I shouldn't have made. I just assumed River was taking me back to my place but the white clapboard house in front of me suggests otherwise. He's brought me to their home.

"I thought I was under house arrest," I say.

River presses the button to turn off the engine. "You are."

I make a show of looking out the window then back at River. "This isn't my house."

"It is now." River steps out of the car and rounds the front to pull my door open. "Welcome to your new home, darling."

I meet his stony look with one of my own. "You can't just make me stay here."

"Yes, I can."

I grip onto the 'oh shit' handle, refusing to get out of the car. "Is that even legal? I'll report you."

River's eyes darken and his jaw sharpens. "I'm trying to catch a serial killer. You are an asset under FBI protection. I can do whatever the hell I want to keep you safe."

We get locked in a staring contest, but I swear River is more robot than human. My emotions are running wild, like a whirlpool in my chest, but River stays cold, sharp.

His gaze drops to my side, where, under my shirt, bandages cover the road rash. He leans in. "You're hurt," he says, "so I don't want to throw you over my shoulder and carry you into the house," his eyes meet mine again and a flicker of heat burns through his cool façade, "but I will if I have to."

"You wouldn't dare."

"Try me."

My core clenches at his words. I don't want to risk him following through, so I scramble after River as he strides to the front door. "How long are you planning on keeping me here?"

River unlocks the door, leaving it open for me to follow him inside.

The guys' house is big. I guess when you've got four FBI agent salaries you can afford to splash out. Polished wooden floors line the hallway and lead into an open plan kitchen and living area. The brown leather sofas where Jude and I sat eating Chinese catch my eye and I take a moment to process that was only yesterday. In less than twenty-four hours, I've told the guys my life story, had potentially the best orgasm of my life, seen a dead body, and got drugged and chased off the road.

It hits me like weights dropping on my shoulders and pretty much all my fight drains away. I close my eyes for a moment, then follow River up the stairs to the right.

He's waiting for me when I make it to the top.

"I don't have a change of a clothes," I say, the words coming out on a sigh.

"Jude's at your house, packing up a bag."

"Of course, he is," I mutter. It's yet another invasion of privacy but River's made it clear he couldn't care less about that. The controlling S.O.B stops outside the first room on the left and ushers me inside.

The lock on the door screams at me. "Do I get a key to that?" I ask.

River's gaze bores into me. "No."

My cheek twitches. I don't like being confined. The urge to run simmers under my skin but my ankle hurts and my limbs are lead.

The room is nice. A double bed with a wrought iron headboard serves as a centerpiece and I sink down onto the navy comforter. Built in wardrobes with dark willow doors line the wall opposite the bed and the dark blue wallpaper with gold highlights gives the room a cozy vibe. As prisons go, I've seen worse.

River looks at me from his stance by the door. "You could just tell me whatever it is you're hiding."

I blink up at him and lift the corner of my lips in a watery smile. I spread my arms out wide. "Home sweet home, right?"

River sighs and shakes his head. He leaves me alone after that, shutting the door behind him. I don't hear the lock turn but the threat's there all the same.

My five-mile radius has shrunk to house arrest and there's a lock on the door I don't have a key to. The message is clear. The more I fight this, the less freedom I have.

28

JUDE

I feel like crap. I don't always take medication for my ADHD but with all the added stress my brain was moving too fast for me to function, so I took a dose this morning. The meds work wonders at slowing down my thoughts, but the downside is I never really feel like myself when I'm on them. I need to book a checkup with my psychiatrist because it's not the same for everyone and I am by no means anti-meds. If my parents had let me have them as a kid, it would have been a game changer. But no, having a neurodivergent son would have been too much of an embarrassment.

Even with the meds, the last forty-eight hours have been hell. No-one's cooked anything for dinner, so I just nuked the leftover Chinese in the microwave and now it looks as pathetic and tired as I feel.

Yesterday, I got back from picking up Freya's stuff and went straight to her new room. I tried to talk to her, but she took the bag off me without saying a word and shut the door in my face. She hasn't left her room since.

I dropped off food this morning and I was going to take her some Chinese, but River proclaimed he'd had enough of her sulking and marched upstairs.

I'm leant over the island, a forkful of noodles halfway to my mouth when the shouting starts. The fork clangs against the marble top as I drop it and race upstairs. I take the steps in threes, bracing myself to a stop against the door frame to Freya's room.

She's kneeling up on the bed, River glowering down at her.

Oz stands awkwardly in the corner, holding a first aid box. His eyes widen at me in the universal plea for help.

I look back at Freya, trying to take stock of the situation. The oversized t-shirt she's wearing swallows her whole and covers most of her pajama shorts. The tartan bottoms stop just above mid-thigh and I have to stop myself from staring at all that bare skin.

She may be small, but her gaze is fierce, and it flashes my way. "Get him out of here," she demands, pointing at River.

Stone encases River's voice. "You don't make the orders round here."

"This is too much!" she shouts.

River grits his teeth. "Your bandages need changing."

"I can do it my goddamn self."

"Oz has medical training. I need him to check for infection."

Freya sits back on her heels. "So, take me back to the hospital, let a nurse do it."

River huffs in disbelief and shakes his head. "I am trying to catch a serial killer; I do not have time to chauffeur you around town like a spoiled little brat."

I suck in a breath.

Freya's mouth drops open, but her shock quickly morphs to fury.

I calculate there's an eighty percent chance Freya tries to attack River if I don't do something so, ever the peacekeeper, I take a step into the room. "Riv, let me talk to her."

His gaze flicks my way. He doesn't want to let this go but I tilt my head a little, subtly nodding to where Freya is gripping the sheets so tight her skin is ghost white.

River finally sees what I'm seeing, and his shoulders drop. Freya's scared. "You've got ten minutes," he says to me.

"Fifteen."

"Fine." He nods.

I step back a little too late as he passes, and I use the moment his shoulder bumps into mine to slip my fingers in his jacket pocket. Once he's gone, I shut the door and use the key I just swiped to lock it. Freya needs to feel safe right now.

I hold the key up so she can see. "He's not coming back in till you want him to."

She deflates a little, sitting back on the bed. The corner of her lip curves up in a way that's just begging me to run my tongue over it. *God, her body distracts me.* "Can I have that?" she asks.

I chuckle and slide the key into the pocket of my jeans. "Sorry Angel, he's going to be mad enough when he realizes I took it from him." I sit down on the edge of the bed.

"Your boss is a tyrant."

I smirk. "Team leader. And he's not normally that bad."

Freya rolls her eyes. "Well, aren't I lucky." She's trying to play it off, but her chest is rising too fast with each breath and one of her hands still has a death grip on the sheet.

I catch Oz's eye then nod at the first aid kit. I read a study about how trauma manifests in behavior and one of the best ways to de-escalate a situation is to remove the trigger and distract.

Oz puts the box down, stepping away from it a bit to lean against the windowsill.

Freya's hand relaxes.

"It's quite impressive really, how much you frustrate him. He's usually all calm and collected and all things serious. You've got a talent for pushing his buttons, Angel. Isn't that right, Oz?" I ask, trying to bring him into the conversation.

He crosses his arms over his chest and nods. "It's kind of fun to watch. I've heard rumors they called him C-3PO during training."

I grin. "Seriously?" Either Oz is making it up or he's kept that one close to his chest. No way am I ever letting River live that down.

"I find a simple 'controlling bastard' works well," Freya chimes in.

I let out a low whistle. "That's quite the dirty mouth you've got," I tease.

Freya blushes, pink spreading across her freckled cheeks. I wonder if she's imagining the same things I am. Her, muttering swear words as I pound into her, driving her to the brink. *Fuck.* Now, I'm getting hard.

Oz clears his throat and, with Freya more relaxed, I force myself to focus on the matter at hand.

"Why don't you want Oz to change your bandages?"

Freya tenses. She pulls her knees in towards her and wraps her arms round them. She looks away from me, staring out the window.

The sun is setting in a beautiful blend of purples and oranges, but Freya's gone somewhere dark.

I share a glance with Oz, worried she's not going to answer when she finally speaks.

"Arthur Maxwell likes to cut," she says softly.

Her words sink into me like a knife. My stomach swirls and it takes everything in me not to react. "Do you have scars, Angel?"

She looks away from the window and back at me, her arms still hugging her knees. "It's not pretty."

I keep my gaze steady. "We're FBI agents, Freya. You think we can't handle a few scars?"

She doesn't answer me, but I can tell she's not convinced. One of the things about profilers is that we're good at reading people. Freya's on the edge of panic.

Every book I've ever read on psychology tells me to be gentle, to tread carefully and I have to force myself to forget the science and listen to my gut. River came on too strong, but he was right about one thing, Freya doesn't need softness right now. She doesn't need to be treated like she's fragile. She needs us to prove that seeing her scars isn't going to change how we see her.

I reach out for her good ankle and tug it towards me. The move unbalances her but she catches herself with two hands on the bed behind her.

"Jude," she says.

I run my hand up her leg, all the way to the hem of her shorts, resisting the temptation to push further.

"What are you doing?"

I ignore her and move so I'm kneeling on the bed then

I place my other hand on Freya's chest, gently but firmly easing her back until she's lying down and I'm looming over her.

Her green eyes burn like a forest fire. "It's more than a few, Jude."

I drop my hand to the bottom of her shirt but when I start to pull it up Freya grabs my wrist with two hands.

I stop. "You think we need pretty?" I ask. "You think after all we've seen, all we've done that we want soft, perfect, fragile?" I ease her shirt up a little bit. "We want tough. Strong. A fighter."

Freya's lips part, her breath warm against my jaw.

"Don't get me wrong, Angel, you're gorgeous. Stunning. But any scars you've got aren't going to take away from that. They'll only add to it. Because in our world, staying alive, is sexy as hell."

She waits a moment but then she lets go of my wrist and gives me a slight nod.

I signal for Oz to get the first aid kit open because even after everything I've just said I know this isn't going to be easy for her, and I want it over as quick as possible.

He sits down on the other side of the bed and gets everything ready. Once he's done, I lift up Freya's shirt. For once my mind isn't wandering anywhere. I am fully focused on the woman laid out before me.

Most of her torso is covered in bandages, so we don't get the full impact at first. A small part of me is hoping it won't be that bad. I've seen countless dead bodies, many of which have been mutilated beyond belief. I can deal with a few scars. But when Oz moves Freya into a sitting position to unwrap the gauze, an uneasiness embeds itself between my ribs.

She winces as Oz peels back the final layer. It must

hurt like a bitch, but she doesn't make a sound. She's trying to be strong but the second the air touches her skin she turns her head to the side and closes her eyes.

To be honest, I'm glad she does because there's no way I can keep the horror that surges through me off my face.

Beside me, Oz goes still, and we both have to take a few breaths. It's bad. Maybe not worse than what I've seen on a corpse but worse than anything I've ever even imagined on someone still alive.

The road rash is red and angry, and still oozing in places but it's nothing compared to the rest of her chest.

He cut her like he made her cut his victims. Eight crosses, four on either side of her torso. Those are the worst scars, the skin raised and pink. You'd have to cut deep to get scars like that.

Or repeatedly cut in the same place.

It would be bad enough if that was all, but the rest of her is littered with thin pink and white lines. The biggest one sweeps in a vicious curve down from between her breasts to the edge of her hip. There's more scarred skin than not and the way some of the lines curve round her side has me thinking her back didn't get away unscathed.

I look over at Oz and see the same rage I'm feeling reflected back at me. We make a decision then and there. A silent promise between us to make her father pay.

Adrenaline buzzes through my veins. I am full of violence right now, but I force myself to be gentle as I cup Freya's cheek and turn her face to look at me. I run my thumb along her cheek bone and her eyes open.

"I was wrong before," I say. "You're not a fighter. You're a *warrior*."

A tear runs down Freya's cheek and this time I don't

resist the urge to kiss it away. My lips press against her soft skin and any doubts I had about how I felt for her burn out. I don't care that it's fast. I don't care that she lied. I don't care about River's rules.

Freya is mine. And I will never let anyone hurt her ever again.

29

FREYA

I've got half an eye on the door, ready for River to come knocking again but the key is still tucked away in Jude's pocket.

Oz's touch is firm but gentle against my skin. The road rash burns as he cleans it, but then I become fully distracted by his other hand. The one holding my waist, keeping me steady as he works.

Tingles run down from the pads of his fingers straight to my core and Jude's heated gaze isn't exactly helping. I'm holding my top up so my breasts are covered but, with the way my nipples pebble under the thin cotton, I may as well be naked.

Once he's finished cleaning my wounds, Oz presses two squares of gauze to my side and gets Jude to hold them in place while he winds a fresh bandage around my stomach. He nears the top and the back of his hand brushes against the underside of my breast.

My core spasms and I squeeze my legs together.

The smirk that appears on Jude's lips should be

embarrassing but all I can think about is how much I want to kiss that smug look right off his cute face.

"I'm going to need you to lift your top up a bit, Freya," Oz says.

I do as I'm told, pulling the fabric up higher until it only just covers my nipples.

Oz reaches round to loop the bandage past my back, the move bringing his face centimeters from mine. His eyes are sharp as they focus on the job at hand. A small frown line pinches the bridge of his nose, and a slight ginger scruff covers his jaw. He looks different without his glasses on. I like the nerdy look they give him, but this version of Oz is good too, less guarded somehow.

"All done." Oz secures the wrapping with a safety pin and takes my shirt from me, pulling it back down.

I thought I would be glad to be covered up again but the second his hands are gone I miss his touch.

Oz turns to pack away his stuff.

Jude rubs my knee and guilt pricks at me for fantasizing about his teammate when Jude and I are... well I don't know what we are.

"You did good, Angel," he says.

I soften. "Oh yeah? What's my reward?"

Jude grins. "Lie back and you'll find out. I think Oz missed a couple of places in his inspection."

I laugh. I'd only been teasing before but I find myself leaning back onto the soft bed.

Jude presses up over me and takes my mouth. I open for him, moaning as his tongue tangles with mine. The low hum that spread through my body while Oz was working ignites but when Jude's fingers trail down to my core, I put my hand to his chest to stop him. I look over at Oz as he snaps the first aid kit closed and stands up.

Jude follows my gaze before turning back to me. "He'll leave if you want."

Oz grunts. "Debatable."

I blink. "You want to stay?" I ask.

Oz takes us in from under hooded eyes. "Aye."

The accent catches me off guard and Jude must read the heated surprise on my face.

"Scottish on his dad's side. The accent comes out in the bedroom," he says.

I glance between them, wondering how Jude knows that. "You two have done this before."

Jude nods carefully. "On occasion. Oz likes to watch."

My stomach sours at the idea of them with other women. I try to shift away, but Jude lowers his weight onto me, pinning me in place at the hips.

His eyes narrow. "We're not saints, Freya, but we're also not players. This isn't going to be a one off, meaningless thing. Sharing you with Oz makes this more serious to me, not less."

Oz moves to the side of the bed and settles in against the wall, crossing one leg over the other. "So, am I staying or going?"

Jude's eyes are clear as they wait for my answer. He's not lying, he wants this and if I'm honest, so do I. I lick my lips. "Stay."

Jude kisses me. "Good girl." He pushes up so I'm no longer pinned to the bed but only so his hand can dip back down to my center. He slides my pajama shorts to the side and drags his fingers through my folds.

I arch off the bed, my nails digging into his shoulders.

"How does she feel?" Oz asks from his vantage point.

"Soaked," Jude answers.

I'm sure my cheeks flush crimson but I get the satisfaction of seeing Oz harden beneath his pants.

Jude is just as talented with his fingers as his mouth and soon I'm squirming beneath him.

"Lift her shirt up."

Jude does as he's told, pushing the material up to my neck until I can feel Oz's gaze on my breasts. God, I didn't know being watched could be this hot.

Jude slides two fingers inside of me and reaches up to play with my nipple. The sensations shoot straight to my core and I want to pull away and push closer all at once.

Jude presses a kiss to the side of my breast. Then sucks till it stings. "If you don't stop wriggling you'll hurt your wounds and I'll have to get Oz to restrain you," he warns.

I gasp as a rush of wetness floods from my core.

Jude's fingers still. "Well, well, well."

"What is it?" Oz asks.

Jude's smile is nothing short of devious. "I think our girl likes the idea of being restrained."

Oz hums. "River will be pleased."

I'm about to ask whether that means what I think it does, but Jude chooses that moment to curl his fingers upwards and my thoughts scatter as I come apart.

"Again."

I'm busy panting, my pussy spasming when Oz's demand registers. "I don't know whether I can-" I start, but Jude cuts me off.

"Shh," he says, "Listen to Oz." His thumb presses down on my clit and I lose the ability to speak, let alone argue.

"Turn her around," Oz orders.

I whine as Jude's fingers leave me but then he's lifting

me by the hips and laying me across the bed, so my head is hanging off the edge. "What – oh."

Oz steps away from the wall and my question falls to the wayside. He stops with his legs either side of my head and I watch, enrapt as he undoes his belt and frees himself. He nods at Jude and my mouth falls open as Jude thrusts his fingers back inside of me.

Oz takes my mouth like an offering, tilting back my chin and pushing his cock inside. The world spins a little as the blood rushes to my head and I grip onto Oz's thighs. The angle opens up my neck so he can slide all the way in, and I choke a little when he hits my throat. It takes a moment for me to adjust to his size but then I swirl my tongue around his length.

He groans, his grasp tightening with the most delicious pressure around my scalp.

Everything in the room disappears and all I know is Oz and Jude. The feel of their hands on my body, the surge of light headedness as I lose my breath only to gasp and shudder around Oz's length. The two of them command a rhythm and I'm swept along with it, the ebb and flow of lust and arousal rising from my scrunched toes to my head, held steady by Oz.

"That's it," Oz coaxes. "Take my cock like a good girl."

Tears blur my eyes. I can't see what Jude is doing but I feel the moment his tongue finds my clit. I moan and Oz must like the vibrations because he thrusts in deeper.

"Fuck. Whatever you just did, brother, do it again."

Jude does, indeed, do it again and I explode for a second time just as Oz pulls out and shoots his load across my breasts.

Jude stays low, licking me clean as aftershocks tumble

through me. He straightens my shorts and pulls me back onto the bed so my head's not hanging off the edge. "Fuck Angel, that was beautiful."

I'm still catching my breath when Oz leans down and presses a soft kiss to my lips. "Did you like your reward?"

I huff out a laugh and smile up at him. "Very much so." I look down at the mess he's made of my chest. "I think I might need new bandages though."

Oz quirks a brow. "You mean I have to undress you again? Such a shame."

Banging rattles the door, breaking the bubble of happiness Jude and Oz built me. "It's been half an hour and I know you took my key, Jude," River calls. "Out. Now."

30
—
ELI

This woman is messing with our team. Not to mention she's becoming a quite literal pain in my neck.

I push up off the stool by the kitchen island and grab the top of my head, stretching it forwards until I hear a crack.

Ever since I saw the wreckage of her motorbike crash the muscles along the left side of my neck have tensed right the fuck up. It brought back too many memories of the time River found me splayed across the road. I swore I'd never ride again and after Freya's crash I was filled with the inexplicable urge to confiscate that bloody bike. Inexplicable because I shouldn't give a shit. She can ride herself to an early grave for all I care because, like I said, she's messing with our team.

Now, she swans down the fucking stairs, both Jude and Oz at her shoulders. Color me surprised.

Not.

Jude's made it pretty clear how he feels about Freya. He thinks she's the one. Oz was never going to be far behind. He and Jude have a connection. I'd say it's like the one I have with River except theirs was born out of solidarity and respect whereas ours was cultivated in pain.

River and I have been by each other's side since we were seven years old. He'd sneak away to my house whenever his parents weren't using him as a pawn in their cons. I was his safe haven until my house became a far unhappier place than his. I know River better than anyone which is how I can tell that he's not as unaffected by Freya as he likes to pretend. We have an agreement though. We all have to be on board when it comes to choosing a woman and I will never choose Freya.

River closes the file he's been scouring and Oz nods at him as Jude helps Freya hop up onto one of the stools. I fight the urge to just walk the hell out.

River's gaze lands on the little spitfire. "Was that so hard?" he asks.

Freya's eyes flare before she puts on a sickly-sweet mask. "No, actually, it turned out to be quite...pleasurable."

Jude coughs in a poor attempt to cover his laughter and I roll my eyes to hide the flush of anger that sweeps through me. "While you've been lazing around in your room all day the rest of us have been working," I say. I slide the folder in front of me and it skids across the island. "Time to earn your keep."

Freya stops the folder under her palm and opens it up. "What's this?" she asks.

River looks up from the new file he's opened. "A list of your father's suspected associates. Names and photos. I need you to go through them and see if you recognize anyone."

"Yes, Sir," Freya mutters.

I sense more than see River go still beside me.

I shake my head. If she's going to throw around phrases like that, soon it's going to be three against one. Me being the only sane person not to fall for a murderer's daughter.

River goes back to his paperwork and for once I can't fault Freya. She's taking this seriously, a slender finger running down the paper as she combs through the list, flicking back every now and again to have a second look at one photo or another.

Jude presses a kiss to the top of her head then leaves her to it, sinking down onto the couch and turning the TV on low. Oz joins him.

I stay at the island.

"You know you don't have to stare at me the whole time," Freya says without looking up from the file. "What do you think I'm going to do? Secretly remove a name?" She nods at River. "Somehow, I think Mr. Perfectionist over there would notice."

"Maybe he just likes looking at you," Jude calls from the couch, a wicked grin tilting his lips. He rests an arm on the back of the couch and gives Freya a slow perusal. "Can't say I blame him."

She rolls her eyes, but the barest hint of a smile teases her lips.

"Stop distracting her," I say, getting up from the stool and joining the others in front of the TV. Normally, I'd be absorbed in the hockey game playing but I spend most of my energy trying not to look at Freya. Ten minutes later the game is entirely forgotten when Freya speaks up.

"River," she says, "I think I've found something."

We're up from the couch in an instant. Ten years

we've been chasing Maxwell, and we might finally have a solid lead. I curl my hand into a fist and tell myself not to get my hopes up, but I rush to the island all the same.

River is more measured as he moves round the island and Freya turns the file to face him.

"He looks a little different than I remember, and my father always called him Uncle Peter not Colin, but I'm pretty sure I recognize this man."

River studies the photo then spins it around to face the rest of us. "Colin Bennet," I say. He's a ferret of man with sharp wrinkles, grey hair, and a thick pair of glasses. "Did you say *Uncle* Peter?"

Freya nods, though the queasy look on her face has me thinking he wasn't the friendly family figure the name suggests.

"I'm not sure my father is capable of having friends, but Peter would come round now and then, and they'd grab a drink and watch the game. I never liked him. He was kind, but the way he looked at me as I got older…"

Every single one of us freezes, our eyes locked on Freya, but she just shakes her head like it's nothing.

"Anyway," she says, "he always brought his dog with him, a little Jack Russell Terrier, named Bella. I think he had a lot of animals. If it's him that is."

"It's him," River confirms. "Colin Bennet is a vet. We flagged him not long before Maxwell stopped killing. Eva managed to find a trace of the drug he used to knock his victims out and we searched local pharmacies, hospitals, and vets. Anywhere that might have given him access to the drug. One pharmacy and two vets were missing some of their stock, Bennet's being one of them."

"I remember him," Jude says. "He claimed one of the local homeless people broke in, but he didn't want to press charges because he volunteered at the local shelter. He seemed like a good guy. Friendly."

"This was back before we knew the Cross-Cut Killer was Maxwell, so we didn't have any way of connecting the two of them," Oz adds.

"But if he was more than just a contact," I say, looking at the photo of Colin on the island, "then there's a chance Maxwell might have gone back to him for supplies now he's started killing again."

Oz's fingers fly over his phone. "Jackpot Potato," he murmurs.

"Jesus Christ," I grumble.

"What?" Oz asks. "It's like Hot Potato but Jackpot Potato."

We all stare at him. "That's quite possibly your worst one yet."

Oz grins at me before turning serious. "Colin Bennet opened up a new clinic in Quantico six months ago."

Freya's delicate neck bobs as she swallows. "Quantico's not a huge place. If he's been living here for half a year, he could have seen me." She looks at River, her eyes widening with a hint of panic. "He could have told my father where I am. That could be why he started killing again. Here of all places."

Images of all the bodies Maxwell's left in his wake flash through my head. The dread hits me out of nowhere, exploding out of me before I can contain it.

"Great," I snap, pushing away from the island. "Nice work Killer, you led a murderer to our town." I flash her a false smile. "Now we get to go talk to his bestie."

"I told you not to call me that, *Elijah*," Freya snaps back, but I'm already walking away.

I don't look back until I reach my room at the end of

the corridor. I can still see her down the hall in the kitchen. Freya's bent forward over the file, her red hair water-falling around her face as she works together with my three teammates. A hint of guilt curls around me. If my mother were here, she'd be scolding me for treating Freya the way I am. But my mother's not here.

And she never will be again.

31

RIVER

We're finally making progress. I report back to Director Syed and make the arrangements for us to see Colin Bennet the next day. Then I spend a sleepless night wondering if Jude's snuck in to be with Freya.

I'm quite possibly losing control of my team. I debate the merits of dragging him back to his own room, but I've already done my nighttime routine and getting up again will only make it harder to sleep. Insomnia is the one thing in my life I can't control but I try my hardest to do so anyway.

I'll leave Jude alone. Freya could do with the company after I forced her out of her own damn home. A small part of me recognizes that my actions may have been a tad extreme but most of me stands by the decision.

Freya is maddening. And stunning, and strong and delicate despite the tough front she puts on. I feel better knowing she's here. We have the best security system in the states. I'm yet to figure out who ran her off the road, but no one is getting in here. And Freya isn't getting out.

I flip my pillow over to get the cold side and stare up

at the ceiling. I keep my room dark to help me sleep. The less I have to distract me the better, but my mind refuses to turn off. I should stop thinking about her but somehow, I don't see that happening.

I still can't quite believe Jude managed to swipe the key to her room off me earlier. It's on me, I'm the one who taught him that move but I was too caught up thinking about a frustrating little red head to notice what he was doing.

I groan. I need to focus. Freya may be a distraction, but she's held up her end of the deal. We finally have a lead.

I close my eyes and run through the details of the case in my mind. Eventually, sleep claims me.

I wake up in the morning feeling minutely more rested than I did before I went to bed. It's only five a.m. so I grab myself a black coffee and a breakfast bar and plan out our visit to Colin Bennet. The others join me just after seven and I brief them around the kitchen island while they eat.

"I want to talk to him," Freya says after I announce Eli and I will be the ones to make the first approach.

I nod. "And you will, but I want to get a read on him before seeing how he reacts to you."

Freya turns her glass of orange juice around in circles on the island. "Are you arresting him?"

"Unfortunately, we can't. Unless he says something incriminating, we don't have enough evidence for it to stick."

Freya looks up at me. "I can connect him to my father."

Eli scoffs as he stacks up the empty plates. "You're an unreliable witness at best and unless you actually saw the two of them partaking in criminal activities, we've nothing to charge him on. You should know that *Detective*."

Freya matches his glare, only softening when Jude places a hand on the small of her back. "We'll catch him out," Jude says. "People make mistakes under pressure and having the FBI turn up on your doorstep is known to have that effect."

"He's right," I say. "We know what we're doing." Freya still looks a little tousled from bed and I find myself wanting to tease her. "We caught you, didn't we?"

Her mouth rounds and my lip twitches as I suppress the urge to grin.

"Oz, I need you here on comms," I say, "the rest of you, go get ready. We leave in half an hour."

32

RIVER

We pull into a small parking lot, gravel crunching under the tires. I did my research this morning, so I know the layout of the place. The renovated old house has two exits, one round the back and the main entrance.

A shiny plastic sign stating 'Happy Vets for Happy Pets' greets us as we head towards the front door.

"Wow, this place is like a walking daytime advert," Eli says. "Can we arrest someone for being corny?"

"Was that a joke, Eli?" Freya asks. "I didn't realize you had it in you."

He shoots her a snarky look and Freya smirks.

"I'm leading a team of children." I sigh.

Jude's head bobs up from his phone. "Hey, what did I do?"

"Freya's not part of the team. She's an asset." Eli may as well have stomped his foot.

"All three of you be quiet. Bennet doesn't know we're coming. I need you focused. Jude, wait round the back exit. Freya, you're coming with us but hang back in the reception area until I call for you."

Everyone falls into position, and I push open the door to the vets.

A bell chimes above my head and a young man behind the front desk looks up. "Hi there, do you have an appointment?"

I flip open by badge. "That won't be necessary. We're here to talk to Dr Colin Bennet."

The receptionist stands up, his glasses slipping down his nose. "Oh, um, he's with a patient at the moment."

I smile but there's nothing kind about it. "It's urgent."

The man wipes his hands on his scrubs. "Right, of course. I'll just um..." He fumbles for the phone, his fingers tripping over the buttons. His voice shakes as he speaks into the phone before replacing it in its cradle. "He's just coming."

A white door to the right opens and I jerk my head at Freya, signaling for her to move out of sight.

Bennet looks much like his photo only with less hair and slightly rounder cheeks. He ushers a dog mum and her trembling poodle out of the room. The dog's nails scratch against the green linoleum floor. "Scotty will be just fine Mrs. Beadle, just keep giving him the antibiotics till the course runs out."

Mrs. Beadle holds Scotty's leash as he scrambles for the door. "Thank you so much doctor."

Bennet waits till she's firmly out the door before turning to face us. It's a subtle power move meant to show us that we're working on his time, not the other way round. It doesn't work of course but the fact that he used it tells me a lot about his character. This is a man who likes to be in charge. He probably gets a thrill out of being a vet and playing savior to all those people.

He strides over to us, straightening the cuffs of his lab coat. Another gesture designed to highlight his authority. This man is a textbook narcissist. "Gentlemen, this is a bit of a surprise. How can I help you?"

I flip my badge again. "Dr. Bennet, I'm Special Agent River Park, this is my colleague, Special Agent Eli March. Is there somewhere we can talk in private?"

"Of course, of course. My office is just through here." He waves an arm and flashes an affable smile that doesn't quiet reach his eyes. He turns to lead the way and I look over my shoulder to check on Freya.

Her head is buried in a pamphlet, but she catches my eye and gives a subtle nod. It's him.

Bennet's office is overly neat even to my standards. In my experience doctors and vets are among the most disorganized of people when it comes to their belongings but everything from the precise rows of folders to the lined-up pencils suggests Bennet isn't as laid back as he's trying to appear.

He rounds the desk and turns to face us. "So, what's this about, Officers?"

"Agents," I correct.

"Oh sorry, I can't say I'm up to scratch on my FBI terminology." He chuckles. "My wife's obsessed with that profiling show, but I must say I prefer something a bit lighter in the evenings."

"Hit a little too close to home, does it?" Eli asks.

Bennet blinks. "Excuse me?"

"Do you know a man named Arthur Maxwell?" I press, getting straight to the point.

A muscle in Bennet's jaw ticks, his smile turning forced. "What's this about, Agent?"

"Answer the question, please."

"Ah, well, I do know him, yes, or rather I did. I haven't seen him since he disappeared." Bennet runs a hand over what's left of his hair. "If this is about the things they say he's done, well, I must admit I find it hard to believe. Maybe I'm wrong, I'm not a profiler after all," he flashes a self-deprecating smile, "but the man I knew, he wouldn't hurt anyone. I don't know where he is if that's why you're here."

"We know where he is," Eli states.

Bennet's bumbling mask slips, his hand tightening around the paper weight on his desk. "You do?"

"He's here in Quantico. At least that's what our two murder victims would suggest."

Bennet regains his composure and shakes his head. "I heard about those poor women on the news. It's terrible. I didn't realize it was the work of the Cross-Cut Killer. How awful." He pauses, as if taking a moment of silence. "I'm still not sure how this led you to me though."

"This is a fairly new practice you have here, how long has it been? Six months? What inspired the move?" I ask.

Bennet's eyes narrow, his hackles obviously raising now it's clear we've looked into him. "My in-laws live out this way. My wife wanted to be closer now her father's fallen ill."

"Must be nice to be somewhere quieter as well. Less chance of any more break-ins."

"I suppose so. I'm sorry Agent, I want to help but I'm really not sure what you're getting at."

My smile is brittle. "I apologize. Let me make things clear. Six years ago, a week before Arthur Maxwell killed and abducted Jennifer Partridge, there was a break in at your veterinary clinic. Four vials of tranquilizer were taken, among other drugs. Now, Maxwell is killing in Quantico. It seems like quite the coincidence that you'd be here too."

Bennet scrunches his face up and shakes his head. He blows out a breath like he's at a loss for words. "Well, I can certainly see why you'd want to check in, but I have nothing to do with those murders. Like I said to the FBI six years ago, it was just a local break-in. One of the addicts from the shelter."

Eli steps forward, planting his hands on Bennet's desk. "But you do know Arthur Maxwell."

Bennet's eyes catch on Eli's hands, and I watch him tense. Apparently, the good doctor doesn't like his space being invaded. "Yes, but I'm pretty sure that's not a crime. I wasn't the only one fooled by Maxwell's façade. If it was a façade that is. I still think you might have the wrong man."

I nod steadily, like he's got me convinced. "The thing is, Colin, I don't like coincidences and there seem to be an awful lot of them around you. We have a witness who can match the times you visited Maxwell to shortly before each of his murders." I pin him with a sharp look. "I don't think there was a break in at your old clinic. I think you took the tranquilizers and gave them to Maxwell, then staged a robbery to cover yourself in case the police came looking."

Bennet loses the innocent act and cocks his head, an amused smile playing at his lips. "That is quite the story, Agent Park. One I seriously doubt any *witness* can corroborate."

I don't bother answering him. I just open the door and

call out into the reception area. "Freya, you can come join us now."

I turn back in time to see Bennet stiffen. When Freya walks into the office he turns as white as his lab coat.

He swallows and tugs at his collar. "Angelica. Or should I say Freya?" He shakes his head, eyebrows raised in shock. "I must say I'm surprised to see you here. And with the FBI? It was only two years ago that you seemed joined at the hip with your father."

I freeze, ice shooting through my veins.

Eli's fingers dig into the wooden desk. He picked up on it too. Bennet just said he'd seen Freya with her father *two years ago*.

Ever so slowly I turn to look at Freya.

She avoids my eyes, staring straight at Bennet. "Time must be getting away from you Uncle Peter," she says, "I haven't seen my father in six years."

Bennet blinks.

My hands drop to the cuffs clipped to my belt. I would deal with Freya later, right now I need to focus on Bennet. "You told us you hadn't seen Maxwell since he went on the run six years ago."

"Lying to a federal officer is a crime, Dr Bennet," Eli adds.

Bennet smiles. He's yet to take his eyes off Freya. "Ah, well, I suppose Angelica is right. I must be getting confused with my dates. I was correct earlier. I haven't seen Maxwell - or his daughter - for six years."

I let my hand come away from the cuffs. He's lying but it still isn't enough to take him in and he knows it. And now I have a bigger problem to deal with. "I see. Well, thank you for your time," I say, cutting the interview short. "We'll be in touch if we have any more questions."

"Of course, let me show you out." Bennet escorts us to the door. He places a hand on Freya's shoulder to stop her. "It was good to see you Angelica and you should know, whether or not your father is guilty of the things they say he is, I'm sure he misses you dearly."

Freya looks sick but I can no longer trust her reactions anymore. To my surprise, it's Eli who takes her arm, pulling her away from Dr Bennet.

"That's it?" Freya asks as we walk back to the car.

"That's it," I say, my voice flat. We climb into the car, Freya sliding into the back with Jude as Eli rounds the hood and I take the driver's seat.

"We barely got any answers," Freya protests.

I twist around in my seat, locking her in place with my gaze. "The only answer I care about right now is how you were with your father two years ago when you claim you haven't seen him since you ran."

She sinks back into her seat and turns away from me, staring out the window.

I turn the engine on and pull away from the vets.

Freya is going to give me answers, whether she wants to or not.

33

FREYA

The last time I was in this interrogation room I picked the lock and fled. The way River's standing in front of the door with his arms crossed tells me he isn't about to forget that. "Is this really necessary?" I ask.

Oz glances at River but carries on setting up the lie detector. He picks up one of the wires and peels back the sticky sheet. "I, uh, I need you to undo your shirt a bit." A blush creeps up under the scruff on his jaw and I find myself curious about Oz once again. He's quiet, doesn't give much away. I'd say he's shy, but it really doesn't translate to the bedroom.

I look up at River from the metal chair I'm sitting on, waiting for an answer but he stays rooted to the spot and stares me down.

I sigh and undo the top two buttons of my shirt.

Oz pulls the material to the side. The back of his fingers brush against my chest. I grit my teeth as he sticks the sensor to my skin, trying not to think about how close his hands are to my breasts. The last thing I need is my arousal spiking on the monitors for everyone to see.

KILLER OF MINE

"Check her hands," Eli says from where he's leaning against the mirrored window. It doesn't bode well for me that we're back in the room they brought me to when I was first arrested.

"Eli, lay off." An edge of frustration leaks into Oz's voice. Half of me is comforted that he clearly doesn't want to be doing this, the other half is just annoyed that he's doing it anyway.

"Check them," Eli presses. "I've seen someone pass one of these by pressing a pin into their thumb to mess with the readings."

I raise both hands, sticking my middle fingers up at Eli. "Happy now?"

Eli's jaw ticks. "Cute. Put them on the table."

The metal surface is cold under my palms and unease creeps up my spine.

River's wrong, I've not told a single lie, but I also haven't told the whole truth. This could end very badly for me.

Oz finishes attaching the sensors and sits down on the other side of the table. He clicks at the laptop a few times then looks over at me. "I need to ask a couple of questions to get your base levels. Answer them truthfully."

I nod.

"What color are your eyes?"

"Green."

"Is Arthur Maxwell your father?"

"Yes."

Oz checks the readings. "Okay, now I need you to tell a lie."

Keep people on edge. Always do the unexpected.

"I have never hurt anyone."

The air sucks out of the room. Three pairs of eyes pin

me in place. I keep my face blank. If they want to know the truth, then I'm not going to sugar coat it. I'll show them the real me.

Maybe it's a good thing we're doing this. My relationship with each of the guys is getting more complicated by the day.

Jude refused to be a part of this interrogation, which I appreciate but he'll still see the results. I don't know whether any of them will feel the same way about me after this. Maybe that's for the best. We should stop before any of us gets too attached.

A small voice in my head whispers it might already be too late for that.

Oz clears his throat, breaking the tension. He nods at River. "We're good to go."

River steps forward and takes the seat next to Oz. "Let's go over what you told us three days ago."

God, has it only been three days?

"Did you kill any of Arthur Maxwell's victims?"

I meet River's eyes. "No."

Oz gives a subtle nod.

"Did you assist in the torture of Maxwell's victims?"

"Yes."

Another nod.

Eli slams his fist against the wall, and I jump at the sound. He storms from the room but not before I catch a glimpse of the torment swirling in his eyes.

Silence settles in his wake.

"Is he okay?" I ask.

River's gaze is cold. "I'm asking the questions."

I push down my concern for Eli and clench my fist. "Get on with it then."

His eyes tighten, his lips a flat line. "You're going to get yourself into trouble, Freya."

I wave my hand at the wires hooked up to my body. "Aren't I already?"

River lifts his chin. "You tell me."

I let out a dry chuckle. "Ask your questions."

"When was the last time you saw your father?"

"Six years ago, before the car crash I used to fake my death."

River looks to Oz who scans the readings before confirming I'm telling the truth.

For once, River's composure slips and he sighs, relaxing back in his chair.

"Happy now?" I ask.

"Then why did Colin Bennet say he'd seen you with your father two years ago?"

I slow my breathing and picture an image of water lapping at the beach. "I don't know," I say. I have to stop myself from watching Oz. I'm not technically lying. I don't know why Bennet said what he did, not for sure.

Oz nods and my eyes close in relief before I can stop them. When I open them back up River's sharp gaze is narrowed on me. *Shit.*

"Let's try that again." He asks the question two more times, but the meditation techniques Carmen taught me pay off and each time shows the same result. But River is nothing if not determined.

He keeps pressing with the questions, going over everything I've told them in the last few days with a fine-tooth comb.

My eyes are blurring at the edges by the time Jude bursts through the door.

"That's enough, River," he snaps.

"She's still hiding something," River argues.

Jude sighs and rubs the back of his neck. "I know." He turns his attention to me and my heart squeezes painfully. It shouldn't hurt that he doesn't believe me. He's right not to. I can't be upset when I'm the one keeping things from them.

I look away and Oz's leg touches mine under the table.

"It's been two hours," Jude says. "You're not going to learn anything more. Not like this."

Something about his tone has me worrying how exactly Jude *does* plan on getting the information out of me.

I turn back to face him and the dark heat in his eyes sends a thrill down my spine. Jude may be angry but he's not giving up on me.

34

FREYA

I ease the door to River's home office closed behind me.
I'm greeted with dark oak and shelves neatly lined with books on criminology and psychology. The curtains are pulled closed, but his desk is lit with a warm glow from a filigreed lamp.

I know I'm pushing my luck. It was only yesterday River had me hooked up to a lie detector and now I'm breaking into his office.

I walk over to the desk and rest my hand on the back of the old-fashioned leather chair. I tug on the top drawer. Locked. I try the others and find the same result. I guess I'm doing this the hard way. I pick out a paperclip from a pot on the desk and re-shape the metal with my fingers.

I'm inserting the makeshift pick into the drawer's lock when the door swings open.

River stops when he sees me, then steps further into the room and closes the door. "Care to explain what, exactly, you are doing in my office?"

I straighten up, folding the paperclip into the palm of

my hand. It doesn't take a genius to figure out what I was doing though.

Yesterday made it clear he doesn't trust me and after this, I doubt I'll be able to sneak back in here, so I shrug and go for the truth. "I want my phone." The hospital released my belongings into River's custody and he's yet to give it back to me.

River's Oxford's clack against the wooden floor as he prowls over to me.

I go to move but he comes up behind me, trapping me between his body and the desk as he pulls out a key.

He unlocks the drawer and slides it open. The wood presses into my thighs, giving me no choice but to step back into his chest. Even through our clothes his warmth heats me, and I realize quite how tall he is. My head doesn't even come up to his chin.

River takes my phone out of the drawer. His arm circles my chest as he holds it out for me. "You could have just asked."

I take the phone from his hand, but River shows no sign of moving. I twist my neck to look up at him and he nods at the phone.

"Go ahead," he says. "I assume you want to contact someone."

I turn back to the phone and unlock the screen. "I thought it would be useful to have a look over Camilla's file again. See whether we could find a connection between her and Posy." It's not entirely a lie. Learning more about the victims could help us locate my father.

I click on my chat with Luke and start typing. "Luke, my partner has the original report, the one with our interview notes on it." I finish typing out my message and go to press send.

"Wait." River's hand squeezes my hip. He bends down and reads the message over my shoulder.

Freya: Hey L, can you send over Camilla's file?

"Okay," River says.

I will my fingers not to shake as I press send. I get a response straight away. "He says there's too much to scan, he'll come round to drop them off in person. Is that okay?" I grit my teeth at having to ask for permission.

"Yes, give him the address and then put the phone down."

I do as he says. "Do I get to keep it?" I ask after putting the phone on the desk.

River's hand travels from my hip to my stomach and his fingers dip under my top. "If you're good." His thumb strokes back and forth over the sliver of bare skin between the bandages and my pants. "Did you let Oz check your wounds this morning?"

My core clenches at his touch and I lean back into his chest. "Yes. He says they're healing nicely."

"Good girl." River twines his free hand in my hair and draws my head to the side, exposing the column of my neck. He bends down and whispers his lips in slow kisses over the bare skin there and onto my shoulder.

My eyes flutter and I swallow air, my chest rising with unsteady breaths. "What are you doing?"

River may have teased. Flirted. But he's never actually crossed the line and I didn't think he would.

He hums against my skin and the vibrations shoot to my core. "Experimenting," he says.

"How romantic." I'm aiming for sarcasm, but my voice comes out husky and aroused.

River undoes the button of my jeans and I jolt a little.

"Shh." He lifts me, spinning us both around so the desk is behind us. "Hands on the wall," he orders.

My hands come up of their own volition, the dark paint cool beneath my heated skin.

River presses the length of his body against my back, crowding me.

I should feel trapped, vulnerable, but instead I feel myself undoing. The stress, the fear, the constant guilt - they all slip away as River surrounds me so completely.

He slides his hand beneath my panties, and his fingers stroke between my soaked folds.

I buck against his touch. Apparently, he doesn't like that.

He hooks a leg in front of mine, locking me in place.

I let my head rest against the wall and a soft laugh tumbles from my lips. "You are such a control freak."

River stills for a moment then he thrusts two fingers inside of me. Pain burns at the edges of pleasure as he curls his fingers and hits a spot that has me seeing stars. His teeth tug at my earlobe. "You were saying?"

I no longer have the ability to say anything.

River picks up the pace, his fingers hitting that spot inside of me over and over as his thumb comes down to push against my clit.

"River." I breathe out his name. "Please."

He slows down.

"Don't stop."

"Shh." River tortures me with his fingers. Each gentle stroke sends ripples of pleasure through me but it's not enough. His touch drives my need to an almost unbearable point and my nails claw against the wall.

"Faster, please River."

He ignores me, his thumb hovering above my clit, just out of reach. "I think we need to set some ground rules, darling. As sweet as it is to hear you beg," he leans close, "You call me *sir* when I'm inside of you."

Heat flushes through me and I scream in frustration. "No."

His thumb pushes hard against my clit. "Yes."

I press my lips together, refusing to give him that much control over me.

River takes my silence as a challenge and picks up the pace again.

I revel in the sensations, my core coiling tighter and tighter as he brings me to the edge. My breathing comes faster. Tingles flood through my body. I press my hips forward into River's hold but it's still not enough. He's holding back.

"River, please."

He stops.

I moan, squeezing my eyes shut. His sexual torture is driving me insane and I finally cave. "Please. Sir."

He presses a kiss to the top of my head and starts moving again. "Good girl."

Heat flushes through me at those two words. My body climbs back up to breaking point and just as I'm trembling on the very edge River drops his lips to my ear.

"What are you hiding from me, Freya?"

I freeze.

He circles my clit. "Tell me what I want to know, and I'll give you what you need."

I cry out and tear my hands from the wall to push him away. I spin around and shove against his solid chest but he doesn't budge. "You son of a bitch!" I go to hit him again and River grabs my wrists, securing them above my head with one hand. I struggle but his hold is iron-clad.

Eventually, I collapse against the wall, trying to catch my breath and make sense of what just happened. "*Experimenting*. Fuck you." A tear runs down my cheek and I hope to God it's too dark for River to see. "What was the hypothesis, *Sir*? If I get Freya horny enough maybe she'll tell me the truth?"

River sighs. "Yes." His free hand comes up and the pad of his thumb brushes away my tear. So much for it going unnoticed. "I concede that perhaps this was a mistake."

"Let me go."

River shakes his head. "You're all worked up, darling. It would be cruel for me to leave you like this."

My eyes widen in disbelief. "What you just did was cruel." I swallow and shrug my shoulders as best I can, trying to appear cavalier. "Besides, I don't need you. I can just go find Jude or Oz. Maybe both. I'm sure they'd be more than happy to help me out. Hell, even Eli might be up for a quick fuck."

I yelp as River spins me around to face the wall again and a sharp sting smacks against my ass. My mouth falls open. He just spanked me.

"Careful, Freya. If you act like a brat, I'll treat you like one."

"With your bare hands, right?" I snark, over my shoulder.

River's laugh is low and delicious, and I hate my body for responding to it. He rubs his palm over where he just smacked. "I'm starting to think I might need to get out my crop for you."

Before I can tell him exactly what I think of that idea someone knocks on the door.

"This better be important," River snaps.

"Some detective is here. He said Freya asked him to bring over Camilla's case files," Jude says from the other side of the door.

River sighs. "I guess your punishment will have to wait." He loosens his grip and I free myself. Before I can grab it, he picks up my phone and slides it into his pocket. "I think I'll keep hold of this for now."

I grit my teeth and walk past him but turn back when I reach the door, my hand resting on the handle. "You act like you're so calm and controlled but you're fooling yourself if you think what just happened here was nothing more than an *experiment*."

It takes two to create the fire we just did. I felt him harden against my back, heard his breathing turn ragged. River's not as unaffected as he likes to pretend and that is the only thing right now stopping me from leaving and going after my dad by myself.

Well, that, and the damn anklet.

35

RIVER

I do not make mistakes. I wait and I plan, and I don't let emotions get in the way. So why the hell am I all twisted up inside because I had Freya trembling beneath my fingers?

It was supposed to be an act, nothing more. A way to get her to talk. Except she's too strong for that and I'm the weak fool who just gave himself a taste of the forbidden.

I can still smell her on me and it's taking everything I have not to storm over to where she's talking with Luke and drag her back inside.

He arrived five minutes ago, Camilla's file in hand and asked to speak to Freya in private. She knew damn well I couldn't say no when, to the outside world, Freya is merely consulting on a case.

Jude joins me by the front window at the bottom of the stairs and peers out at Freya and her partner. *Ex-partner.*

"Would it help if I told you he was gay?" Jude asks.

I work my jaw, determined not to let my emotions leak out. "Why would that help?"

Jude stares pointedly at where my hands grip the windowsill. "Your jealousy is showing, River." He grins like a small child. "You like her. Despite your whole 'she's off limits' rule."

I cut him a look. "You mean the rule you've so flagrantly ignored?"

"Oh yeah? What happened in your office just now?"

"That's not the same," I deny. "It was an interrogation technique. Nothing more."

Jude doesn't answer and I turn away from the window to find him staring at me, his mouth parted in horror.

I close my eyes. "I may have miscalculated."

Jude runs a hand over his afro. "Jesus fucking Christ. No wonder she looked so pissed. I know technically I'm the genius here, but you'd think even someone as emotionally stunted as you would realize seducing someone is not a morally okay way to get information."

I tuck my hands into the pockets of my suit pants, so he won't see them trembling. My voice stays cool. "Not pulling any punches I see."

"You hurt Freya," he snaps. "What do you expect?"

He's right and the guilt sits like a bad meal at the bottom of my stomach. It's the same feeling I'd get after my mum told me to knock on someone's door and ask for help. The same prickling sensation on my neck and the same flush of shame as I'd ask to use their toilet only to unlock the window so my dad could break in later that night.

When my parents finally got walked away in cuffs, I told myself I'd never break another rule. I'd never manipulate or lie or con anyone ever again but that's exactly what I just did to Freya.

She was right to be mad, and I need to take my own advice.

"I'll apologize," I say. "Freya *is* off limits. It won't happen again."

Jude shakes his head. "It never would have happened in the first place if you weren't attracted to her. You like her but you're trying not to because you don't know how to trust."

His words punch into me. "I trust you. And Eli and Oz."

"Do you though?" Jude fiddles with one of the stones he keeps in his pockets, turning it over in his fingers. "You know everything there is to know about the three of us but Freya's got secrets. She'll share them when she's ready. Until then you either trust her or you don't."

Outside, Freya places her hand on top of Luke's. I wonder whether I can have him transferred. I make a mental note to deepen my research on him, then I turn to face Jude. "Are you done with the sage advice?"

"One more thing." Jude nods towards the window. "The woman you're so desperately trying to control just walked out of sight."

I snap my gaze back to the window. Freya and Luke are gone. With her anklet on she can't get far but I find I don't like having her out of my sight.

I stride past Jude and head for the front door, thinking up an excuse I can use to get her back inside as I go.

Maybe Freya's right. I am a control freak. But life is chaotic and unfair. If I don't control it, everything will collide and I'll be that lost little boy again, watching his parents get driven away in the back of a police car.

I won't let that happen.

36

FREYA

It feels good to see Luke again, like some sort of normalcy is returning to the crash course my life has become.

I wish we could just shoot the breeze for a while longer, but I don't know how much time River will give us. "Did you bring it?" I ask.

Luke nods and reaches for his pocket.

A place my hand on his, stopping him. "Not here." My eyes flick to the window. Even through the glass, River's stare has goose bumps pricking my skin.

Luke's sharp gaze analyzes the situation. "What's going on, Freya? Do you need me to get you out of here?"

I shake my head. "It's complicated, but I'm fine. Thank you for coming."

"Hey, just because you ditched me for the FBI doesn't mean I'm going to ignore an SOS."

I give him a wry smile. "I'm just glad you remembered."

Early on when Luke and I were made partners we got into a sticky situation during an undercover op. After, we made a series of codes based around our names. Each nickname means different things. "L", the nickname I used in my text to Luke means: 'All okay, need burner phone'. I didn't exactly think I'd be using it to get one over on the FBI, but I'm no longer convinced I can trust River to help me catch my dad. Not before he puts me in a 6x8 cell at least.

I sneak another glance at the window. River's distracted talking to Jude so I take Luke's arm and guide him further down the street. "Come on." It's fairly quiet out here and the cars parked on the paved drives shield us from view.

"Seriously, do you need to get out of here? Because I parked down the road in case we needed to pull a Bonnie and Clyde."

I stop walking and tug up my trouser leg. "As tempting as that sounds my fancy new piece of jewelry might get in the way."

Luke's eyes widen. "Is that a tracking anklet?" He looks back at the house. "What the hell is going on, Freya?"

I cover up the anklet again. "I can't explain. I'm sorry, I know it's not fair. I wasn't even supposed to show you the anklet, but I'm fed up with lying to everyone."

Luke catches his lip between his teeth then sighs. "Is this because you're Maxwell's daughter?"

I gape up at him.

He rolls his eyes. "I'm a detective, Freya. You're the right age. You've told me nothing about your childhood and you have a weird obsession with the Maxwell case. I put two and two together a while ago."

I press my lips together and fight back the tears

pricking my eyes. "Thank you. For never saying anything."

Luke takes out the burner phone and slips it inside Camilla's case file before handing the folder over to me. "You're my partner. I've got your back."

I angle myself away from the house and use my body to shield my movements as I transfer the phone from the folder and into my bra.

The second I turn back around the front door opens and River storms out. He glowers at me like I've committed yet another crime by moving out of his sight.

"I better go." I take one last look at Luke as River strides over to us. "I'm going to catch him. Maxwell," I say.

Luke nods and rocks back on his heels. "I know you will just... be careful, okay?"

I say goodbye to Luke and brush past River before he reaches us. "Don't worry," I say, "Your asset is still here."

River scowls and follows me back into the house.

Inside, the five of us go over Camilla's file, looking for any connections between her and Posy. We find nothing. It's a good couple of hours before I'm able to head to my room and get some time to myself.

Once the door's closed behind me I take out the burner phone and snap a photo of the tracker anklet.

Always have an escape route.

I type in the one number I have committed to memory and send the image to Carmen. If anyone can figure out how to get the tracker off, it's her.

37

ELI

Jude's making us play happy fucking family. It's something he does every now and then when the cases get hard. Pizza and a games night. No work talk allowed.

I sprawl out on the armchair and take another swig from my beer.

I think he started them for Oz. The online world is a dark place and Oz can get lost in it. He goes quiet, quieter than normal. I don't blame him; he's seen some messed up shit, but Jude's like a goddamn golden retriever puppy, dropping a ball at your feet until you come play with him. So, I'm used to these games' nights. What I'm not used to is Freya being a part of them.

We're in the midst of a game of Monopoly and rather aptly, Freya's in jail. She leans over the coffee table and throws the dice, rolling yet another double. She grins and moves her little metal top hat out of jail.

"Apparently your knack for escaping prison translates to the game world too."

She cuts her eyes to me, and I can't decide whether I

feel bad or whether I like seeing her fire. She brings out the worst in me but I'm starting to realize I don't entirely hate that. Given how much she unnerves me it's only fair I return the favor.

Freya gets over my little jab too soon for my liking, grinning and curling her fingers for money when River lands on her property.

None of us have ever beaten River at Monopoly. He's got a brain made for strategy but Freya's putting up a good fight. She's trying to get Jude to form a coalition with her, pointing to each of her delicate fingers in turn as she checks off her reasons.

I'm not sure Jude's even listening. He's just watching her lips move as she speaks. Dusty pink against smooth cream skin.

Oz shoves a bowl of popcorn into my stomach. "You're staring," he mutters.

I give him the finger before stuffing a handful of popcorn into my mouth.

My game plan is to exclusively buy up properties that Freya wants so she can't get full color sets. It's petty but I'm chasing the small flush of satisfaction I get every time I take away something she wants. My mind runs away from me, imagining her spread out on my bed, tied to the headboard, and screaming bloody murder at me because I won't let her come. I could edge her all night and it still wouldn't be punishment enough. Not that she knows what she's done.

The dice clatter against the board bringing me out of my head. River buys yet another hotel and in the next move Freya lands on it. She steadily counts out the money she owes, careful not to give him the satisfaction of reacting. Something happened between the two of them and for once I might not be the only one in the room Freya's mad at.

It's not until forty minutes later that she finally breaks. Oz, Jude, and I are all bankrupt, but Freya's been hanging in there, the luck of a cat keeping her from landing on the deluge of properties River now owns. Her fortune runs out when she comes to a stop on River's most expensive property.

River smirks. "Face it, darling, I win." He goes to take off the houses from Freya's last remaining spaces and she lunges across the coffee table.

"Don't you dare," she says but her threat loses its edge when Jude catches her around the stomach and pulls her back onto the sofa. Her t-shirt rides up and Jude's fingers find her belly. She squeals, her legs kicking until Oz traps them across his lap, a grin chasing away the shadows from his eyes.

Freya's laugh sends blood rushing to her cheeks and her fiery hair tangles around her face like a lioness' mane.

My cock hardens beneath my jeans, and I curse it to high heaven. It would be easier to hate her if she weren't so darn gorgeous. Her smile is infectious. Even River, the most stoic man I know, is hiding a grin behind his fingers as he takes a sip of Cognac.

He flicks one of Freya's little green houses up in the air and catches it.

Jude's still tickling Freya and she finally relents. "Fine, fine. You win. I surrender."

The mood shifts at her words, the room electrified with sexual tension.

Freya falls quiet as three pairs of heated eyes zero in on her. Four if you count me.

Freya swallows.

Given his off-limits mandate, I expect River to be the one to put a stop to whatever the fuck this is but it's Oz who clears his throat.

Jude blinks and lets go of Freya, subtly adjusting himself as she sits back up.

Freya brushes loose popcorn crumbs off her lap. "I, uh, should probably go get some sleep. This was fun though. Thank you."

She stands up but hesitates before leaving. "I don't remember the last time I hung out with people like this." Her smile is sad. "Actually, I'm not sure I ever have." She walks away before any of us can figure out how to respond.

Guilt twinges under my skin. I don't like the reminder that though Freya may be a criminal, she's a victim too.

We clear up in silence, each of us stewing in our own thoughts. I'm stacking the glasses in the dishwasher when Jude decides to share his with me.

"You need to apologize to her."

The glass clatters against another as it slips from my fingers a little too soon.

"I get why you're mad, I do. But you don't understand what she's been through."

Something in his voice has me looking up from the dishwasher. "What *has* she been through?"

He shakes his head. "It's not mine to share but trust me Eli, whatever wrong she's done, she's already paid the price."

I run a hand through my hair, wishing I had my hat on to hide behind. "I don't know how to talk to her. To *be* with her."

"She wants the same thing you do. She might be the only one who can make sure we get it. But I've got a bad feeling." Jude puts his hand in his pocket, turning his stones over between his fingers. "If we push her away, she's going to run."

Oz joins us and takes over stacking the dishwasher. "We'll finish up here." The words 'go talk to her' are left unsaid and it occurs to me that maybe this game night wasn't for Oz, but for me.

I go upstairs and rap my knuckles against Freya's door.

"Come in," she calls, her voice muted by the wood. She does a double take when she sees it's me. "Oh, I thought you were Jude."

"Sorry to disappoint."

"Yeah, you really should be." She crosses her arms, but her words have no heat.

I shut the door behind me and lean against it.

The guest room has never really been used before. The only one of us with family that might visit is Oz and he tries to keep them as far away from this world as possible. I'm used to it just being this empty room but somehow Freya has filled it. A hairbrush and a tub of body cream sit next to her glass of water on the bedside table and some of her clothes are strewn over the end of the bed. She feels at home here.

I clear my throat and drag my gaze back over to Freya. "I did actually come here to apologize. The way I treated you in the hall the other day was not okay."

Her breath leaves her in a rush, and she sits down on the end of her bed. "Oh yeah, what about all the other times?"

I dip my head. "I'm angry. I...have a right to be. But I put my hands on you. I crossed a line that I never thought I would cross and for that I am truly sorry."

She watches me, not saying anything. Then she turns to look out the window, the stars white sparks against the dark sky. She shrugs a little. "I didn't say no. And I don't quite remember but I think I might have tried to hit you."

The air huffs out of me. The knot inside my chest I've been carrying since that day unravels. "You did."

She turns back to face me. "Then I guess I'm sorry too." She stands up and crosses the room till we're only a foot apart. "Will you tell me why you're so angry?"

I take her in. My eyes trace from her bare feet, over her sleep shorts and her oversized t-shirt and stop at her delicate face. She looks so innocent like this. You'd never think she once took a knife and carved into flesh. "No," I say.

She nods, like she knew that's what my answer would be. "You should probably go then."

My jaw tightens. "What if I don't want to?"

She bites her lip. "You do. You may be sorry, but you still don't like me."

I push away from the door and step into Freya's space, pulling her lip from between her teeth with my thumb.

She blinks up at me and I lean down till my face is inches from hers. "I like you too much." I thread my hand through her wild hair and tug her head back till my lips whisper against hers. "I hate how much I like you."

Freya's breath shakes. She licks her lips, and her tongue catches the edge of mine.

I almost groan out loud.

"Why?" she asks.

My hand tightens in her hair and her pupils dilate. "Because liking you," I say, "is the biggest fucking betrayal in the world."

Freya places her palm on my chest, her eyes creasing. "To who?"

I suck in a breath, not liking how my heart's tripping in my chest. I press my hips into Freya's and spin us both around until she's backed up against the door. I push my hand, still locked around her hair, against the wood, trapping her head to the door. "That's none of your fucking business."

She opens her mouth to respond but before she can, I kiss her. Her nails dig in through my shirt, but she doesn't push me away and that tells me everything I need to know.

"Besides," I say pulling back, "I don't think you want me to like you." She opens her mouth to speak but I don't give her a chance. I crash my lips back against hers in a violent kiss.

She matches me stroke for stroke, our tongues battling it out for dominance. She's not going to win.

I switch which hand is holding her hair and shove my fingers underneath the elastic waist of her shorts. We both groan as I find her heat. I've got two fingers inside of her before she pulls away from the kiss, panting.

"What are you talking about?" she asks.

"You've got Jude," I say, slowing my pace and curling my fingers back and forth. "He gives you softness, protection." I move my hand to her neck and collar her, squeezing just enough so she can feel the pressure. "River needs control. He'll set the rules."

I drop my eyes and watch as I pull my fingers out. They're coated in her juices. I lift them to her lips. "Oz likes to watch, choreograph, but he's gentle too." I slide my fingers inside her mouth, staring at her till she swirls her tongue around them, licking them clean.

My cock is rock hard, pulsing against the zip of my jeans. I'm not sure whether this woman is angel or demon. A soft pop fills the air as my fingers slide out of her mouth.

"What will *you* give me?" she asks, her voice husky.

My thoughts darken and I squeeze her neck harder as my hand drops, and I shove three fingers into her sweet pussy. "Pain," I say.

She chokes on her moan, her eyes tightening from the burn of my fingers.

I pump all three in and out of her, the anger I feel pushing my touch to the edge of violence.

I place my thumb on the underside of her chin and force her head back. "Fear," I breathe against her lips.

She blinks rapidly, her mouth stretching open.

"The thrill of not quite knowing if I'll go too far." I withdraw from her cunt and press one finger against her rosebud.

She goes still.

I hold her steady. "You've got darkness in you, Freya. Sweet and soft alone isn't going to do it for you. You need more. You need m-". I break off my words and pull away from her.

She sags against the door, and I stumble back another step. We stare at each other, both too rattled for words.

My chest heaves with each breath and I'm so turned on it hurts but I can't do this. I can't. Not with her. It's one thing to find a release, but where I'd been going with my little speech didn't feel like just sex.

I cannot have feelings for Freya.

She twists away from the door and buries her forehead against the wall. "Go," she chokes out.

So I do.

38

FREYA

I stay with my forehead pressed to the wall until my breathing finally calms and my legs stop trembling.

I want Eli to storm back inside. To collar me, throw me down on the bed and take me hard and rough. I also never want to see him again.

My lips tingle. I can taste him on my tongue. Desire edged with anger. It's intoxicating.

I drag myself away from the wall and drink from the glass on my bedside table.

The water's cool but it does nothing to break the heat writhing through my body. I draw the curtains, get into bed and stare at the ceiling. I want to know who Eli thinks he's betraying. I want to know why he hates me so much. I want to be able to stop thinking about him.

I close my eyes but it's no good. Eli's words, his touch, sparked a need deep inside me and I'm too far gone to show any restraint. I curse his name and let my hand drift down to my hips and underneath my shorts.

I'm still wet. My fingers find that small bundle of nerves, but no matter what I do I can't seem to find release. It's like my body got tempted by the devil himself and now it's demanding nothing less.

I groan and curl up on my side.

A soft knock has me turning towards the door and I scold my traitorous heart for hoping it's Eli.

It's not. Jude eases the door open and pokes his head inside. "Are you okay?" The soft yellow lighting from the hall glows against his skin.

"No," I confess.

Jude opens the door wider, a single eyebrow arching as he takes in the rumpled sheets. I have no doubt my skin is flushed, my eyes wild.

"Tell me he didn't leave you hanging."

My mouth parts. I don't know how to answer that. He doesn't seem upset but...

Jude closes the door and comes to kneel on my bed. He peels the covers back from my body, his eyes locking on the way my nipples pebble under my shirt. He brushes the backs of his fingers over the tips, and I jolt. A deep moan tumbles from my lips.

"Poor thing," Jude says, "he's left you in a right state."

Before I can stop him, Jude lifts my shirt, bunching it up under my chin. He dips his head and takes a nipple in his mouth, sucking hard. Sensation shoots straight to my core, and I arch into his hold.

"Jude," I pant. I push at his shoulders till he sits up and almost laugh at the sulky look on his face. Then I remember what I was going to say. "Eli and I, we kissed."

Jude's face is blank.

"We did more than that," I add.

"Good." Jude smirks. "I might be a little jealous if he'd managed to get you this worked up with just a kiss." He dives back down, squeezing my other breast and pinching the nipple between his teeth. *God this man is trying to kill me.*

I thread my fingers through his curls and drag his head up. "Aren't you mad?"

Jude's face softens. "Short answer: no." He trails a hand down my stomach, sending shivers skating across my bare skin. "I'm a little too busy to give you the long answer right now but I promise we'll talk after." His fingers dip between my folds. "Now lie back like a good girl and let me take care of you." He flicks my clit and I lose my grip on his hair.

His words should be patronizing. My pride bristles at being told to be a good girl but I can't deny the way my core clenches.

I don't think I've ever been taken care of before. I'm not sure I realized how much I yearned for just that until these guys came into my life.

I let my head drop onto the pillow and watch as Jude slowly drags my shorts down my legs and flicks them to the side.

He places a soft kiss at the top of my mound before coming back up.

I lift myself a little as he pulls the shirt over my head. He throws that to the floor too and then I'm lying beneath him, completely naked.

Oz took the bandages off this morning and nasty grazes cover my left side, but Jude doesn't seem to care. He takes my breasts in his hands again, playing with my nipples, then pinching until my back arches.

My core pulses and I squirm, lifting my hips as I try to find the pressure I'm desperate for. "Please, Jude. Please."

"Shhh, I know what you need." Jude unbuttons his

jeans and pushes them down over his hips. He groans as he pulls himself from his boxers and strokes the length of his cock.

I try to reach for him, but he swats my hand away. "Nuh-uh, what did I say?"

"Lie back," I repeat.

He raises a single brow, waiting.

"Like a good girl." I sigh and settle back against the bed.

"Better." Jude lifts me by the hips. He pulls me down the bed until the insides of my thighs are pressed up against his hips.

I gasp at the sensation. I try to move against him, but he holds me still. "Your shirt," I say, "take it off."

Jude smirks. He leans over me and takes my bottom lip between his teeth, giving me the slightest nip. "Stop trying to top from the bottom," he scolds, but then he sits back and pulls off his shirt.

His skin is so smooth compared to mine. The ridges of his muscles define his stomach like they're carved from marble, and a fine scattering of dark hair covers his chest.

I reach out again and this time he lets me. He's so hard. I brush my thumb over his nipple.

He shivers.

I grin and do it again and then I get bold. My hand drops to his cock and I draw my fist up, reveling in how something so hard can feel so soft. My fingers hit something even harder, and my eyes widen. I brush my thumb over the metal bar near the tip of Jude's cock. It's about an inch wide, a curved barbell piercing. "Oh my god," I whisper.

Jude smirks. "Trust me, Angel, you'll love it."

Shock has my heart beating faster. Out of all the

guys, Jude is the last one I'd expect to be pierced. Eli, sure, but not Jude. I stroke his shaft, playing with the piercing.

"That's enough of that now." Jude grabs my wrist. He picks up my other hand and presses them both into the mattress either side of my head. "Keep them there," he orders.

I do what he says, staying perfectly still as Jude slips on a condom and lines himself up.

He cups my face in his hand and brushes his thumb across my cheek. "You ready?"

I nod.

"I need your words, babygirl. I'm about to ruin this pretty little pussy so I need to know you're on board with that."

"Yes," I say. "Fuck me, Jude."

His gaze darkens and he thrusts into me.

My eyes roll back in my head, and I gasp. I'm so wet he slides all the way in, to the hilt, and I've never felt so full before. His piercing hits my g-spot and a delicious burn tingles from where I'm stretched around him.

He holds still for a moment, waiting for my eyes to find him before he starts to move. Each thrust sends waves of pleasure from the top of my head to the tip of my toes.

Jude said to keep my hands against the bed, but he never said anything about my legs. I cross them behind his back and pull him closer, lusting for more.

He gets the message and pounds into me harder. His grip tightens around my hips so hard I think I'll bruise. He takes full control, moving me against him in a relentless rhythm. It's not as vicious as I imagine Eli would be, but Jude leaves no doubt that he's the one in charge right now.

"God, you're beautiful. You feel so good, Angel. Look at you, taking me so well."

His praise ripples through me, and I squeeze around his cock. "More, Jude, please. I need more."

"Shh. Hush now. I've got you, babygirl." His hand drops to my pussy, and he grinds the heel of his palm against my clit. He's so deep inside me. Every thrust pushes my core against his palm and senseless moans fall from my lips.

"That's it, come for me Angel, let me feel you fall apart."

My chest heaves in heavy pants. My eyelids flicker. Every part of me coils so tight I feel like I'm about to explode. "Jude–Please, I need... I'm going to-"

He steals my words with a kiss. "I know, I know. Just let go, baby. I've got you."

His words send me cascading over the edge and I come harder than I ever have before. Pleasure pulses in my veins as Jude guides me through my orgasm, chasing his own release. Aftershocks pulse through me and he mutters a curse before burying himself deep and following me over the edge.

Our heavy breaths fill the room as we come down from up high. The weight of Jude's body grounds me.

My fingers find his hair and I play with the coils. "Well, that was pretty incredible," I say once I've regained the ability to form sentences.

Jude chuckles. "*You* are incredible. Stay there." He gently pulls out of me and deals with the condom before getting back into bed and gathering me in his arms.

We lie there, simply existing with each other for a while before my brain starts to whir.

"What did you mean about the long answer?" I ask.

"Is it like with Oz? How you don't mind sharing?" My words keep tumbling out. "Because you should know I've also kissed River. Or he's kissed me. I didn't know whether I should say. We never said this was exclusive but-"

Jude kisses me.

"Do you just do that to shut me up now?"

Jude grins. "Calm down, Freya. To answer your question, yes, it is like with Oz. We probably should have talked to you about it sooner, but I didn't want to freak you out."

"Okay." I draw out the word.

Jude shifts us till he's leaning against the headboard and I'm resting against his chest. "A long time ago, the four of us decided we didn't want to have serious relationships. We'd seen too many of our colleagues' marriages fall apart because of the job we do."

"So, you're saying you just want a fling?" Hurt curdles inside of me even though it has no right to be there. Before I can spiral Jude smacks my butt.

"Will you shut up and listen, please?"

I stick my tongue out at him but stay quiet.

"We knew there'd be a time when casual would no longer be enough for us so one night, when we were kind of drunk, we came up with a plan. One woman for all four of us. That way, between us, we'd always have time for her, and if one of us died on the job, she'd never be left alone."

I push up against his chest so I can face him. "That's kind of morbid, you know?"

"Welcome to the Serial Crimes Unit, Angel," he says dryly.

"It's also kind of sweet." I trace patterns across his chest as I digest what he's just told me.

It's not like I haven't heard of polyamory. I like to read a good romance as much as the next girl, but that's all it's been. Fiction. Considering it in real life feels far more complicated. "So, what does that mean for us, exactly?"

Jude rolls me onto my back and holds himself above me. "It means you're not just mine. You're ours."

My body heats again at his words but it's not that simple. "You say that like I don't have a choice."

Jude shakes his head. "You've got a choice. But you should bear in mind I am very good at getting what I want."

I press my hands to his chest but can't bring myself to push him away. "What about River and Eli? They hardly seem like they'd be on board with this."

"They'll come around. Both of them want you Freya, they just need to get over themselves and realize you're it for us."

I feel like I should say something, but my thoughts are a mess. Jude is talking like this is forever, but I've never been that good with permanence. Never let anyone get that close. Let alone four people.

I can't deny how the guys make me feel though. Lying here with Jude, I'm at peace in a way I'm not sure I ever have been before. River and his team are bossy and protective and infuriating but for the first time ever, I feel like I belong.

"You don't have to make a decision now. Just think on it, okay?"

I nod my head. "Okay."

Jude kisses me and resettles us on the bed, making me the little spoon.

It doesn't take long for him to fall asleep and I'm well on my way to dreamland when the burner phone Luke gave me buzzes. I lean over and take it out from the bedside drawer. A message from Carmen flashes on the screen.

Unknown: Sorted, let me know when and where.

I swallow. The tracker weighs down my ankle like it's pinning me to the bed.

Jude stirs.

I shove the phone back inside the drawer and snuggle up against him. Not for the first time, I wish my life wasn't so goddamn complicated.

39

ELI

I turn up at the morgue with two cups of coffee in hand and my Stetson pulled low over my face. My neck is surprisingly ache free, but I barely slept last night and it shows. I was seconds away from doing something stupid, like going back and begging Freya for forgiveness, when I saw Jude slip into her room.

I spent the rest of the night imagining what the two of them were doing and being equal parts jealous, angry, and turned on.

I turn the corner and force a smile across my face. "Knock knock," I say, leaning against the open door.

Eva strips off her gloves and rushes over to me. "I could kiss you," she says, grabby hands reaching for one of the coffees. She takes a long sip and hums in satisfaction.

Eva is undeniably attractive. Gorgeous black hair she keeps braided in cornrows and a body with curves for miles. Normally a sound like that from her lips would have me hot as hell, instead it's got me thinking about Freya and what it would take to make her moan like that.

"You're here early." Eva's voice drags my attention

back to her. She takes another sip of coffee, shrewd eyes analyzing me over the top of the cup.

I shrug, stroll into the room and kick back against the counter. "I had some time."

The morgue is a cold place with tiled walls, linoleum floor and an entire wall of refrigerated drawers where the bodies are stored. I wonder again what the fuck it says about me that I feel relaxed here.

"And who doesn't like to spend their free time watching an autopsy?"

I grin, ignoring the dripping sarcasm. "Exactly."

Eva rolls her eyes and snaps on a fresh set of gloves.

She pulls the sheet covering Posy Winter's body back. I remove my hat and take a moment to imagine her as she would have been, before the brutality of her murder. Raw anger coils in my gut. I'm well versed in keeping it contained, at playing the light-hearted flirt, but that all goes out the window when it comes to this case. The past few days I've been like a different person and it's starting to wear on me.

I close my eyes and fight against the feeling that I've failed Posy. That I've failed all the ones who came before her.

"Come on Posy," Eva whispers, "Help me catch the son of a bitch who did this to you."

I open my eyes.

Eva gives Posy's hand a light squeeze before beginning her observations.

Slowly, the heaviness of the situation lifts, and Eva and I fall into familiar chatter. She lasts a full five minutes before asking the question that's on her mind. "So, you going to tell me about her?"

"Her who?" I say, because apparently, I'm twelve years old.

Eva flashes me a look that says 'seriously.' "Her, the cute detective who's supposedly consulting on the case."

"She's not cute. She's vicious." I have to consciously relax my grip so I don't crush the take-away coffee cup.

"I thought you liked women with claws."

"Yeah, when they scratch my back, not when they tear my fucking soul to shreds."

Eva straightens up, a stunned smile gracing her face. "You actually like her. Like more than just a fling."

I grimace. "I can't like her."

Eva nods. Her gloved fingers tap a rhythm against the edge of the metal table. "You know," she says, "technically I'm a doctor. Patient confidentiality applies."

I look at Posy. "All your patients are dead."

"Well, apparently so's your soul, so we should be good."

I laugh and a tiny bit of the weight I'm carrying slips away. This is why I came here. Eva has a way of helping me get my thoughts in order. I knew I was going to tell her everything, I've just been putting it off.

I place my coffee down and grip the counter behind me until the metal edge hurts my fingers. I swallow, my throat dry and force myself to say the words that haunt me. "Freya's real name is Angelica Maxwell."

The blood drains from Eva's deep brown skin. "Maxwell as in-"

"Yes."

"Holy shit." Eva wets her lips and blinks. "Did she..."

I shake my head. The urge to defend Freya hits me out of nowhere. "She says she hasn't killed anyone but she-" I break off and try again. "He made her..." *Shit. Now I can't even speak.*

Horror pulls at Eva's face as she figures out what I'm trying to say. "She's the protégé, the one who cut the crosses."

I nod and fight the pressure building under my eyes.

Eva's hand flutters to her chest. "Oh God, Eli. Your mom."

My breath hiccups out of me in a broken sob. I press the back of my hand to my mouth, like I can physically hold back the pain. I've been trying to do just that since I was fourteen because Maddie Briggs wasn't just Maxwell's seventh victim.

She was my mother.

"How can I like her, Eva?" My eyes find Eva's across the room, pleading for answers she doesn't have. "She cut into my mother's body. She tortured her. I should hate her." I push away from the counter and clench my fists. "I need to hate her."

I pace over to the wall and lean against it, resting my head on my forearms.

Eva comes up behind me and rubs circles on my back. "But you don't."

I press my lips together and shake my head. "I really don't."

"Not hating Freya doesn't make you a bad son, Eli."

I don't answer.

Eva sighs and carries on rubbing my back. "How old was she when Maxwell took your mom?"

I work my jaw and do the math in my head. *Fuck.* My heart cracks a little at the answer. "She'd have been seven."

"She was just a child, Eli." Eva's voice hardens. "A child raised by a monster. She didn't stand a chance."

I turn around so I'm facing Eva and slump against the wall.

"Deep down, I think you know she's not to blame. You wouldn't like her otherwise." Eva presses a finger into my chest, right where my heart sits. "More than like her."

I can't quite find the words to agree. Logically, I know Eva's right, but it still feels like a betrayal. It's been sixteen years. I've failed to catch my mother's killer and now I'm falling for his fucking daughter.

Eva takes a step back and crosses her arms. "I'm going to say something now and I need you to not break anything in my lab. I don't want any holes in my walls, and I don't have time to stitch up your knuckles."

I brace myself then nod for her to continue.

"What would your mother have said if Maxwell was forcing Freya to cut her?"

I've imagined my mother at the mercy of Maxwell countless times. None of them hurt as much as the visual of a young Freya holding a knife to my mother's chest.

I screw up my face and stop myself just short of snapping at Eva. Because I know exactly what my mom would have said. "She'd have told her to do it." My voice comes out hoarse. "'Better her be the one hurting than a child' she'd have said." I can't stop the tears now, but I refuse to make a sound.

Eva pulls me into a hug and holds me until I hug her back.

"Maybe you found each other for a reason," she says when we break apart.

I'm not sure I believe in fate like that but I'm glad I came to Eva. Her question may have hurt but it was what

I needed to hear. My anger for Maxwell and the grief from losing my mother were clouding my thoughts. Things won't be simple between me and Freya. I still hate that she has secrets. I still don't fully trust her. But Eva's right. My mum wouldn't see my feelings for Freya as a betrayal. She wouldn't want me being cruel to her. If anything, she'd want me to look after her. To make sure she was okay after being raised the way she was, having to do the things she did.

I wipe my face dry and grab my Stetson of the counter. "I should let you get back to your job. We've got a killer to catch."

Eva nods. "I'll call with the results as soon as I have them."

I pick up my coffee and stop at the doorway. "Thank you, Eva."

She smiles at me. "Anytime, Eli."

I'VE JUST ARRIVED BACK at the house and parked on the drive when Eva's name flashes up on my phone. I press to answer, and she comes through on the car's Bluetooth. "That was quick," I say.

Silence hangs heavy for a moment before Eva speaks. "I'm not finished yet, but I found something, and I thought I should tell you sooner rather than later."

A stone sinks down into my stomach. "What is it?"

"When I looked back over the old cases, part of the reason I was able to tell the crosses on the chest were made by someone different to the laceration across the throat was because I suspected the crosses were made by a left hander. Maxwell is right-handed." Eva pauses.

Unease trickles down my spine and I grip the steering wheel as she carries on.

"I didn't know for sure, but this time, because of the writing on the chest, it was easier to see. Eli, whoever cut into Posy's chest, it wasn't the same person who cut her neck."

I don't say anything. I can't. Because the only thought in my head is that Freya is left-handed.

40

RIVER

Eli crashes into my office like a wild bull. It's not often he gets like this nowadays, but it's been happening more since Freya came into our lives. Part of me wonders whether bringing her in like this was the right decision or whether I've just made everything harder for my team.

"Where is she?" Eli demands, vibrating with anger.

I stand up from behind my desk, keeping my movements slow. "Freya?"

Eli snarls at me. "Her name's Angelica and she's a fucking liar."

I blow out a breath between rounded lips and hold my hands up in the air. I've seen Eli at his worst. I've peeled him off the tarmac after he tried to bury himself in drugs, but I've never seen him look quite so vicious. "What happened?"

Eli's cold eyes bore into mine. "She's the one who carved into Posy Winters' chest."

My heart trips. I go still, my body freezing while my brain plays catch up. My first instinct is to deny it. To rage

KILLER OF MINE

at Eli for daring to accuse her of something like that but I hold it back. My feelings for Freya are getting in the way of me being objective just like I knew they would. I should have kept more of a distance. I shouldn't have brought her back here. I squeeze my hand into a fist then force myself to let it go. To lock my emotions away and focus on the facts. "That doesn't make sense."

Eli steps in towards me, his nostrils flaring. "I've just been with Eva. The throat laceration was done by someone right-handed - Maxwell. The cuts on the chest were made by a left-hander."

I shake my head.

Eli grabs my shoulder. "Think about it. Posy was missing for two days before her body was left in the park. Freya could have gotten to her before we put the tracking anklet on."

I run through the past four days in my head. Analyzing every detail, every interaction I've had with Freya.

I don't do this. I don't doubt myself because I don't make mistakes. But I let Freya in and now I'm paying for it.

A fist clenches around my heart and my blood races. I rub the aching spot on my chest. "She took a lie detector test."

"We didn't ask the right questions. Come on, Riv. You've been saying all along that she's hiding something." Eli drags a hand through his hair, his face contorting. "She played us all." A broken edge seeps its way into his voice and that's all I need to pull myself together. If Eli's right, this will kill Jude and Oz. Maybe me too. But right now, I have a job to do. If I've made a mistake, I will fix it.

"Look at me, Eli." I wait till his eyes lock with mine.

"We don't jump to conclusions. We analyze the evidence, and we find proof. Freya wants to catch her father. She's telling the truth about that. Things might not be as clear cut as they look."

Eli's throat bobs. "And if they are?"

I hold his gaze. "If Freya laid a hand on either of the most recent victims, then the deal is off. She goes to prison."

Eli follows me out of my office, his presence a caged inferno at my back.

We find Freya in the kitchen. Her hair glimmers under the golden glow of the low hanging light above the island. She's pouring cereal into a bowl but stops the second she catches sight of us.

She eyes me warily. "What's the matter?"

"I need to ask you some questions," I say.

She leans back against the sink and folds her arms across her chest. "Same old, same old then."

"This isn't a joke," Eli snaps.

Freya gives him a blank look, then turns back to me. "Ask your questions."

"Are you left-handed?" I already know she is, but I want to see if she'll confirm it.

Her eyes tighten. "Yes."

"Did you have any contact with Posy Winters or Camilla Banks before we found their bodies?"

Freya uncrosses her arms and grips the counter by her hips. "You know I didn't."

"Yes, or no?" Eli pushes.

"No." Freya's voice is firm, but I hear the thread of hurt in her reply. "What is this all about?"

"The autopsy suggests Arthur Maxwell was not the person who made the cuts on Posy and Camilla's chest."

Freya's hands slip from the counter. "And you think it was me."

"Did you, in any way, harm Posy Winters?"

She doesn't deny it but the look on her face has me doubting myself once more. Resignation slumps at her shoulders and for once her tough mask falls away. She looks tired. Not like she hasn't had enough sleep but that bone weary tiredness of life. I could kick myself for making her feel like that, for taking away her fight.

"I have to ask, Freya, it's my job," I say, silently begging for her to understand.

Freya sucks in a sharp breath. Like giving oxygen to embers, her fire roars back to life. The flames flare in her eyes. "Actually, River you don't. You could just trust me."

Eli scoffs. "Why would we trust you?"

"Because I'm here!" Freya shouts. "Because I've done nothing but try to help. Because I've told you everything I possibly can. I've said aloud things I never wanted to tell a soul. I've relived the life I faked my death to escape from, for *you*. So you can do your fucking jobs and catch my father."

Her words tear at me but Eli's like a devil on my shoulder. A voice in my head whispering that she hasn't actually answered the question. She hasn't denied it.

"Freya, I need to hear you say it."

Her laugh is hollow. Exhausted. "You're a profiler, River. You know I'm not a killer. You know I didn't touch Posy. If I had, I wouldn't be here, sleeping with your teammates. You'd have me behind bars. If you won't trust me, at least trust your instincts." She moves around the kitchen island and goes to walk past us, but I cut her off.

My hand curls around her bicep.

"My instincts are telling me you're hiding something.

They've been telling me that all along and I've ignored them. I can't trust you when you're keeping things from me."

Freya places her palm on my chest and my hand around her arm spasms. My entire body is magnetized to her touch.

I've had to make difficult decisions doing this job but never before has my heart so completely disagreed with my actions.

Freya's soft voice envelops me. "Trust isn't about knowing everything. It's about believing in that person anyway."

Every cell in my body is telling me to let this go. To promise Freya that I trust her. But I force myself to do my job. "Answer the question."

Pain cuts across Freya's face before she hides it. She snatches her hand back and stares me dead in the eyes. "No. I didn't." She yanks her arm out of my hold, striding past me.

"Where are you going?" Eli calls.

Freya holds up her middle finger. "Screw you, Eli." She heads for the front door and the sight of her walking away has me panicking.

"Do not leave this house," I order, steel in my voice.

She stops at the door, her hand resting on the knob. She shakes her head then looks back at me. "Screw you, too." She opens the door and steps outside.

Eli and I stand in silence, staring at the front door, until Jude and Oz jog downstairs.

"Why did I just see Freya walk out by herself?" Jude asks.

I grind my jaw. "She's upset."

He looks between Eli and me. "What did you do?"

"I'll explain later. Oz, give her five minutes then pull up her tracking details and follow her."

Oz nods at me.

I turn around to face Eli. For the first time since we brought Freya in, a shadow of guilt darkens his features. We lock eyes. *We just fucked up.*

Freya's right. My instincts are telling me she didn't have anything to do with Posy and Camilla's murders. She had no motive, little opportunity, and underneath her tough exterior, I honestly don't think she wants to hurt a soul.

She could have run again, instead she offered her help. And I may have just ruined our best chance at catching the man who killed Eli's mother.

41

FREYA

Like the criminal Eli and River think I am, I swiped the spare key to Jude's car this morning.

I felt guilty at the time, but now I'm glad I did it because it only takes me twenty minutes to get to the mall. I messaged Carmen when I was stopped at a traffic light telling her to go ahead with the drop off. I almost backed out after last night with Jude, but she messaged again this morning and wasn't taking no for an answer.

Carmen's dislike of authority borders on anarchy. I'm amazed she hasn't busted me out of here herself.

It feels weird being at a mall, like it's too normal a thing to be doing after the week I've had. I check the time on my burner phone and look around the busy food court. I've no doubt River will have sent one of the guys after me. I won't have long before they catch up.

My foot taps a rapid beat against the tiled floor. I'm trying to focus on my surroundings - the lines of people at each food station, the smell of junk food in the air - but River's words play over and over in my head. Each replay cuts into me like the scars on my body. I knew he didn't trust me, not fully, but I didn't think he'd go so far as to accuse me of hurting Posy. I blink away the image of his face.

A young boy with Beats headphones slung around his neck scans the food court. He's just the sort of kid Carmen would use for a drop off. I straighten up, ready to push off the pillar I'm leaning against, when a thin figure in a black hoodie and sunglasses stops next to me. *Carmen*.

I throw my arms around her before I can stop myself and she stumbles back a step. Carmen is a tiny thing really and still appears around my age even though she's ten years older.

She hugs me back fiercely then grabs my shoulders and looks me up and down. She pulls the sunglasses low on her face and pins me with a disapproving stare. "What the hell sort of trouble have you got yourself into this time, kid?"

"You weren't supposed to come yourself," I say. "What if someone sees you?"

Carmen waves a hand through the air. "I'm a ghost. Disappearing's what I do best remember?"

I bite my lower lip, sudden tears pricking at my eyes. "I missed you." I hadn't seen Carmen since I enrolled in the police academy six years ago. Part of keeping my identity a secret meant cutting ties with her, but prior to that I lived with Carmen for almost a year. She's the closest thing to a big sister I have.

Carmen hooks her arm around my neck and tugs me close for another hug. "You too, kid."

I bury my face in her shoulder, breathing in the sweet scent of the Twizzlers Carmen's so addicted to.

She taps my anklet with the toe of her boot. "Tell me

again why I can't just break this thing off you right now and get you out of here?"

My laugh comes out as more of a sob and I pull back from the hug, shaking my head. "I have to do this. They're my best chance at catching him."

"They fucking collared you," Carmen growls.

"It's not a collar when it's on your ankle," I point out.

"Potato, po-tah-to. You're still on a leash."

"That's why you're here."

Carmen eyes me for a moment then sighs. She slips a shiny black device from the pocket of her hoodie. It's about the size of a memory stick and every government in the world would go to extreme lengths to get to the mind that created it. It's a good thing Carmen's as good at hiding as she says she is.

She flips the device over in her fingers and shows it to me. "Press this button and hold it to your anklet for twenty seconds, then you're good to go."

I fold my palm around the key to my freedom and slip it into my jeans. "Thank you."

"Anything goes wrong, you call me. I'll get you out. I can have you a new identity within hours."

The idea of starting over again, of letting Freya Danvers die, sours my stomach. Maybe before, when all I'd have been leaving behind was Luke, I could have done it. Not that I don't care for Luke, because I do, but I have a feeling leaving the guys wouldn't be so simple.

For the first time in my life, I feel like I have a real family. A place to go home to. Even as mad as I am at River and Eli right now, every cell in my body rebels against the idea of never seeing them again.

The hair on the back of my neck tingles and I spin around, scanning the mall. My heart kicks at the sight of

Oz making his way through the food court. "You better go," I say, turning back to find an empty space, Carmen already melting away into the crowd.

I lose sight of her. It's better this way but I keep searching the food court just for one more glimpse of the woman who saved my life.

Oz doesn't make a sound, but I sense him coming up behind me. His body is a wall of heat at my back, and I lean against his chest. His arms circle me, and his hands link together over my stomach. The move is sweet, comforting. It's also a way of stopping me from running. There are layers to Oz I'm only just starting to peel away.

"How mad is River?" I ask.

Oz kisses the top of my head. "Next question."

"Are you taking me back?"

Oz hums. "I could. Or I could take you on a date."

I twist in his arms and hook my hands around his neck. "A date?" I ask, a smile playing at my lips.

"One dish from every food stand. What do you say?"

I laugh. "Won't you get in trouble?"

Oz bends down till his lips whisper against my ear. "Hearing that laugh is worth it."

42
OZ

You know, I can't remember the last time I ate at a food court. Sure, I've had my fill of takeaways but usually I'm eating them with one hand while I work at my laptop. Jude's always saying I don't get out enough but until Freya came along, I never really had anything to go out for.

"You ready?"

I look up from the array of dishes we've collected to a grinning Freya. I've never seen her so carefree. If I'd have known food was the key to her heart, I'd have been feeding her gourmet meals every day. Any concept of me being neutral ground when it comes to Freya went out the window the second I saw her scars. I'm as far gone as Jude. She's it for me. Which is why I'm sitting at a crappy table in the middle of the food court instead of taking her back home.

The desire to have her all to myself, just for a little while, roots me to the chair. So, for once in my life, I ignore my phone buzzing with messages from River and focus on Freya.

She holds up a container with fried dough balls in one hand and one with dumplings in the other. "Sweet or savory?"

I take a dumpling. "Savory, obviously. Who eats sweet first?"

Freya's lips twist like she's got a secret. She puts the containers down and snags a sugary dough ball.

I shake my head. "You're off your rocker."

Freya licks her fingers, but sugar still clings to the edges of her lips. "Off my what?"

"It's something my granddad used to say. It means you're mad. Cuckoo. Bats in the belfry. Nutty as a fruitcake."

Freya laughs, her eyes crinkling around the edges. I feel it in the rapid beat of my heart.

Needing to touch her, I reach over and swipe the sugar off her mouth. I bring my thumb to my lips and taste her sweetness.

Freya's eyes fall to my mouth. Her breath hitches.

I'm tempted to abandon the food and whisk her away to the nearest room with a lockable door, but as much as I want to devour her, I want this too.

I want to talk with her, to play with her, to just simply be in her presence.

Every new thing I discover about her is like finding an easter egg in a video game. A little hidden secret, that only I've discovered. The way she took me for my word and picked a dish from every single food stand. Challenge accepted, her grin said. The way her eyes lit up when I used old British phrases. How normally she sits with both feet on the ground, ready to run but when she's relaxed, like right now, she pulls one leg up onto the chair. I could spend days getting lost in the details that are Freya.

My phone buzzes against the table.

Freya's foot comes down to the ground.

My life revolves around screens, but I would give my phone up in a second if it meant Freya never again felt like she had to run.

"Is that River?" she asks.

I turn over the phone and look at the latest missed call. "Yeah."

Freya pushes the dough balls away and wipes her hands on a paper napkin. "We should go back."

"What did he say to you?" I ask because I'm not taking her back without knowing what she's dealing with.

Freya goes quiet. Just when I think I'm going to have to coax it out of her she speaks up.

"He asked me if I'd been the one to carve my name into Posy Winters' chest."

I turn to stone. Each breath a fight against concrete. "He did what?" I ask, my voice cold.

Freya shrugs. "I have a history, I guess." She's trying to play it off, but her lip twitches and she won't meet my eyes. "If I hadn't done what I did when I was younger…"

"No. You did what you had to do to survive. Don't let River, Eli or your own damn brain trick yourself into thinking you had a choice, because you didn't."

"Didn't I?" Freya's clouded green eyes pierce into me. "I didn't fight him. I just did what I was told."

I want to pick her up and hold her but she's clinging to her chair so tightly, I don't think softness is going to get through to her right now. Instead, I lean back and cross my arms. "Take off your shirt, look in a mirror and tell me again you didn't fight him."

She stares at me, a hundred emotions flitting across her face, but she doesn't back down.

I snatch up my phone and start typing.

"What are you doing?"

"Telling Jude exactly what River and Eli did and making it clear I'm on his side if he wants to go a few rounds with them."

Freya sighs. "Boys have too much testosterone."

That shocks a laugh out of me. I put my phone down again and run a hand over my mouth. "All right."

I pick up the plate of hot wings and hold it in front of Freya. "You're the one who picked Fireball level spice, so you get to go first."

Freya's smile finds its way back and my chest loosens.

"You're on." She reaches for a chicken wing and takes a bite. She chews. Swallows.

"And?"

"Totally fine." Her words are nonchalant, but a steady blush rises up her neck to her cheeks. "Yep, all good. Easy peasy lemon–" Her eyes bug out. "Holy shit."

I laugh as she stuffs two dough balls in her mouth and screws up her face. When she's wiped the tears out of her eyes, she pushes the plate towards me.

"No way José," I say, holding up my hands.

Her mouth drops open. "Traitor!"

"It's just like my granddad used to say. Why learn from your own mistakes when you can learn from others."

Freya scowls. "I'm eating *all* the dough balls," she says, tucking the basket in towards her chest.

I eye the copious amount of food on our table. "I think I'll survive."

It takes us about two hours to stuff ourselves as full as we can. In some sort of unspoken agreement, we steer clear of any heavy talk about the case or Freya's past.

Instead, I tell her about my family. The five siblings I have and my parents who are embarrassingly proud of their FBI agent son. We're all good now, but I caused them my fair share of grey hairs when I was a teen in trouble with the law for hacking into government sites. I tell her that's how I got recruited, aged seventeen, and the impressed look in her eyes has me feeling a hundred feet tall.

I may have made some mistakes when I was younger but if they led me to here, with her, I'd make them all over again.

Eventually though, our plates are empty, and I have to take her home.

She follows me back in Jude's car and by the time we pull up to the house and she climbs out onto the drive, all the tension that our dinner drained away is back.

She slips her hand into mine as we walk to the front door.

I turn the keys in the lock and push it open.

River is sitting on the armchair in the living area, in direct view of the door. He closes the book he's reading and lifts his gaze. His hard eyes skate over me and settle on Freya.

She sucks in a breath.

"Come here," he orders.

Freya's hand spasms in mine but she doesn't move. Even though Freya's mad at River, she couldn't help talking about him over dinner. She might be scared of her feelings for him, but she's not scared *of him*, so I decide to let this play out.

"Freya," River growls. "You have five seconds to do as your told. Five, four..."

I know what she's going to do before she does it. I also know River needs to get over himself and having to chase her might well be just the thing to push him over the edge. So I let go of her hand.

"Three—"

Freya legs it up the stairs.

River stands up. He strides towards the stairs, pausing when he reaches me. "Is she okay?" he asks, a tinge of regret in his voice.

I nod. "She's strong."

"Good." River starts up the steps.

"Have fun, brother," I call after him.

43

FREYA

I didn't run because I'm scared. Not really. Okay, maybe a little bit. But River can look damn intimidating when he's in dominant mode. Mostly, though, I ran so I had time to hide the device Carmen gave me. I've just tucked it at the back of my bedside table drawer when River opens the door to my room.

I turn to face him.

He leans against the door frame, blocking the exit with his legs. His strong arms are crossed over his chest, and he gives me a look that has me feeling like a child for running. "Are you going to behave?"

Heat flares through me at his question. *Fuck this shit. I'm mad at him.*

I look over my shoulder at the window.

River tenses. "Don't be stupid."

"Sorry, Sir." I give him a half smile then run for the window. I reach my arms up like I'm going to pull it open but the second River lunges after me I change directions. I launch myself over the bed towards the now unobstructed doorway.

Tricking people is easy, Angelica, it's all about the misdirect.

River curses but I'm already in the corridor. Fool on him for thinking I'd be stupid enough to jump out of a second story window.

My plan is to lock myself inside Oz's room. I'm halfway down the corridor when a strong arm hooks around my waist.

I scream as I careen towards the floor but River twists us at the last second.

He takes the brute of the fall on his back, landing on the oak floorboards with a thud that rattles my bones before rolling us, so I'm trapped beneath him.

Fool on me for thinking I could get away.

I hammer my fists into his chest. "Are you insane?"

River pins my wrists either side of my head and presses his forehead to mine. "Stop running from me," he growls.

He's straddling my hips. I try to pull my hands free, but he squeezes my wrists in warning.

My anger is drowned out by a flush of arousal. My panties dampen. *Damn it,* apparently my body hasn't caught onto the fact that we're mad at him. I wriggle beneath him and turn my head to the side. I freeze.

Oh shit. My stomach clenches, my eyes widening. I quickly look back at River but it's too late.

He glances over to the side. His jaw hardens. "Freya, why is there a phone on the floor?"

I lift my shoulders in a restricted shrug. "How the hell should I know?" Except I do know. It's because I'm an idiot who remembered to hide the key to my tracker but forgot to stash the damn burner phone. It must have fallen out of my pocket when River tackled me.

River keeps my hands pinned but sits up. "Where did you get it from?"

I press my lips together. I can see his brain working, thoughts flicking through his mind.

He finds what he's looking for and his dark eyes settle on me. "Luke," he says with a sigh. "When he dropped off Camilla's file. Son of a bitch."

"River–"

"No. Enough," he cuts me off. "I thought I owed you an apology. I was going to say I should have trusted you more. Now, I'm not so sure." River lets go of my wrists only to settle one hand loosely over my collarbone. It's like a switch flicks in my brain. He's not holding me down with any force, but the touch is so dominant I couldn't move if I tried.

River runs his other hand over my body. Down my arms, across my chest. It takes me a moment to realize he's searching me, but there's nothing professional about it this time.

My breath hitches when he strokes his hand over my breasts. He stills for a second and I feel him harden against my stomach. "You're not going to find anything," I say.

"Quiet." He uses both hands now, circling my ribcage and dragging them down, over my stomach, to my hips.

I arch into him.

He lifts up to free my right leg, keeping my left trapped between his. Patient, determined fingers undo my laces and slip off my boot. He spreads my leg out to the side and runs his hands up my calf, my thigh, right to the top of my leg.

I'm wearing jeans but I may as well be naked for the

fire his touch leaves behind. I wet my lips and drag in some more air.

River switches to my other leg. "You were gone all afternoon. What exactly were you doing?"

Seriously? He wants to talk now? "Why don't you go ask Oz, he's the one you sent after me."

"I told you not to leave the house. You didn't listen."

"Yeah, well Oz didn't listen when you told him to bring me straight back. Aren't you going to punish *him*?" I have no doubt that's what this is. A punishment. River's slow, sensual touch as his fingers explore every inch of my body is nothing short of blissful torture.

He pushes my knee out wide and runs a fingertip back and forth along the crease between my upper thigh and my core.

I tilt my head back. My chest heaves with every breath as need coils deep inside of me. "I hate you," I pant.

River smirks. "Don't worry. Oz is getting punished as well."

I quirk a brow. "Oh yeah, you going to chase him down and pin him to the floor too?"

River gives up all pretense of searching me and starts to stroke me over my jeans.

My nails scrape against the wooden floorboards.

"No. Oz's punishment is that he doesn't get to have you tonight."

It's hard to concentrate right now but I force my eyes to meet his. "You can't control who I spend my nights with. What are you going to do, lock me in my room?" As much as the unspoken threat has been there, he knows I can pick locks.

"No," River says. "I'm going to lock you in my room."

I go still.

River stops his ministrations.

"I thought there were rules against that." I'm well aware Oz and Jude have been breaking them, but I didn't think River would cross that line.

River lifts one shoulder. "I'm in charge. I can make new rules. The only time you seem to listen to me is when my hands are on you."

"So, what? You're going to fuck me into submission?"

River leans back down till his face hovers above mine. He presses a soft kiss against my lips. "You'll have a hard time picking the lock when you're pinned to the bed with my cock."

Holy shit. He's going to fuck me into submission.

River doesn't wait for my response. He just picks me up, throws me over his shoulder and carries me to his room. He opens the door at the end of the corridor and drops me onto his bed.

I've not been in River's room before and once I've righted myself, I look around. Everything is dark and neat. All the furniture is a rich walnut apart from the bed which has an elegant, yet masculine black metal frame and navy silk sheets. There's not a single item of clothing lying around, and I have a feeling if I opened his wardrobe it would look like one of those show homes.

River catches my chin between his thumb and fingers. "Pay attention."

I look up at him.

"Good girl." His lips touch my forehead. "Now strip."

My mouth drops open but if I'm honest this mix of gentle and bossy is really doing it for me. Not that I'm ready to let River know that just yet. "Do I get a say in this?"

River takes the cufflinks out of his shirt, steady hands rolling up his sleeves. He drops the cufflinks on the chest of drawers to the side of the door. "Pick a safe word, darling."

Holy moly. I mean, I kind of knew that's where this was going, but what River said in his office about getting out his crop, comes back to me. The word 'punishment' suddenly seems a lot more frightening.

I must get lost in my mind for a little too long because River closes the space between us, one hand collaring my throat. He lifts me ever so slightly, so I have to sit up straighter on my knees.

Stern, heated eyes stare down at me. "When you're in my room you do as you are told without hesitation. If I ask you a question, you answer it. If I tell you to do something, you do it. Leave the brattiness at the door."

"What if I didn't come through your door voluntarily?"

River chuckles softly. "That's five."

His words send a shiver through me because I know exactly what he means. "With your bare hand or the crop?" I taunt.

"Keep talking and you'll find out. Ten. Add that to the ten you're already getting for running and that's before I've taken into account the burner phone–"

"Melon," I blurt out. "My safe word is melon."

"See, that wasn't so hard now, was it?" River releases me and steps back. He crosses his arms and with his shirt sleeves rolled up I can see just how strong he is, the ridges of his muscles sharply defined. He tilts his head in a slight nod.

I know what he wants but I'm not sure how he's going to react when he sees my scars. I trust Jude and Oz not to have told him which means he doesn't know what he's asking me to do right now. How much trust I'm about to put in him. I swallow and pull my t-shirt over my head.

River doesn't make a sound. Doesn't move a muscle. But I swear the room gets colder. He scans my body, like he's cataloguing every crisscross mark, every raised angry slash. His cheek twitches. "Your father?" he asks.

I nod.

River's voice cracks. "We'll catch him Freya. I promise you that."

I don't answer. I just step off the bed and unbutton my jeans. I strip till I'm standing naked in front of River.

He's still fully clothed and the power shift in the room is surprisingly seductive. Vulnerability prickles at my skin but the way River's gaze strokes over me, the heat in his eyes, reminds me I've got power of my own here.

He steps towards me like he's in a trance, the palm of his hand caressing my hip then dipping low to brush over my ass.

I reach up and twist my fingers through his hair at the back of his neck. I graze my teeth over my bottom lip then guide him down for a kiss.

He's an incredible kisser, leading just enough to show me he's in charge but letting me explore his hot mouth. A satisfied hum settles in my chest, but I pull away, trailing the tip of my tongue along his jaw till I can whisper in his ear. "Do you really think I'm going to let you spank me?"

River's hand drops to my pussy and he draws a single finger through my folds. I'm so turned on my knees almost buckle, and I grip his shoulder to keep steady.

"Are you really going to pretend you don't want me to?" he counters.

The challenge settles in his eyes, and I stare up at him. "I don't."

River tuts, his fingers playing with my soaked pussy. "Such a pretty little liar." Too fast for me to react, River hooks his foot around the back of my ankle and takes my legs out from under me. I'm falling back onto the bed, but before I make contact River grabs my hips and flips me onto my front.

I bring my arms up, the air knocking out of me as I land on my stomach.

The smack comes before I can stop it. A sharp stinging pain that pulses through me and settles in my core. I push up on my arms and glare at River over my shoulder. I open my mouth, but he cuts me off.

"Unless the next word out of your mouth is going to be melon, lower your head back to the bed and shut up."

For approximately three seconds I think about disobeying, but River's eyes darken. He goes still, like a snake about to bite and raises a single brow.

I grit my teeth and lower myself back down.

"So you can obey. Good girl."

The praise sends heat rushing through me then River's palm hits my ass again. The initial contact isn't so bad, but the pain continues to radiate and each spank smarts more than the last. I stay angry for the first five. By the tenth I've melted into the duvet. Five more and my ass is on fire and I'm squirming with need.

River rubs his hand over my burning skin, and I groan into the bed.

"You have no idea how many times I've pictured my

handprint marking your skin like this," River says, his voice a little gruffer than usual.

I close my eyes and hide my smile in the bedsheets. No way am I admitting that knowing River's been thinking of me makes my chest glow. "I'm so glad one of us is happy," I say dryly.

River chuckles. The mattress dips as he climbs onto it. He lifts me further up the bed and rolls me over onto my back. "You did well, darling," he says then presses a soft kiss to my lips.

Even the silk sheets feel rough against my bruised skin and every reminder sends another wave of arousal through me.

"Does that mean you're going to hurry up and fuck me now?"

River pinches my hip. "Language."

I hiss and swipe his hand away, but he just smiles, amusement lightening his eyes.

"You know patience is a virtue," he says.

I scowl. "Patience is for suckers."

River laughs and the vibrations roll over me.

I moan and reach up to cup his face. "River, please. I need you."

He takes my hand and presses a kiss to my palm. "I like the begging, but you'll get what I give you." He takes my hands and curls them around the metal bars of his headboard. "Don't let go."

Before I can protest, River ducks down between my legs and runs his tongue over my center.

I squeeze the bars, my back arching. This is no gentle seduction. River eats me like a man starved, his tongue pushing inside of me then back out to flick over my clit. He alternates between the two, pressing his tongue flat against me until I feel like I'm about to come apart then he stops and gets off the bed.

I lift my head. "What...Oh." River's undressing.

I take a moment to admire him and all that smooth olive skin as he removes his shirt. Then he unbuckles his belt and oh lord. I have however long it takes him to put the condom on to wonder exactly how he's going to fit before I'm being pulled down the bed and River's thrusting inside of me.

I cry out.

He stretches me open, burying himself so far inside me I'm fuller than I've ever felt in my life.

"You're...big." I choke out.

River smirks. "You can take me." He draws out, slowly, then slams back into me.

I see stars.

River sets a ruthless pace and I realize the spanking wasn't my only punishment. His hand comes down to collar my neck and it's all too much. The sheets against my reddened ass, the feeling of him inside of me, stretching me, the unbridled force of this man and his hand around my neck. I come violently.

My core ripples around him as he keeps up the pace, carrying me through my orgasm and building me up for another.

"Again," he growls.

I shake my head, my chest heaving.

River tightens his hold on my neck. He presses his thumb under my chin, forcing my head back. "Again," he orders.

I have no choice. My body listens to its master, and I come for the second time, clamping around him.

River thrusts into me a few more times then stills,

spilling himself into the condom. His head bows as he holds himself above me on his forearms.

My eyes flutter open and closed. I twine my fingers in River's hair, playing with the black strands as I catch my breath.

River presses a kiss to my forehead. "Stay there."

I shudder as he pulls out, aftershocks cascading over me.

His footsteps pad against the rug next to the bed as he disappears into his ensuite to deal with the condom, then returns to the bed. He climbs in beside me and positions us so I'm the little spoon. "Give me your hand."

I'm all floppy and satisfied and my brain is still in a bit of a haze, so I do as he says without thinking.

He raises my arm above my head. A soft click and the feel of cool metal around my wrist snaps me out of it but when I try to pull my arm back I can't. River's cuffed me to the bed.

"Can't have you running on me again now, can I?"

I twist onto my back and stare at him in disbelief. I'm about to lose my mind on him when his eyes drop to my chest. I go to cover myself with the sheets, but River stops me.

He props himself up on one elbow and settles his hand on my stomach. His thumb brushes back and forth over the long scar across my tummy. "I'm sorry I asked you what I did. I know you wouldn't do that, not if you had any choice."

I sigh. This man is not used to apologizing, but he's done it anyway. For me.

I let myself relax back into the bed. Well, as much as I can with my arm cuffed above my freaking head. "I'm sorry I ran. It's kind of my default setting."

"Promise me you won't do it again."

I break eye contact with him, staring at the ceiling. It's painted a dark blue instead of white.

"Freya."

I don't want to lie to River, not after what we just shared. "I can't do that," I whisper.

River sighs and lays his head on the pillow. We lie there in silence for a bit, and I wonder whether I've just ruined everything. Living here, with the guys, I'm so close to having all I've ever wanted but I can't seem to let myself take it.

I'm debating what I can use to pick the cuffs when River speaks again.

"My parents were con artists."

I stay still, not wanting to disturb the fragile trust he's giving me.

"For a while it was all I knew. They started using me in their cons as soon as I was old enough to speak. Probably before that but I just wasn't aware of it. My whole childhood was one lie after the other. If it hadn't been for Eli..." River sighs and I risk rolling onto my side to look at him. Frown lines etch into his forehead, his pain a visceral thing. "Trust doesn't come easy to me Freya, but when you have it, you've got it for good."

I glance up at the handcuffs securing me to the bed. "I take it I still don't have it."

The corner of River's lips kicks up. "Maybe I just like seeing you in my cuffs."

I roll my eyes.

River goes serious again. He lifts up and leans over me, till we're nose to nose. "We'll get there," he says. "I don't like that you're hiding things from me, but I understand that sometimes secrets need to be kept for a reason."

It's as good as I'm going to get and, for the first time, I wish that I could tell River everything.

If only it were that simple.

44

JUDE

I took my meds again this morning to help me focus so I'm able to stay relatively still as we sit across from Kyle Winters, Posy's husband.

He looks like he's living his worst nightmare, which I guess he is. He got called home early because his wife of six months was murdered by a serial killer. Even for a soldier who's seen unknown horrors it doesn't get much worse than that.

On any other day he'd probably be good-looking, but right now his face is mottled and red where he's been rubbing his hands over his mouth and his eyes are full of torment.

"They wouldn't let me see her." His breath wrenches through him. "Posy's parents had already identified the- her, and they said I shouldn't- they said it was better if I didn't."

River sits forward in the floral armchair in Kyle's sitting room, resting his elbows on his knees. It's too casual a pose for him but he's doing it to put Kyle at ease. "If you need to see her, we can arrange it," he says.

Kyle blinks and his eyes clear. The furrow in his brow tells me he didn't think any of us would understand but River stood by Eli's side as he identified his mother's body. He knows.

"Thank you," Kyle says. He straightens up and shakes his head. "You must have questions."

We do, but we have to be careful how we go about them. Kyle's in a fragile state.

We didn't want to overwhelm him, so Eli and Freya are in the kitchen making tea while River and I ease into the interview. So far there've been no shouts from the other side of the small bungalow, so I presume Freya and Eli have yet to kill each other. Even on my meds I'm fidgety. My eyes keep checking the door, my thoughts drifting to Freya. I'm pretty certain, after River kidnapped Freya to his room the other night, that he's on board with making her ours but Eli is still an unknown. He's... volatile.

I'd be happier if Oz was with them, but he stayed back at the house to go through some new footage we'd got from the park where Posy was found. Besides, the fact that River and Freya are on steadier ground seems to have made Eli back down for now.

River slips a photograph of Camilla out of a folder and places it on the coffee table, facing Kyle. "Do you recognize this woman?"

Kyle wipes his hands on his fatigues and sits forward. He studies the photo like it's a blueprint. Like maybe he can find his wife's killer in the contours of Camilla's face. He shakes his head. "I'm sorry, no."

River takes the photo back. "That's okay. Her name is Camilla Banks. We know you've been on tour for the past three months. Is it possible your wife knew Camilla?"

Kyle screws up his face. "I guess. Not well though. We'd FaceTime as much as we could. She was struggling to settle in here, it was a big change, and we don't know many people in the area. If she'd made a friend, she would have told me."

Military families move a lot for work, but I get a brain itch. Oz's mom calls it intuition, River calls it a gut feeling. The scientific explanation is that my subconscious has picked up on signs my conscious brain has missed. "If you have no family or friends nearby, why did you move here?" I ask.

"Uh." Kyle leans back on the sofa and runs his hand over his mouth again. "I guess there's not much harm in telling you. We kept it pretty quiet because Eleanor's family situation is complicated, but we came out here to be closer to her. To Eleanor. She's Posy's sister."

River looks up from the folder. "Our records show Posy was an only child."

Freya slips back into the room then and hands a steaming mug to Kyle.

He smiles in thanks and wraps his hands around it. "She is and she isn't. Posy was adopted. Eleanor is her biological sister. They found each other on Ancestry last year. 100% DNA match. Surprised the hell out of us."

Freya freezes on her way out. She starts moving again after a heartbeat, but I know she's put together the same thing I have.

"They were identical twins," River confirms.

Kyle nods. "Spitting image. I took their first photo together. Said it looked like someone had pressed copy and paste." Kyle grinds the heel of his hand into his eye. "Sorry."

I catch River's eyes. "Camilla was a twin. Identical."

"Is that why this happened?" The mug trembles in Kyle's hands. "The killer, this Maxwell person, you think he's targeting twins? Why would he do that?"

"We don't know yet," River says, "but this changes things. Knowing the connection between the two victims could help us find him."

River and I ask the rest of our questions to cover our bases, but we've already found what we've been looking for. Oz and I have been scouring through Camilla and Posy's lives for days trying to find a connection. They looked nothing like each other, led completely different lives, there was nothing to connect them. Until now.

The question is, why is Arthur Maxwell suddenly targeting twins?

45
OZ

I replay the video for the one thousandth time. I don't get screen fatigue in the same way as most people, computers have always just felt natural to me, but seriously, even I am reaching my limit on how much longer I can watch this video.

The park on the screen is dark, lit only in an orange haze from a couple of street lamps. The navy van is barely visible against the backdrop of the field. It drives past once, then disappears off camera. I click the trackpad and drag the little round button across the line, skipping ahead until the van comes back on screen.

This is ridiculous. I run my hand over my beard, huffing into my palm. The footage is from a doorbell cam belonging to a house across the street from the park where we found Posy. The Uniforms noticed it while canvassing and the family were more than happy to share the footage. But it's useless.

I've done everything I can to enhance the video, but the lighting is too bad and the angle is all wrong. It doesn't show the playground so I can't even be sure that the van is the one Maxwell used. But it appears around the right time and doesn't stay for longer than ten minutes.

My eyes are gritty, like I've got sand in them, and my shoulders ache from being hunched over my laptop. I should have gone into River's office, used that baby soft faux-leather chair of his, even if he does get snippy when we adjust the height.

I crack my neck and groan in relief then I force myself to close the laptop.

There's nothing more I can do and while we haven't got a number plate, I've at least managed to narrow down the make of the car. It's not much but hopefully Freya and the guys will have gotten something useful out of Posy's husband.

I rap my knuckles on the top of my laptop in frustration. I'd thought having Freya on board would make a difference this time, but the case is grinding to a halt like it always does. Arthur Maxwell is a psychopath, but he's also got genius level IQ, higher than Jude even, and he knows how to hide.

I wonder how long it will be till the guys get back. The clock on the oven says it's almost five o'clock.

I slip off the stool, the surface of the island smooth under my hands as I push away. I'm frustrated and tired and I need a break.

There's a drive through Starbucks just down the road so I decide to distract myself by getting Freya a white chocolate mocha. It was one of the drinks we ordered when we bought half the food court at the mall. I snuck a sip and promptly regretted it, but Freya loved it and the sounds she made while drinking it have haunted my dreams.

I leave the kitchen and swipe the keys off the hook in

the hall. I'm checking my phone as I open the front door and I almost walk straight into Freya.

She takes a step back, lifting the cardboard drinks tray she's holding up in the air, so I don't crash into it. "Woah," she says, "don't hurt the coffee."

I chuckle and run my hand over my face again. "Sorry, I wasn't expecting you back yet."

"Where are you heading?"

I tap the coffee tray. "Great minds and all that."

She smiles. "Well, I guess we can go back inside then."

I hold the door open and step aside for her to pass. She peers around for a moment before heading to the kitchen. "Where are the guys?" I ask, following after her.

"They decided to go to the office to sort some stuff out. I got them to drop me off here first." Her ginger curls swing in the air as she smirks at me over her shoulder. "Can't have you getting too lonely now, can we?" She puts the coffees down on the island and I snag her hand, pulling her in towards me.

"Oh, yeah? You going to keep me company, Mo Leannan?"

She tilts her head to the side. "What does that mean?"

A blush heats my cheeks. I hadn't meant to say that, not out loud. "It's uh, what my father calls my mother. It means 'my love'."

Freya blinks. She goes blank for a second and I panic that I've made things too serious, but then she bites her bottom lip and drags me over to the island.

She picks up one of the takeaway cups and hands it to me. "Hazelnut latte for you and..." she takes out the other cup, "white chocolate mocha for me." She takes a long sip and hums to herself.

I shake my head. "There's something wrong with your tastebuds."

"Maybe you should check them out." She sticks her tongue out at me then hops up onto one of the stools.

I take the one next to her. My drink's a little cool, like it's been waiting around a while, but the caffeine is like water to my drought ridden brain.

"So did you get anything useful out of Kyle?" I ask, in between sips.

Freya pulls a face.

"What?"

She studies the marble specks on the island. "Nothing, it's just, can we talk about something different for a bit?" She peeks up at me from under her eyelashes.

I frown, not used to seeing her act this demure. I catch her chin between my fingers and lift her head. "Hey, what's the matter?"

"Nothing. I was just kind of hoping we could have some more 'me and you' time. Like at the mall."

Oh. I hold back my smile. "You want to go on another date?" Something niggles at the back of my brain, but Freya bites her bottom lip again and all I can think about is doing just that myself. It takes me a moment to realize nothing is stopping me from doing what I want, and I lean in to kiss her.

At the last second, she dodges, her lips murmuring in my ear instead. "Finish your coffee, Oz. Then maybe we can go upstairs."

She scoots back and drinks some more of her horrid concoction.

I hold her gaze, take the lid off my coffee and down it

in one. Then I stand up and offer her my hand. Or that's what I try to do. Instead, the room spins. I grab the back of the stool, but I stumble, and it topples over.

"Oz!" Freya jumps up and crouches down next to me.

I blink. She's all hazy. *How did I get on the floor?*

"What..." the word comes out slurred.

"Oz, look at me. What's wrong?"

"Dunno." The ceiling turns upside down. "Dizzy."

Freya hooks her arm around my back. "Okay, we've got to get you to the hospital. Can you walk?" She pulls me up and I stumble again but I manage to catch myself on the island.

My eyes snag on the empty coffee cup. My heart drops to my stomach like a bomb. I try to focus on Freya. "What did you do?"

She cringes. "I don't know what you're talking about." Freya loops my arm over her shoulders, and I have no choice but to lean on her. The floor is made of water. I keep sinking into it and my thoughts are getting washed away by the waves. I close my eyes for a second.

When I open them, we're outside and Freya's resting me against the car as she opens the door.

"Come on now, in you get," she says.

I frown at her, because this is Freya, and I must be wrong. She wouldn't hurt me.

It's getting hard to think, so I do as I'm told even though my brain is screaming at me. *Why won't it shut up?*

I'm lying across the back seats. Breathing is hard. Sluggish. The car starts growling at me. I swat it away. I want to sleep now. I'm drifting off when Freya's words from earlier float to the forefront of my mind. *"They decided to go to the office to sort some stuff out."*

That's what's been niggling at me. We never call it the office. It's always The Lair.

I told Freya that the other day and she laughed so much. She loved it.

I have this overwhelming feeling that maybe I shouldn't be sleeping right now but my eyes are too heavy to keep open. Oh well. Maybe one of the guys will wake me up.

46

FREYA

I think I have to tell them the truth.

I stare at the houses blurring by as River drives us home. Ever since Kyle mentioned Posy had a twin, I've been trying to figure out what to do next. These guys are some of the smartest in the country, if I don't tell them soon, they'll work it out by themselves.

A creeping sensation tiptoes up the back of my neck and my leg jitters like a sewing machine.

Eli scowls at my knee, like I'm deliberately disturbing his space just to wind him up. He's been nicer to me the last couple of days but every now and then I find him staring at me, his eyes hot with anger and lust. Like he wants to hate-fuck me.

I'm no longer sure I'd be so opposed to the idea. I could do with being thrown around a bit. A rough and hard tangling of bodies. Maybe it would get rid of the nervous energy bubbling inside of me.

The closer to home we get, the more on edge I become. I'm not sure when I switched to thinking of the guys' house as home, but the realization does nothing to help my panic.

At first, I think the panic is just because of what Kyle revealed but I've always been hyper-alert to my surroundings and as we drive up to the house the unease sinks and twists like smoke in my stomach.

Oz's car is gone.

I sit forward, peering out the window. "Did Oz say he was going to The Lair?"

I glance over at Eli. He's staring at the empty space on the drive. "No.

River pulls the car to a stop and Jude unclips his seat belt. "He's probably just popped out for a moment. Maybe he found something on the tapes." There's nothing to suggest Jude is wrong but his voice is hesitant, like he's trying to convince himself.

We walk to the door in silent, purposeful strides. Inside, River calls out for Oz.

There's no answer.

My heart trips over itself and I push past the guys into the kitchen. "Oz?" I call. Nothing.

His laptop's closed on the island. Two takeaway coffee cups sit beside it.

River comes up behind me, his body a wall of warmth at my back. "River…" I say, my voice wavering, my eyes not leaving the cups.

"I know," River says. He takes out his phone. The dial tone rings quietly through the room, once, twice, and then a louder ringing takes over.

I jolt and drop to my hands and knees, reaching under the couch for where Oz's phone must have fallen. I decline River's call and the room falls silent.

Jude and Eli jog back into the kitchen. "He's not in his room," Jude says.

"Nor the office." Eli runs a hand through his tousled hair.

River nods at the island. "Two cups. Someone else has been here. Clear the whole house."

Jude and Eli draw their weapons and split off again.

"Can you track his car?" I ask.

River nods and taps at his phone.

I walk back over to the island. There's writing on the coffee cups, messy lines like when the barista scrawls your name but... I pick up the cup, turning it around to see the scribbles on the side. It takes me a second to realize what I'm seeing. When I do, dread coils round my chest like a snake. A throbbing pressure builds under my eyes, and I have to bite my lip to keep quiet.

This is my fault.

"Freya, prints!" River snaps at me, and I drop the cup.

"Shit, sorry, I forgot." It's a rookie mistake, not wearing gloves when handling evidence, and it's one I think River knows I wouldn't ever make. But he's too worried about Oz to pick up on my lie right now. It was a risk I had to take because the writing isn't just random scribbles, it's a code. A code only I and one other person understand.

The message is simple and to the point. An address followed by a threat: *come alone or he dies*.

I step away from the island and rest against the back of the couch, sitting on my hands so River doesn't see them tremble.

He pockets his phone and paces across the room.

"Anything?" I ask when he starts paying too much attention to the coffee cups.

He turns to face me. "The techs are tracing the car now."

I nod. I have a feeling even if they find it, it will be too late. The first thing you do after kidnapping an FBI agent is dump the car.

I force myself to swallow. There's a lump in my throat made up of all the words I should say right now. All the confessions River's been wanting me to trust him with. All the truths I should have already told him. Maybe if I had, this could have been avoided. Maybe we'd already have my father behind bars and Oz would be safely here with us now. Maybe.

For twenty-three years my life revolved around one person. Every decision I made, every lie I told, every person I pushed away, it was all to keep a single promise. Nothing was more important. And then River, Jude, Oz and even Eli crashed into my life and now I have four more people to think about. Four more lives to protect.

If Oz is hurt, I'll lose it all. Everything. And my promise will mean nothing. Because River will not forgive, and he might be the one person I can't outsmart. But if I want to keep Oz safe, I'm going to have to try.

I wait until Jude and Eli re-enter the kitchen. The guys form a huddle, the three of them a well-oiled machine that will do anything to save their teammate.

I use their focus to my advantage and slip out of the kitchen. I keep my feet quiet on the stairs and gently close the door to my room behind me.

The device Carmen gave me is hidden in the drawer of my bedside table. I dig it out and pinch the thin black device between my thumb and forefinger and hold it to my tracker. A long beep sounds and the light flashes off a second before the mechanism unlocks.

My ankle feels bare without it. Like I've lost my anchor.

I scribble a quick note and place it on the bed underneath the tracker. Then I head to the window.

When River was chasing me, I never intended on jumping out the window, but I think, back then, part of me wanted to be caught. I scouted this house for escape routes the first night they brought me here. If I'd really wanted to outrun him, I could have done it.

The window's not ideal but there's a drainpipe running down to the ground and it's sturdy enough to hold my weight. I think.

The climb out is awkward. I have to stand on the window ledge and stretch all the way over to the right to grab onto the drainpipe. My fingertips hook around the frame of the window, but I can feel them slipping. I grip on so hard that pain twinges my forearm and my right hand latches around the drainpipe only seconds before I lose my grip. My body swings outwards like a barn door and I grunt as my side hits the wall.

I slide a little ways down the drainpipe before I secure my hold and brace my feet against the clapboard. By the time I get to the bottom, my heart is racing a mile a minute and sweat coats my skin.

I take one last look at the house I've started calling home. If I go now, that's it. They'll never forgive me. But I'd rather be sitting in a prison cell with Oz alive, than be the reason River, Jude and Eli lose a brother.

47

JUDE

I can't breathe. The adrenaline has chased off any positive effects of my meds and my hand jitters relentlessly against the wall.

The techs have arrived and I'm doing my best not to glare at them, but I don't like them here. In our space. Collecting evidence. Taking pictures.

River keeps glancing at me, caution in his eyes. He knows I'm spiraling but he doesn't have the time to coddle me right now.

I need to pull it together. For Oz.

I've never been that close with my brother. When I was younger, I used to imagine what it would be like to have a sibling I could play with, talk to, anything to make the stifling formality of home that much more bearable.

My parents set my brother and I against each other as soon as we could walk. Everything was always too much of a competition for us to have any sort of healthy relationship but the day I met Oz it was like we'd known each other since birth. And I'm terrified.

We found traces of some sort of powder in the bottom

of one of the coffee cups. The techs are testing it now, but I know what they're going to say; Oz was drugged and kidnapped.

I hit the soft side of my fist against the wall. I want to tear the whole county apart looking for him, but I know mindless searching isn't going to help anything. We need to work the case.

River's taken charge, shelling out orders and burying his emotions like he always does. Eli's snapping at anybody that does the slightest thing wrong. We're all falling apart, and it takes me far too long to realize Freya hasn't come back downstairs.

She's probably just trying to stay out of the way, but the second I notice she's gone, it becomes unbearable to have her out of my sight.

I signal to River that I'm going to check on her then head to the stairs. When Freya is upset, she hides. Or runs. I've learnt this about her. She's used to dealing with everything by herself but she's part of a team now and she needs to understand she's not alone anymore.

I rap my knuckles against her door. "Freya? Can I come in?"

I'm patient for about ten seconds before I open the door and I realize my mistake.

I didn't think my heart could beat any harder. I didn't think I could feel worse than I did when I learned Oz was missing. I just plain *didn't think*.

If I had I would have cuffed Freya to my wrist to make sure she couldn't ever leave my side. I wouldn't have been so caught up in my own thoughts that I didn't notice her panicking. I would have realized finding Oz gone would make her do something stupid.

But I didn't. And now her window's open and her

tracking anklet is sitting on her bed like a heart-rending goodbye.

"River!" I yell. "River, get up here now!" I keep shouting for him till my voice is raw and River and Eli's footsteps are pounding down the hall.

"What the fuck is it?" Eli demands.

I turn to them, Freya's anklet hanging from my fingers. The note she wrote crumpled in my fist.

River turns to stone. "That's not possible."

"We underestimated her. This can't be a coincidence," Eli says, walking over to the open window. "What if she had something to–"

"No," I cut him off. I don't care how bad it looks that she's run, Freya would never do anything to hurt Oz.

"Why now then? Why did she run, *now*?"

River kicks the bed.

I jump, my eyes darting his way. Normally, River's anger is a quiet, controlled thing, but right now he looks like he could throttle someone.

"We were distracted," he says.

I shake my head. "She left a note." I pass him the piece of paper.

He scans it, then looks to the heavens, drawing a deep breath in through his nose. "When we find her, I'm going to tie that goddamn self-sacrificing brat to my bed and never let her go."

Yeah, we're in agreement on that.

Eli raises an eyebrow. "Self-sacrificing?"

"She's going after, Oz," I say. "She said it's her fault he's been taken and she's going to get him back."

"And she couldn't do that *with* us?"

I run my tongue along my teeth. "Apparently not."

River reads over the note again, his eyes narrowed. "She knows where he is."

My heart flips. "What?"

River hands the note back to me. "She doesn't say she's going to find him, she says she's going to *get* him."

Eli walks over to me and reads the note over my shoulder. "Could just be a turn of phrase. How would she know?"

"Another phone?" I ask River.

He shakes his head. "I've been checking since I found the first one and she's not been out of our sight since the mall." River huffs out a frustrated breath and stalks from the room.

Eli and I follow after him. "Where are you going?"

He jogs down the stairs, paces into his office and takes out all the case files we have on the Cross-Cut Killer. He spreads them open across his desk, sifting through them like there might be a map with an 'x' marking exactly where to find Freya and Oz. "None of this makes sense. It's like we've been playing catch up ever since Freya came into the picture. We're missing something."

I round the desk and help sort through the files, re-reading the notes from Freya's interviews.

Eli stays by the door. He opens it a little then closes it again and repeats the process till River snaps at him. "Stop dicking about and come help."

"Eli?" I say, when he shows no sign of moving.

"The door." Eli looks back at us. "There were no signs of a break in and there were two coffees on the island. *Two.* Who would Oz trust enough to let them in the house? To share a drink?"

River straightens. "An agent?"

I shake my head. Oz isn't exactly an extrovert, we're pretty much his only friends. Well, us and Freya.

The sounds in the room fade away until all I can hear is my breathing. Everything ceases to exist except a single train of thought. I follow it like a string through a maze, gathering the different papers I need to find the center. The interview with the vet. Luke's account of what happened the night Freya was chased off the road. The autopsy photo of Eli's mum, Madison Briggs. "Like birthday candles," I mutter. There. The puzzle piece that doesn't fit.

"Jude... Jude." River's voice filters through my brain and I blink back to the present. "What is it?" he asks.

I look up at them. "Maddie was the first victim with the crosses, yes?"

River nods.

Eli's fist clenches and he shifts his gaze, glowering at the wall. I hate that he's having to see his mother like this yet again, but I needed to check.

"Freya said her dad made her start cutting his victims when she was seven. One cross for every year like some sort of twisted birthday candle, were her words. So, why," I say, tapping my finger on the photo, "are there fourteen crosses?"

Both Eli and River look at the picture of Maddie. I turn the other papers to face them. "The vet, Colin Bennet, said he'd seen Freya with her father two years ago. The night Freya was drugged, Luke said he thought she'd come back already but Freya swore she hadn't. Posy and Camilla have nothing in common, except for the fact they are both twins. Identical twins." My breath shakes past my lips as I finish telling them what I've only just put together. "Freya has a twin."

Eli tears his eyes away from his mother and I gently turn the photo over. "How is that even possible?" he asks. "Oz did the deepest dive on every aspect of Maxwell's life. There is no record of a second daughter."

"I don't know how Maxwell did it, but I'm certain he did. This is why she was lying to us. She's not protecting her father."

"She's protecting her sister," River says.

Before we can figure out what to do with this information there's a knock on the door.

A tech with silver rimmed glasses and short spiky hair pokes her head inside. "We've got a lock on the car. Uniforms were nearby, they're there now."

I step forward but she shakes her head, her eyes creasing in a grimace. "He's not there. It, uh, doesn't look good."

48

OZ

The Freya who's not Freya looks down at me. Cloudy green eyes study me like I'm a lab animal. She's got the same freckled face as Freya, the same ginger curls that drop like a churned-up waterfall down past her shoulders. It's not her though. It's not *our* Freya.

I'm in a warehouse. The space is cold and damp. The large open area is pretty much empty apart from a table with chains hooked round it a few feet away.

Sweet Jesus, I'm trying not to think too hard about that table.

My body is still heavy from the drugs. I push against the concrete, inching myself up the metal beam my hands are tied behind. The room spins as I move, and I swallow the urge to vomit. I tilt my head back. The cold metal helps push away the grogginess.

The Freya who's not Freya is still studying me.

"What's your name?" I ask, my voice a little slow. Each breath an effort.

She cocks her head. "Angelica."

"No," I say.

"Yes." She's stubborn, like a child having a tantrum.

I lean forward as far as my binds allow so my face is inches from hers. "You're not her."

"Aren't I?" she asks. "I'm never really sure."

I grit my teeth. "What is that supposed to mean?"

She pushes out of her crouched position and circles me. She trails her finger around the beam like in her head she's on some sort of carousel ride.

"He raised us as one. Did she tell you that?" She shakes her head. "Of course not, she likes to pretend she's only one person when actually she's two. She's me and her and I am her and me."

My head is still fuzzy but I'm pretty sure that's not why this woman sounds insane. Like actually, potentially clinically insane. "So, you're Angelica," I say, deciding to play along.

She smiles and drops to sit cross legged in front of me. "You can see me though, can't you?"

I give a slow nod.

"How do you do it?"

"Tell you apart?"

She bobs her head up and down. "No one else ever could. I used to get worried the teachers would catch on. That I'd do something she wouldn't do, and they'd know and then he'd be angry and not let me out again." She runs a fingertip down my leg, her nail scratching on the denim of my jeans. "I liked being let out."

Her finger climbs back up my leg, over my chest, only stopping when she reaches my neck. "I'm supposed to cut you here."

I go still.

She slices her nail across my throat. A sharp scratch tingles in its wake. "He's shown me lots of times, but I still can't do it." She smiles again. "That's why you're here though. I'm going to fix it."

Yeah, I don't like the sound of that, so I try to keep her talking. The guys will be looking for me by now. I just need to buy time. "What happened to you after Freya – your sister, left?"

Angelica frowns. "He didn't let me out for a long, long time. He said I was dead."

"He said *you* were dead? Or he said your sister was dead?"

She wraps her hand around my neck and pushes my chin up with her thumb. "You're not listening," she snaps. "There is no her and me. If she was dead, I was dead."

"Okay, okay." I swallow. Her thumb digs in so much even that small action hurts. "I'm sorry," I say.

She lets go of my throat and runs her fingers through my hair.

I hate it. I hate having her hands on me because it's too much like when Freya touches me. And she is not Freya. She is not mine. "What's the plan here, Angelica?"

She smirks. "Don't worry, I'm not going to hurt you." Her hands drop to my chest, and she starts unbuttoning my shirt.

My entire body goes rigid.

A scrape echoes through the warehouse as Angelica picks something up off the floor and then she's pointing the tip of a knife to my bare chest. "We're just going to wait right here for *Freya* to come rescue you."

Her words do little to reassure me. I very much doubt this woman's version of 'not hurting' is the same as mine, and I really, really do not want Freya anywhere near her. Based on what I know so far about Angelica, I'm strugglingly to understand why Freya was so determined to protect her.

"She never told us about you, you know," I say. "She wants to keep you safe."

The tip of the knife pierces my skin. I suppress a grimace.

A bead of blood appears on the silver blade. "She left me."

"I don't think she wanted to."

Angelica lifts the knife up. She watches my blood run down to the hilt. "You're not supposed to break a promise. I haven't broken mine. That's why he's mad."

"Your dad?"

She sits back on her heels. Nods.

"Is he here?"

She shoots forward, pressing her finger to my lips, her face centimeters from mine. "Shh, you can't tell him."

"Where is he?" Getting kidnapped might be worth it if I can get a location on Maxwell.

"I'll take you to him once I've fixed it."

"What do you have to fix?"

She twirls the knife towards herself. "Me. I'm broken. She made me promise not to kill anybody, but daddy doesn't like that."

I sink into the beam as I realize just how much weight Freya's been carrying. I mean Jesus, she's the only thing standing between her sister becoming a serial killer.

My heart squeezes for this girl whose world has been twisted and distorted at the hands of a monster. How Freya got out with her mind intact, I'll never know.

"We can get you away from him," I say. "We can keep you safe."

"No." She slices the knife across my chest lethally fast

and two sharp lines burn into my skin in a large cross. "No. No. No. I will fix this!"

Sweat gathers on my brow. I clench my hands behind the beam as warm blood runs down to my waist.

"How?" I bite out. "How are you going to fix it?" I know I'm not going to like the answer, but I ask the question anyway.

"She's the reason I can't kill anyone but if she's dead, then so is my promise."

I breathe through the pain and the fear and try to work with Angelica's logic. "If you kill her, you'll have broken your promise."

She just shakes her head. She dips her finger in my blood and finger-paints a stick figure on the concrete. "No, I won't. She made me promise never to kill another person. But Angelica isn't *another* person. She's me." She draws her finger across the neck of the stick figure and smiles at me like she's solved a puzzle. "I never promised I wouldn't kill myself."

Doing the job I do, being taken like this has always been my worst nightmare. Being the victim, instead of the hunter. I didn't think anything could scare me more.

I was wrong.

I don't care what happens to me. I will do anything. I will take all the torture. I will die if it means Freya is safe.

So, I force myself to hold Angelica's gaze, to keep her eyes on me and not on the stupid, reckless woman who just stepped into the warehouse.

49

FREYA

I'm standing in the shadows. I haven't seen my sister in six years, but all I can look at is Oz. Blood runs down his chest from the all too familiar shape of a cross. It takes everything in me not to rush over to him.

Never let anyone get close, they'll be your downfall.

Oz has got his eyes locked on Angelica, but I know he knows I'm here. His hands are clenched into fists behind the beam he's tied to, and I can practically hear his thoughts screaming at me to leave before she notices but it's already too late.

"Hello Angelica, or is it Freya now?" my sister asks. She turns round to face me. "What? Not even a hug hello for the twin you abandoned?" This is why I hate being called Angelica. It was never just my name, it was always ours. For some reason, out of all the horrible things my father has done, that one always unsettles me the most. He didn't raise us as two children, he raised us as one. But no matter how we were brought up, she's still my sister.

"I couldn't find you," I say, the words lurching from my chest. I'd looked so hard for her. For him. I was never doing it to catch my father. I was doing it to get my sister out.

She spins the base of the knife on the tip of her finger. It's a trick we learnt in the endless hours we spent locked away in the basement. I'd leave for school in the morning and when I got back, she'd show me how good she'd got. There wasn't much in the basement, but we were always allowed knives. It was like he thought letting us play with them would make us just like him. I guess, for my sister, it did.

"I'm here now," I say. "Let Oz go."

She shakes her head. "I'm supposed to kill him."

We are truly identical, and there's something indescribably unsettling about seeing yourself talk about murder so casually. It's like when you have a nightmare only to realize you are the monster.

I shrug off the crawling sensation on my skin and take a few steps towards her. "I don't think you will," I say. "I don't think you can."

We were only ten when I made her promise to me she would never kill anyone. Maybe I'm just clinging to some foolish hope, but I don't think she's broken that promise. Not yet.

She crouches down and presses the point of the knife into Oz's chest. "You left me. You broke your promise, what's to say I haven't broken mine?"

Oz catches my eye and shakes his head.

"Let him go and I'll stay here with you. I'll let you do whatever you want to me-"

"Freya," Oz growls.

"But you have to let him go," I finish. My eyes are on Angelica, but Oz's glare burns into my skin. If we both get out of this alive, I'm in so much trouble.

Angelica throws the knife up in the air and catches it. She cocks her head to the side and purses her lips like she always does when she's thinking. I see the second she makes her decision but I'm too far away to stop it. The hilt of the knife slams into Oz's temple, and he sags forward.

"No!" I run towards him, skidding onto my knees. I cradle his face in my hands. I don't realize how stupid it is to expose my back to Angelica until pain explodes through my head and everything goes dark.

MY EYES ARE SANDY. A heavy throb beats behind my forehead and I want to bury myself in my comforter and go back to sleep.

I try to curl up onto my side, but I can't. I can't move at all. Panic slithers through me and I force my eyes open.

Dark. Musty. I'm in a warehouse. The warehouse. *Oz.*

My stomach swirls and I try to sit up but I can't. My sluggish heart speeds up. My breath comes in choppy waves. *Why can't I move?*

I lift my head and look down my body. I've been stripped to my bra. Grimy silver chains shackle me to a metal table. The weight of them presses into my hips, my legs and around each of my wrists.

"I'm sorry I hit you."

I turn to the voice. Angelica's sitting on a fold-out chair, her elbows on her legs and her chin resting in her hands.

"Where's Oz?"

"Is he your boyfriend?"

I tug at my wrists making the chains rattle against the table. "Angelica, where is he?"

She launches up off the chair and presses her knife to my sternum. "It's rude not to answer a question."

I don't bother pointing out she just ignored mine. My sister's mind fragmented a long time ago. I'm normally better at getting through to her but it's been a while, and I can't think straight until I know where Oz is. "He's..." I wet my lips and try to slow my breathing. I think of Jude and River and even Eli. "I don't know what he is, but I care about him. A lot."

She frowns. "You used to only care about me."

A tear pools in the corner of my eye because she's right. For the first seventeen years of my life, she was all I had.

Angelica traces the knife over the crisscross scars on my chest. "We're not matching anymore."

The meaning of her words sinks in, and I close my eyes. I knew he wouldn't have stopped his abuse but her confirmation tears through my chest.

"Look."

I open my eyes. She's taken off her shirt. Just like us, our scars are identical, and my gaze instinctively finds the new marks. The ones she has but I don't. More tears well in my eyes. "I'm sorry," I whisper.

She shrugs. "It's okay. I can fix it now."

"No. No!" I try to lean away from her, but the chains are too tight. I can't do anything as she brings the knife to my chest and cuts.

The first slice is the worst. It's been six years since I've felt pain like this, and I couldn't hold my scream in if I tried.

Any ability to reason with her slips away as she carves

into my skin. She cuts over old scars, setting my chest on fire. The pain consumes me. I am nothing but hurt and memories as flashbacks invade my mind.

> *Warmth spreads through my pajama bottoms as he walks towards me, bloodied knife in hand.*
>
> *"Your turn, sweetie."*
>
> *I shake my head. "Please Daddy, please don't. I didn't do anything."*
>
> *"I know you didn't, sweetheart, but your sister did. You know the rules. If I cut her, I cut you. Identical in every way, remember?"*

The knife cuts into my hip, the pain even worse against the bone and I slip away again.

> *"That's it. Good job, sweetie." He runs his rough hand through my hair. His hands are always so steady. Mine's trembling as I make the second cut.*
>
> *"Nice and steady. Once you've finished your sister's cross, she'll do yours, okay?"*

"Stop, please, stop. Angelica!" I thrash my head against the table until the pain dulls and I'm sucked back inside my memories.

> *I drop the knife on the floor. "I'm not doing it. I won't do it anymore."*
>
> *The woman tied on the table behind me sobs.*
>
> *My dad sighs. He picks up the knife and holds it out to me. "Why must you be so stubborn? Every cut you refuse to make, I will give to your sister. Would you rather that?"*

I think of Angelica down in the basement. Of how blank she looked the last time I cleaned up our wounds. I'm fifteen now and I'm not blind to what's happening. Every cut takes pieces of her away from me. Makes her more like him.

I take the knife.

I don't know how long I'm lost. When the cutting stops, sweat coats my skin and my stomach is slick with blood.

"That's better," my sister says. "Now we're the same again."

"Why did he punish you so much?" I ask once I'm able to form words again. After we hit our teens, it was usually me getting us punished. By that point, Angelica enjoyed doing the things our father wanted us to do.

"He's mad at me because I won't kill anyone. I do everything else, everything up to that point but I- I just can't."

Despite the pain I'm in, relief floods my body. I've spent the past six years hoping and praying she hadn't crossed that line. "That's a good thing, Angelica."

"No!" She backhands me. "No, it's not. I'm supposed to kill. I'm nothing to him if I can't kill."

I work my jaw and turn back to face her. "I can get you out," I say. "We can leave, right now, both of us and you never have to see Dad again."

She shakes her head. "I don't need you to solve my problems anymore. You got me into this mess. You made me promise not to kill anyone, but if you're dead, my promise dies with you."

My body goes cold. "That's not how promises work," I say.

Angelica shrugs. She smiles sadly and rounds the table till she's standing behind my head. "I guess we'll find out."

The knife, still slick with my blood, rests against my neck and I realize this might actually be it. Even in the midst of being tortured I think a part of me believed that the guys would find me. That somehow with River's bossy ways, Jude's genius, and Eli's pure determination, they'd get here in time, and everything would be fine.

They'll find me. I'm sure they will. I just might not be alive when they do.

50

RIVER

The fire fighters get the last of the flames extinguished and reel in their hoses.

I stand with my feet rooted to the dead grass. I'm clinging onto my professionalism by my fingertips right now. The emotions I'm suppressing tie themselves into knots in my stomach as I stare at the carnage.

Oz's SUV has been reduced to a burnt-out shell. The front half of the roof and the windscreen are missing, and the leather seats are charred to a crisp. The smell of smoke and the fire's lingering heat still clogs the air.

One of the local cops walks on up to us and sticks out her hand. "Officer Whitely. I take it you're the SCU agents?" Officer Whitely is short, with a blonde bob sitting under her hat.

I dip my head, detaching myself further from the pain as I take her hand. "Special Agent River Park, these are my colleagues Special Agents March and Elroy."

Denise shakes hands with Eli and Jude before turning back to me. "Someone saw smoke from the highway. Fire brigade realized the number plate matched your BOLO and called it in." She hooks her thumbs in her belt and shakes her head at the smoking SUV. "I'm just glad no one was inside."

So were we. The car was abandoned just off the side of the highway in the middle of an expanse of dry land. Unfortunately, the location doesn't give much away. It's not near a parking lot or a gas station which means whoever took Oz probably had a car waiting for them at this spot.

I pull my gaze away from the burnt SUV and get my head in gear. "Eli, talk to our press contacts, put a call out for witnesses who might have seen anything that could help us." Eli nods and takes out his phone.

"Jude, check it's safe with the fire brigade then bring forensics in to access the scene. I'm going to talk to Ramsey."

Jude doesn't move. He just keeps staring at the car. I can almost see the horrors he's imagining reflected in his eyes.

"Jude," I snap, bringing his attention back to me.

He blinks a few times then screws up his face. "Shit, sorry."

I put my hand round the back of his neck and squeeze. The ADHD makes Jude feel everything so much more intensely. I'm usually better at grounding him but all I've been able to think about is Oz and Freya. "I know. I know, Jude. We'll find them," I say.

Jude presses his lips together. He draws in a breath through his nose and nods. "I'm good. Go. I'm okay."

I hold onto him a second longer, scanning his face to make sure he's telling the truth. Satisfied, I let go and head over to the fire crew.

I catch Ramsey, the arson investigator, as he's hopping

out of the truck. We've worked together a number of times in the past and he's good people, ex-marine, but I can't help thinking Freya would deem him even grumpier than me.

"I haven't even looked at the scene yet, Park. Come back later."

"Can't do that. We're on the clock."

He gives me a look. "When are you not?"

I keep pace with him as he walks to the SUV. "Give me your gut feeling," I say.

"I need to collect evidence, analyze. You know, do my job." He drops his bag on the ground and takes a look at the damage.

"The person who did this has Oz, Ramsey."

He stops what he's doing and looks back at me. People call Ramsey angry and brutal, but I see the softening in his eyes that most would miss.

"At least give me your best guess," I press.

He runs a palm over his rugged, mountain man beard. "We're looking at a small bomb. The fire spread but I don't think the aim was to create a large amount of damage. The blast area is concentrated around the navigation system. If I were a profiler, I'd say whoever did this wanted to take out the GPS tracker."

"That's why we couldn't find the car straight away."

Ramsey nods. "Now let me get to work and I might find you some real evidence." He doesn't wait for my response before turning his attention back to the car.

I give him his space. I'm walking back over to Jude when I spot the tracks in the dirt. They've been somewhat disturbed by the fire fighters and the cops, but they look recent. I call a couple of techs over and get them on it, with any luck we'll be able to identify the make of tire and, from that, narrow down the type of car we're looking for.

It's been four hours now since we came home to find Oz missing. Just under that since Freya went off on her own to bring him home. Part of me hopes she's having better luck than us. The rest of me doesn't want her to find him, because I know what it means for her if she does. Freya's twin took Oz for a reason and every profiling instinct in my body is telling me he was just a means to an end. A way to get Freya away from us. Ever since I've met her, Freya's sparked my protective instincts, but apparently, I need to get better at protecting her from herself.

"River!" Jude's shout breaks me from my reveries. He runs towards me, his phone pressed to his ear, his eyes wide and alert. "I've got him. It's Oz." Jude chucks me the keys and we sprint back to my car.

Eli catches up with us and hops in the back while Jude rides shotgun and I drive.

"Where am I going, Jude?"

"He's at a gas station- Oz, Oz no, stay where you are. Oz, listen to me."

Eli grips Jude's headrest and leans forward. "What's he doing?"

Jude shushes him.

My hands tighten on the steering wheel, and I turn onto the highway. We leave the worst of the smoke behind, but a gray haze still hangs beneath the cloudy sky. I want to put my foot down but there's no point speeding anywhere until I know where I'm going.

Jude sits up straighter, his face screwed up in concentration. The air is sucked out of the car. All of us waiting. "Yes sir, he's my friend. No, don't call the police, we're

FBI and we're on our way to pick him up now. If you could just give me your address..."

We need to get to Oz. I know Jude's spoken to him, that he's alive, but something's wrong. If Oz was in his right mind the first thing he'd have done is give us his location.

Finally, Jude rattles off an address and I step on the gas.

"Yes, sir," Jude says. "Thank you, sir. We're on our way now. Just keep him there please. I know. I know. Thank you."

Jude ends the call. He stares out the windscreen, his leg jigging up and down. "Can you go faster?"

I'm already going over eighty miles per hour. Still, I press down on the accelerator.

"How bad is it?" Eli asks from the back.

Jude shakes his head. He's taken a couple of his stones out of his pocket and is rolling them between his fingers. "He wasn't making sense. The gas station attendant had to take the phone back off him. He said he looks like he's been attacked."

"But he's alive," I say. "He's alive and he's safe." It's a reminder for myself as much as them.

Jude echoes my words back to me and eventually the stones return to his pocket.

Eli clears his throat. I look at him in the rear-view mirror. "Was there –" he swallows and tries again. "Was there any sign of Freya?" His hand grips his seatbelt, like he's using it to hold himself together.

"Oz kept saying she was there, that she'd been with him but..."

"He doesn't know she has a twin. He might have

thought –" I cut myself off because Jude doesn't need to hear that right now.

"No." He hits the door with the side of his fist. "He would have known. He wouldn't believe she'd do that."

I don't say anything. For Oz's sake I hope Jude's right, but if he is, that means Oz really did see Freya. Only, now, she's no longer with him.

The second I pull up to the gas station I realize it's so much worse than Jude said. Oz is inside, hammering at the doors, a gun clenched in his hand.

I yank on the hand brake and get out of the car. As I get closer, I see the owner through the window and curse.

He's standing a few feet away, aiming a shotgun at Oz's head.

I draw my own weapon but keep it down at my side and signal for Jude and Eli to do the same.

I catch eyes with the shopkeeper and hold up my badge.

He nods and reaches behind the counter. The doors open and Oz stumbles out. His hair is matted with dried blood and his chest is crimson red.

I holster my gun and grab hold of him to keep him steady.

He's hugging his torso with one arm and his pupils are blown. "Freya. Freya." He sways in my hold.

I reach for the gun he's holding. "Let go, Oz. Give me the gun."

"I've got to go back," he says but his words are slurred.

"I know, I know. We'll get her Oz, but you've got to give me the gun." I let out a breath when his grip loosens, and I can ease the gun from his grasp. I pass it off to Jude.

Eli glowers at the shop owner and I look over to see

he's joined us outside and is back to pointing his bloody shotgun at Oz.

"I don't know what he's on," the old man rumbles, "but he bulldozed into my store and asked to use the phone. When I wouldn't give him a gun, he launched himself over the counter and took one for himself."

"Lower your weapon," I order.

His eyes flick over to me.

"Now."

The owner grits his teeth but lets the shotgun fall to his side. I know I'm being harsh, this man did us a favor keeping Oz inside the store, but I have no patience for anyone threatening my family.

"He's not high," Eli adds, apparently just as annoyed as I am. "Can't you see he's got a head wound?"

Oz tries to lunge away from me, muttering under his breath.

I pull him back. "Oz, look at me. Look at me!"

He's all over the place but eventually he gives me his eyes. They're blinking rapidly. "She has Freya. Angelica has Freya. I need to go back."

Jude stands at my shoulder. "Angelica *is* Freya, Oz."

"No, no she–" Whatever Oz is about to say gets lost as he falls forwards and throws up on the tarmac. He drops to his knees and I hook his arm over my shoulder, hoisting him back up. "Eli, you drive. He needs to go to the hospital."

"You're just leaving?" The store owner calls out.

"Yes," Eli snaps.

Between the three of us we get a dazed Oz into the car. We speed out of the gas station, leaving the owner standing on the concourse with his arms thrown out wide.

Oz lies sprawled across the back seats, his head in Jude's lap. "Freya," he mutters. "She's got Freya. She's going to kill her."

My stomach drops like an anchor. "Do you know where she is?"

"Warehouse." It's all he says before he rolls onto his side and pukes again.

51

FREYA

One cut across the throat. Deep and fast.

Angelica screams in frustration. A vicious, angry sound. The knife nicks my throat then clatters against the ground as she throws it away.

I gasp, letting my lungs fill with a breath I didn't think I'd get to take. Each inhale makes the fresh cuts on my chest burn but I'm still alive. *I'm alive.*

Angelica's hand settles on my sternum, and I grunt in pain. She leans down till her face hovers over mine. "Take your promise back. Tell me you didn't mean it and that it's okay for me to kill."

Tears sting my eyes. I shake my head and one falls loose. It runs down the side of my face. "I'm not going to do that."

Angelica shrieks, her breath hot and angry against my skin. She stands back up and the air shudders out of me.

She paces back and forth before facing me again. Her hands move to my wrists and the chains holding me loosen. Hope flutters beneath my chest but the scars on my body keep it trapped.

"What are you doing?" I ask.

The chains clank against the metal table as Angelica works. She wastes no time, unlocking each of my restraints till the only thing holding me to the table is my fear of my own sister.

"Get up," she orders.

I ease myself to sitting. The edge of the table is slick with blood. I swallow down my own vomit and wipe my hand against my pants. My eyes flick to the door over Angelica's shoulder.

She looks over at it then back at me. "Go on, then. Do it."

I shake my head. "You're not just going to let me go."

She shrugs. "If you can get past me, you can leave." Her arms hang down by her side. She's going for nonchalance, but I know how to read my own twin. Her face is set, her eyes cold.

"I know what you're trying to do. You think if I fight you, you'll be able to kill me because that's self-defense." I stay sat on the table, my legs hanging over the edge like a teenager at school. "I won't do it."

"So, you're just going to stay here?" Her eyebrows raise. "I called Dad when you were out. He's missed you."

Everything inside of me locks up. I force myself to keep my face blank but the idea of seeing my dad makes me want to puke.

Angelica keeps pressing. "Besides, don't you have a boyfriend or three to get back to? I wonder whether they'd still be waiting for you if I told them all the things you've done."

The sharp underside of the table bites into my fingers. "They already know."

She huffs out a laugh and bends down to pick up the knife. "You're fooling yourself if you think they actually care for you. They're just using you to get to dad. They had you tagged, like an animal."

"This won't work." She's trying to goad me into fighting, but I barely have the energy to hold myself up. Everything she's saying I've thought myself a hundred times over. On paper it makes no sense for the guys to like me. I'm everything they fight against. But I can still feel Jude's fingers on my cheek. I can hear Oz's laugh and see the maddening heat burning in River's eyes. Even the cocky cowboy likes me. He doesn't want to, but he does.

Angelica tilts her head to the side. "Are you in love with them? Because they won't love you back."

I meet her gaze. "You don't know that."

She cocks an eyebrow and says just two words. "Madison Briggs."

Maddie's face flashes through my mind. Her curly blonde hair and her shaky smile. She was the first one he made us cut. I bite my cheek. "What about her?"

Her mouth rounds. "Oh. You really don't know."

My heart kicks up a storm under my ribs and the adrenaline has me hopping off the table. I take a step towards Angelica before I stop myself. My hands clench into fists. "Know what?"

She laughs, a breathy, disbelieving sound. "Maddison Briggs: wife to Eddison March and mother... to Elijah March."

My limbs go cold. It feels like the rest of my blood drains from my veins. "No." The word trips past frozen lips. "No. No." I keep repeating it, like my body thinks if I say it enough it won't be true, but my mind is connecting the dots. The way Eli flirted with me outrageously... until he found out my true identity. The moment in the hall with his hand around my neck, pure hatred in his eyes. How he told me that liking me was the biggest fucking betrayal in the world.

"Oh my god." My hand covers my mouth. Tears prick my eyes, but their sting is just a fraction of the pain I deserve.

I tortured Eli's mother.

I watched her die.

Angelica moves closer to me. She runs her hand though my hair like I used to do to her when we were kids. "Shh," she says. "Listen. Do you hear that?"

I hold in my sobs and listen. The rumble of tires against gravel. An engine humming before switching off.

Angelica smiles. "Daddy's back."

A deafening bang punches through the warehouse and the door behind Angelica slams open.

Eyes gleaming with victory lock on me.

He's here.

52

ELI

I crack my neck again, but the ache is trapped deep in the bone, a hundred times worse than usual. I can't even ask for some pain meds because the nurses are mad at us. We've turned Oz's hospital room into an investigation room, and they keep glowering our way every time they come to check on him. I guess having the window and walls covered in crime scene photos isn't viewed as conducive to healing.

Any other time I'd be charming the hell out of those nurses but right now the only thing I can think about is finding Freya. We've just passed the six-hour mark since Jude found her gone and my chest keeps getting tighter. *Fuck*. I shouldn't feel this way.

Oz has a minor concussion exacerbated by the drugs in his system, but he's going to be okay. None of us wanted to leave him alone though, hence the angry nurses. He confirmed Freya was at the warehouse with him and her twin, but he doesn't know what time she arrived or how long he was out before waking up near the gas station.

I look over at him in the hospital bed. He's propped up against the cushions, working with River to try and remember everything he can about the warehouse. Dark circles hang under his eyes and butterfly strips hold together the cut on his forehead, but he looks a lot better than he did before.

Jude comes back in holding a plastic cup filled with ice chips for Oz. He keeps going on pointless errands because he can't stand still right now.

Jude's like my opposite when it comes to being stressed. He buzzes with energy; I go quiet and mean. I don't like the cruel side to me. It reminds me too much of how my dad gets when he's missing mum. My head's been so screwed up lately that the darkness has been right at the surface. Freya's reaction when we accused her of hurting Camilla and Posy was what finally jolted me out of it.

Eva was right, I care for Freya and part of me still hates that, but I've been trying my best to make amends for the way I've treated her. If we don't figure out where she is soon, I might never get a chance to make things right.

I run a hand over my face. We should have kept a closer eye on her. We knew she was a flight risk. What really worries me though, is how reckless she is. I know where her type of recklessness stems from, it's what happens when you don't value your own life. I've seen glimpses of the way she views herself and it's not good. She may attest her innocence, but she feels guilty, and I'm scared it's going to be the death of her.

River's phone buzzes against the bedside table. He checks the screen and puts it on speaker. "Ramsey, tell me you've found something."

Ramsey keeps it short and sweet. "Traces of paint."

"What does that mean?" I ask.

"Most likely that the bomb was made in a location with a lot of paint about. They found traces in the tire tracks as well."

River's eyes snap to Oz. "A warehouse?"

"Could be. It would offer plenty of space and they're usually in secluded enough areas in case something goes wrong."

"Thanks, Ramsey." River hangs up.

Jude's already opened his laptop and is tapping away at the keys.

Oz holds out a hand. "I can do it. I'll be quicker."

Jude shifts away and shoots him a scowl. "You're not supposed to look at screens."

Oz is right though; he would be quicker. It's taking Jude a while, so I turn back to the crime scene photos of our kitchen that we Blu-Tacked to the wall.

I scan the pictures the techs took; a few strands of Freya's hair; a scuff on the floor; Oz's drugged coffee cup. There must be some clue as to where Freya's twin took Oz. If Freya could find her then– *Fuck.*

I spin around to face the others. "How did Freya know where to go?"

Jude looks up from the screen. "Are we sure she didn't have another burner phone?"

River shakes his head. "I would have noticed. And," he clears his throat, "I may have placed a jammer in her room."

Oz quirks an eyebrow. "She's going to love that."

"Okay so how then?" I ask again. "How did she know exactly where to go?"

When we got back to the house, Jude and I went

upstairs to look for Oz. River and Freya stayed in the kitchen. "Think back," I say to him. "What did she do when we found Oz missing? What did she see?"

River's eyes flick up to the corner as he thinks. His jaw hardens. "The coffee cup. She picked up the coffee cup."

I grab all the photos of the coffee cups off the wall and place them on the bed on Oz's blanket. We pour over the images.

"Wait, wait," Jude says. "Those scribbles on the cup, I've seen them before." Jude goes back to his laptop and pulls up another image. He turns the screen to face us.

"Is that Maxwell's old house?"

Jude nods. The image is of a wall in the basement, covered with non-sensical scribbles. It was almost six years ago that we found the house and by the time we got there Maxwell was long gone.

Jude scrolls through more photos, close-ups on the lines. "The markings are too repetitive and structured to be random. We figured it was a code but it's complex. The shapes aren't just replacing letters, there's an added element to it that we couldn't figure out. Oz and I spent a while trying to solve it, but seeing as we thought Freya was dead and we already knew Maxwell's identity, we decided it wasn't worth our time."

I hold the photo of the coffee cup up to the screen. *Holy shit.* "It's the same code."

Oz sits forward, wincing a little as he does so. "Jude, have you found a list of warehouses yet?"

Jude clicks onto a different tab. "Five abandoned warehouses that were used for storing paint or for processes that involve paint and three that are temporarily out of order due to maintenance."

My eyes flick to the clock over by the door. The second-hand ticks like a countdown to a bomb. "We don't have time to search all eight locations."

"We might not have to." Oz watches Jude. He's traded the computer for a scrap of paper, scribbling out the code from the coffee cup. "Part of the message has to be a unit number, right? That gives us a starting point. If we input the eight different addresses we have, the correct one should act as a key for the code."

Jude's curls fall around his face as he works. The speed at which his brain functions never fails to amaze me. He whizzes through the different options, inputting them into a program on the computer that's connected to the rest of the code we gathered from the basement.

On his fifth attempt the shapes on the screen translate into English. He looks over the rim of the laptop at Oz and grins. "Jack-and the bean stalk-Pot."

"Oh, that's a good one."

I groan towards the ceiling. "Address, Jude?"

"Right, sorry." He taps a couple more keys and our phones ping with the address.

"230 Miller Street," River reads. "It's fifteen minutes away. Let's go."

Oz pulls back his blankets.

Jude's eyes widen. "Woah, what are you doing?"

Oz stares at River. "I'm coming."

River works his jaw, but Oz doesn't back down. "Fine, but you're staying in the car."

53

FREYA

I'm scared. I want to run. I want to run faster and farther than I ever have before, and it takes the amount of self-control I thought only River had to stay rooted to the cold concrete floor.

I've played out this moment over and over again. The day I find my father. I wanted it to happen, I've been hunting him and now he's here. Twenty feet away from me. Only I didn't find him. He found me. And I underestimated how bone-crushingly terrified I would be.

I'm trembling from the inside out, like my organs are fighting to escape my body because they remember exactly how much pain this man can cause. My breath stutters in my chest as I struggle to find oxygen.

He takes a step towards me and his army boot hitting the concrete has me scrambling back. I grip the edge of the metal table Angelica chained me to. I'm not a rising star detective right now, I'm a little girl in her living nightmare and the monster is coming for me.

He moves closer.

Angelica takes hold of my hand but I don't fool myself

into thinking it's an offer of support. She's merely preventing me from running.

Arthur Maxwell stops in front of me, his dark brown eyes taking me in.

I'm in my underwear, my chest dripping with blood from Angelica's handiwork. He smiles at the sight and gives my sister a nod of approval.

The cold air chills my skin.

I force myself to focus on him. He looks different than before. Not so much that I don't recognize him, but he's clearly had enough work done that facial recognition wouldn't. Brown hair slicked back, eyes blue instead of hazel. His cheeks are rounder, his nose smaller and he's grown a short, neatly trimmed beard. It all makes him look softer, less like the killer I know he is.

My dad raises his hand and I flinch.

Nothing happens.

Always do the unexpected.

I open my eyes to see his hand waiting inches from my face. He picks up a strand of my hair, stuck to my cheek with sweat, and tucks it behind my ear. "Hello, daughter of mine."

I don't know whether it's from pain or fear or both, but I turn to the side and throw up. Spots of vomit splatter against his boots. I wipe my forearm against my mouth and stand up.

Maxwell's perfect new face twists in disgust. "Your tolerance is far too low." He nods to my chest. "A few cuts are nothing. We'll have to build your stamina back up."

My vision blurs and I flash back to my childhood. To days in that basement as my dad cut over the crosses in my skin, opening them up again every time they began to heal. I'm getting dragged under into the memories and it's only when they start talking about Oz that I'm able to ground myself.

"Where's the agent?" my father asks.

Angelica tips up her chin. "I dealt with him."

"What?" his voice drops low, quiet and the threat in it has me trembling.

"He talked too much. I wanted to be alone."

Maxwell narrows his eyes. He looks around the warehouse, like he's realizing he might not be as in control as he thought.

A flutter of hope unfurls under the pain in my chest as I follow his thoughts.

"Despite all my efforts to perfect you, Angelica, you can't kill. So, what exactly, does 'dealing with him' mean? Tell me you did not let him go?"

Angelica's grip on my hand tightens. "He's not in any state to do anything."

Maxwell slaps her across the face. Her head snaps round from the impact and for a moment our eyes meet. I stare at her, tears clouding in her eyes.

"You stupid girl." He takes out his knife. It's his favorite one. Seven inches long with a bone handle and glistening steel. The steps for disarming an armed suspect run through my mind. I could take that knife from him, I know I could, but I don't make a single move.

He presses the tip of the knife to Angelica's neck and tilts her chin upwards. Her green eyes go blank. She stares up at him. "Wait here," he orders.

She nods.

He turns to me. He presses the flat side of the knife against my cheek. I try to go to that blank place. The one my sister finds safety in. Instead, I find myself thinking of Jude. Of him spinning on his chair. Of Eli flipping his

Stetson. Of Oz watching me with heated eyes and River holding me steady.

My father smiles at me, soft and gentle. "Don't worry, I'll be back for you." And with that he twists the knife and cuts a line of fire down my cheek. It's not much more than a scratch compared to the damage Angelica has done to my chest and I manage to stop myself from screaming.

Maxwell turns away and heads to the back of the warehouse. I watch him go, willing my feet to chase after him, to wrestle the knife off Angelica and launch it into his back. Then he slips out the door and I'm too late.

54

ELI

It takes us ten minutes to get to the warehouse because River gives me the keys and if there's one thing I'm good at, it's driving fucking fast. Jude called SWAT for back up, but we've beat them to the scene and there's no way I'm waiting.

The warehouse is nothing much. Corrugated metal with rusted corners and a small door to the side.

Jude, River, and I, draw our weapons and pause outside the door. Freya's voice carries through the metal and my shoulders drop a fraction. Except then I hear his voice and I explode. The man who killed my mother is on the other side of that door.

"Eli, wait!" River calls but I'm too far gone to listen. I kick down the door and storm inside, gun raised.

The warehouse is cold. Empty. I scan the shadows for Maxwell but he's not here. *Why isn't he here?* My heart stutters in my chest. I blink rapidly.

"Eli." Freya's voice breaks on my name and my vision settles on her. Tears and blood track down her face and I'm so focused on the blood covering her chest that it takes me a second to see the knife at her throat. Freya's twin really is identical to her, it's easy to see how Oz was fooled.

She's got her arm banded around Freya's waist, using her as a shield as she presses the knife to her throat.

"He went out the back," Freya says.

My feet move, already taking me to the back door behind them but then the knife at Freya's throat draws blood.

"Nu huh, you don't want to do that," Freya's sister warns.

I go still as a fucking statue. My instincts are fighting with each other, pulling me in different directions. This is the closest I've ever been to the man that killed my mother and logic is telling me to go after him, to sprint to that back door. Jude and River can take care of Freya. This is my shot.

Except I can't move.

I can't leave her here with a knife at her throat.

I'm not sure when my priorities shifted. When protecting Freya became more important to me than catching Maxwell. But the realization tears at my heart. I feel like I'm betraying my mother all over again. And yet I still can't fucking move.

River edges in front of me and Jude stops by my side. "Let her go," River orders.

I shake myself and step to the side, raising my gun.

"Don't shoot, don't shoot!" Freya shouts at us.

Her twin smirks. "You should listen to my sister. She's always been protective. She won't let you hurt me." She sounds just like Freya.

"Let her go and I won't have to," River commands.

"Angelica," Freya whispers, "just do as he says." Oz

told us she called herself Angelica but it's still weird to hear in person. *Does she think she's Freya?*

"No!" Angelica digs the knife in, and a trickle of blood runs down Freya's pale neck.

River's hands tighten around his gun.

"River, don't," Freya begs. "She won't hurt me."

"She already has." He bites the words out, his eyes dropping to the cuts marking her bare stomach.

"River, look at me."

He does as she asks. I keep my gaze on the knife, watching for the slightest of movements.

"I need you to trust me," Freya says. "Don't shoot her. She won't kill me."

Jude lowers his gun a fraction. "Are you sure?"

The knife shifts a little as Freya swallows. "I'm sure."

I take my gaze off the knife to look at her eyes. I've spent every day since Freya came into our lives studying her. I may have been wrong about her intentions, but I know when she's fudging the truth and right now, she's lying through her fucking teeth.

"River," I warn.

"I know."

Jude lifts his gun again but none of us have a clear shot. They're the same height and we can't shoot Angelica without risking hitting Freya.

Angelica rests her chin on Freya's shoulder. "Oops, too slow." She tilts the knife.

Freya closes her eyes.

The back of the warehouse explodes. The sound smacks against my ears, smoke fills the air and then the SWAT team, led by Oz, swarm inside.

Angelica whips around and a gunshot cracks through the room. She cries out and drops the knife. She falls to her knees, gripping her shoulder and Freya stumbles towards us.

I holster my gun and rush to her, catching her in my arms when she sways. "Eli, I'm so sorry." The words slip from her lips before her eyes flutter closed.

55

FREYA

I'm back in the hospital. My chest is covered in bandages once again and my arm is hooked up to an IV. I lost more blood than I thought from the cuts Angelica made which is why I apparently passed out in Eli's arms.

The guys have all pulled up chairs around my bed and it feels like the first time I sat in their living room and told them my story. Only this time there's not going to be any half-truths or hidden lies.

They didn't catch my father. Instead, they found one of the SWAT team dead, his throat cut and his vest missing. That's how he'd slipped away, by pretending to be one of us. We got Angelica though. My sister is locked in a cell somewhere and if I ever want to see her again, I have to come clean.

River's sat to my right. He leans back in his chair, his hands locked together in his lap. Waiting.

I take a sip of water and fiddle with the plastic cup. There's no easy way to explain the mess that was my childhood, so I just dive right in. "My father raised us as one person." I look up at the guys. "He gave us the same name, the same scars. He said being identical would be our greatest weapon. The perfect alibi."

Jude taps his fingers against the arm of his chair. "One of you commits the crime while the other is out in public."

"Exactly. No one knew we were twins. He only registered one child and he never let us out at the same time. We'd take it in turns to be 'Angelica'. One of us would go to school, eat dinner, sleep in our proper bedroom, while the other stayed at home, locked in the basement. We switched out every day. I always thought someone would notice but they never did."

My fiddling breaks the rim of the cup. "It's partly my fault, I never got close to anyone but it's hard to make friends when you don't know what you said to them the day before."

Oz reaches out and gives my foot a quick squeeze over the blanket. "None of this is your fault," he says, the slight Scottish lilt seeping into his voice. "You were a child."

That's what Carmen used to say to me. Well, with an added swear word or two. She'd like Oz. "I wanted to tell someone, but he used us as insurance against each other. He said if one of us told he'd have to kill the other one to prove we were lying." I close my eyes. My father is a manipulative shit. As I got older, I realized even the way he phrased it was designed to control us. He didn't say he would kill my sister, he said if I messed up, he'd *have to,* like it would be my fault.

"I take it there's still no sign of him?" I ask River.

He shakes his head.

"I told you he looks different now, right? He's had plastic surgery."

"You said. We'll get you to sit down with a sketch artist when you're feeling better."

Eli sits froward. He rests his elbows on his knees and passes his cowboy hat from hand to hand. "What did your sister want from you?"

The doctors have pumped me full of painkillers, but Eli's question makes every new cut burn.

I put my cup down and pull my knees up to my chest. "You have to understand, Angelica isn't like me, but she is a *good* person." I catch Eli and River glancing at each other, and my fist tightens around the blanket. My voice hardens. "When we were six years old I let one of the women my dad brought back escape."

Jude's eyes widen but I shake my head.

"She didn't get far, and he knew one of us had helped her." I run my teeth over my bottom lip and take a shaky breath. I've never told anyone this before, not even Carmen. "I got scared and my sister took the blame. When one of us got punished we both did - we had to stay identical you see. But this time, after he cut us, he took Angelica down to the basement." My chin trembles and I force myself to lift my head, to look at each of the guys. "He left her there, in the dark, for three weeks. She was six. Terrified and alone, while I was upstairs living like a normal child. I got to go to school every day, sleep in a proper bed." My smile is sad, bitter. "I made a friend. Her name was Olive and we said we'd be friends forever. It was the best three weeks of my life." My voice cracks.

I brush a tear off my cheek with the back of my hand, but I can't find the breath to carry on. It feels like my lungs are being turned inside out. I close my eyes.

The bed shifts beneath me and then I'm being carefully lifted forward as a warm, solid body settles behind me.

"I've got you," River says, his lips soft against my ear. His hands hold my arms, careful not to touch where it hurts.

I rest my head against his shoulder and gradually learn to breathe again.

Jude drags his chair closer and links his fingers through mine.

I take a deep breath and carry on. "When he let her out, she was different. Empty. It was like she'd made herself numb to everything. I tried to bring her back, but she wouldn't talk to me for months and when she finally did, I knew she wasn't the same. She still protected me fiercely, but it was like I was the only person she cared about. Everyone else was fair game. I tried to make her see that what our father was doing was wrong but..."

Oz squeezes my foot again. "The psychological damage of being isolated for so long at such a young age would be almost irrevocable. There was likely nothing you could have done."

I meet his gaze and nod. Logically, I know he's right, but I was the one who let the woman escape, I was the reason Angelica got punished and it still felt like my mistake to fix. "When we were nine, she told me she liked cutting them, his victims. I made her promise to me, there and then, that she would never kill anyone."

Oz sits back and adjusts his glasses. "She said your father was mad at her because she couldn't take the final step, she couldn't kill."

I run the pad of my thumb over Jude's knuckles, grounding myself through his and River's touch. "I guess she thought if I was dead her promise would be null and void."

"Freya, look at me." River's chest vibrates against me.

I tilt my head back.

He uses the side of his knuckles to lift my chin till he can look me in the eyes. "Do you realize that at nine-years-old you single-handedly stopped your sister from becoming a serial killer?"

I swallow. "You don't understand. It's my fault she's like that in the first place. I shouldn't have let her take the blame." I try to shake my head, but he holds my chin between his thumb and forefinger.

"She protected you," River says. "Just like you've spent the last eighteen years protecting her. It's what we do for family. You got her out, Freya. You got her away from your father. We'll make sure she's looked after."

I pull away from him, twisting in the bed so I can face him properly. "Why? Why would you do that? She's dangerous, she kidnapped Oz, she –"

"Is your sister," Jude cuts me off.

River nods. "And you and her are not the problem, your father is. And now we've got your sister, maybe she can lead us to him."

I look at each of the guys. They nod, determination set in their eyes. Even Eli is in agreement.

I don't know how to process everything I'm feeling right now. I've never had people care for me the way they do. On top of the blood loss and the torture, the emotion overload is too much to take. So, I lie back and bury my face in River's chest.

He presses a kiss to my head and runs his knuckles up and down my back.

I close my eyes and just let him hold me.

56

FREYA

Another woman is missing.

Isabella May.

She's an identical twin and Jude just got word she hasn't been seen in over twenty-four hours. I should be looking for her but instead I'm sitting on the edge of my hospital bed. I'd already be half-way out of this place if it wasn't for the imposing man towering in front of me.

I poke River in the chest. I blink, it's like touching rock. *So not the time for this, Freya.* Shaking my thoughts clear, I raise my eyebrows at him. "As attractive as you look being all glower-y and stuff, we don't have time for you to be an over-protective control freak, right now."

River grabs my finger. His hand is warm, solid. "It's not even been twenty-four hours," he tells me, like I've forgotten I spent yesterday reliving my childhood.

"And how long do you think it will take for my father to figure out Angelica is not coming back? To kill Isabella?" I counter. "He's not going to hang around River, he will leave, and we will lose our best chance at catching him."

River's face remains hard, unbreakable. "You're injured. You need to rest. We'll interrogate Angelica again and find–"

"All four of you have already spoken to her and got nothing." I flatten my palm over his shirt. "Let me talk to her."

River's mask cracks a little, fear radiating from his eyes. "She hurt you. I–" He swallows. "I don't even want you in the same *state* as her, let alone the same room."

My shoulders drop. I like that he wants to keep me safe, I really do. But this is never going to work if he wraps me in cotton wool. I push gently against his chest until he steps back then I stand up. "I'm a detective, River. My job is dangerous, but I am good at it. I know how to protect myself."

"I know you can protect yourself. My worry is that you'll choose not to again." He looks down at me, disapproval carved into the rigid lines of his face. "You put yourself in danger yesterday to save Oz."

I run my hand up his chest and cup his cheek. "Wouldn't you?"

His eyes flutter shut, his brows knitted in pain.

"It's what we do," I press. "Every day we put ourselves in danger to protect others."

He opens his eyes. His jaw clenches under my hand and I brush my thumb over his cheekbone. "I don't like it," he says through gritted teeth.

I give him a sad smile. "You don't have to like it. But you need to let me do it. She'll talk to me."

He growls. "You're my asset. You're supposed to do as you're told."

I laugh. "Did you ever really think that was going to happen?"

His hands drop to my hips, and he tugs me towards him.

I fall into his chest as he grumbles against my hair. "Never."

I smile against his shirt.

Angelica's being held at my old station. Technically, to keep my cover, I'm still employed here and just on loan to the FBI. I figure quite a few heads would have turned when River walked in with my twin in cuffs.

Ruiz's dark eyebrows skyrocket when she sees me and all four of the guys, walking towards the interrogation rooms. She kicks Luke's chair, and he looks over at me, a question in his eyes.

I nod to let him know I'm okay. I need to get a drink with him soon. Now River and the guys know everything, I can finally tell Luke the truth. With any luck, we can toast to putting my father behind bars too.

I'm pretty sure Angelica will talk. I have a feeling she's been refusing to speak so that she gets to see me. It may have been six years since we've seen each other but a twin bond forged in abuse is not easily broken.

River stops me outside the locked door to the interrogation room. "Are you sure you want to do this?" He scans me up and down.

I don't exactly look the part. I'm wearing joggers and one of Jude's t-shirts that's baggy enough to fit over my bandages. The cuts still ache but I'm on a heavy dose of painkillers and after a night of sedated sleep my mind feels surprisingly clear. "I've got this," I tell River.

He nods at the guard who unlocks the door with a key

attached to her belt. River, Jude, Eli, and Oz go into the viewing room. I take a deep breath and walk inside.

Angelica's shoulder is bandaged where Oz shot her. Her right wrist is cuffed to the table while her left arm rests in a sling across her chest.

"You came." She smiles at me. It's a simple, innocent smile like the one she gave me when we were eight and I snuck us outside to play together in the garden.

The metal chair scrapes against the floor as I pull it out and take a seat across from her. I eye her sling. "Are you alright?"

She shrugs with her good shoulder. "We've had worse."

I meet her eyes, a carbon copy of mine and nod. *We really have.*

"What happens now?" she asks, and she doesn't sound like the manic woman who cut into me yesterday. She sounds like a scared young girl.

I rest my hands on the table. The cold metal chills my skin but I don't pull away. "Now, I apologize," I tell her. I can practically feel River's glare through the two-way mirror behind me. I wet my lips and focus on my sister. "I broke my promise. I swore I would never leave you and I did and I'm sorry. I shouldn't have done that, and I am so proud of you for not breaking yours."

She frowns and pushes at her cuticles with her thumb. "I wanted to. I tried to."

"I know, but you didn't."

Her eyes laser in on me. "Maybe I did, maybe I'm lying. I'm good at that."

She is, but not to me. I take her hand and stop her from scratching her fingers to shreds.

She goes still.

I let out a steady breath. "I need you to tell me where dad is."

She shakes her head, short sharp jerks.

"Angelica."

"No. No. I won't. I can't."

"Yes, you can."

"No!" She screams and stands up, sending her chair crashing to the floor.

I get up and hold up my hand to the mirror, stopping the guys from coming storming in.

Angelica yanks at the cuff locking her to the table. She pulls hard, the metal cutting into her wrist as she throws her head back and forth, her eyes squeezed shut.

I round the table and grab her arm. "Stop it. You're going to hurt yourself."

She doesn't listen to me, wrenching her body away from the table.

I hook my arm around her waist and pull her into me. "Allie, please stop," I beg, calling her what I used to before dad caught on to the fact we'd given each other nicknames. "Please, Allie."

She sucks in a breath and lets out a pained keen. She crumples against me and presses her forehead into my shoulder.

I hug her to me as she sobs, my top dampening with her tears. I cradle the back of her head with my hand and whisper into her ear. "You never have to see him again. He can't hurt you anymore. I won't let him. You did it," I say, "you got out. We both did." Pressure grows under my eyes, and I realize I'm crying too.

We sink to the floor, gripping onto each other so tightly it hurts. We cry for what feels like hours, the two of us a storm cloud releasing all the pain our father gave us. We are tied together with rusted chains. Our lives fused with matching scars. Her cuts bleed in time with mine. No-one else knows what we went through. No one else lived it.

My sister is damaged, I know that, but deep inside her is the other half of me and my hold around her shaking body is a promise: I will never let her go again.

When our tears have dried and my muscles ache from holding her so tightly, she twines her fingers with mine and gives me an address.

57

FREYA

The bulletproof vest is heavy. My chest burns from the weight of it pressing against my cuts but according to River it was wear the vest or be left behind.

We drive over a bump and I suppress a wince. I have a feeling if River sees how much pain I'm in, he'll insist on taking me back to the hospital. And there's no way I'm missing this.

"We're approaching now. Pink house on the right," Jude says from the driver's seat.

I press my forehead up against the window and look out. The bungalow is quaint. Pretty. It's the sort of place you'd expect a sweet old couple to live, not the country's most wanted serial killer.

Green vines of ivy climb up the pink walls and a warm glow emanates from the porch lights in the early evening dusk.

We're only half an hour away from my house. The thought of my father living so close crawls up my back like that deceptively innocent ivy.

Jude doesn't slow down as we near and I catch sight of

the SWAT team vehicles in the wing mirror. "Everybody ready?" River asks.

We all nod and River twists in the passenger seat to look at me. "You sure you want to be here for this?"

I hold his gaze, steady, determined. "I'm sure."

He nods. A glimmer of approval flickers in his eyes despite the fact I know he'd rather I was tucked safely away. His faith in me strengthens my resolve and I draw my gun.

Jude grinds the car to a sharp stop and kills the engine.

"Let's go," River calls.

We push the doors open and climb out. The back-up vehicles pull up behind us, the SWAT team pouring out in full combat gear. River and the team leader exchange signals and the SWAT guys go ahead.

Our approach is quiet. Two of the SWAT team position themselves in front of the door and silence hangs over us like a thunder cloud. They count down on their fingers, three, two, one...

The battering ram slams into the door and we explode into action. The door splinters and SWAT swarm inside, their shouts filling the air like cracks of thunder.

We follow after them, River leading us as we move seamlessly, the perfect team. It feels like I've been part of this group for a lifetime, not a couple of weeks. We lift our weapons, watching each other's backs as we clear the different rooms of my father's hide out. I grip my gun tighter each time, mentally bracing for seeing him again. He's a smart man, he'll come peacefully once he sees he's outnumbered, but my father doesn't need a knife to cut me. His words will do just fine.

We stop in the living room. Floral sofas and a coffee

table with a white laced cloth have me questioning whether this is the right place but then I remember how good my dad is at living a double life. For seventeen years, to the outside world, he was a caring and loving father. To me and my sister, he was a monster.

I'm so hyper-focused it's not until Harper, the SWAT team leader, joins us in the living room that I realize why we've stopped. We've searched everywhere. He's not here.

I lower my gun. "No. No, he has to be here." Panic threads my voice and Harper's gaze flicks over to me before returning to River.

"There's a basement," she says.

My body revolts. Bile pushes at my throat but I swallow it down, already moving.

"Freya, wait," River orders.

I don't listen. I'm already out of the living room, my feet eating up the space covered by patterned rugs.

Two of the SWAT team stand guard in the hallway. One of the rugs has been pulled back to reveal a trapdoor secured with a padlock. Part of the wood has been sawn away, so the padlock is hidden flush against the floor. I wonder how many people have walked through this hall not knowing what lies beneath it.

I don't know whether it's the look on my face, or River and the guys at my back, but the SWAT agents part as I approach. I nod at the one with the lock cutters and he snaps the padlock between the metal blades.

I drop to my knees and remove the broken lock. The SWAT guys aim their weapons at the trapdoor and I wedge my fingers in the recess, gripping the edge of the panel. I take one second to compose myself, then I pull it up.

It's dark down there. Jude lets out a breath when no one shoots up at me. My eyes adjust, revealing a thin set of steps leading down. I look back at River.

His jaw is sharper than I've ever seen it, his eyes dark, but he nods.

I pick up my gun, take the torch offered by the SWAT guy and slowly descend. The light from the torch cuts through the shadows as I scan the basement.

The beam catches on crimson blood. A body slumped against the wall.

I gasp but force myself to finish the sweep before coming back to the middle of the wall and the woman tied up there. I holster my gun and skid onto my knees in front of her. My fingers tremble as I ease the cloth gag from between her teeth. Her chest is cut up and her head lolls to the side. I press my fingers to her neck and a sob falls from my lips when I find a pulse.

"She's alive," I say as the others join me. "She's alive." Someone flicks a switch, and a bare bulb floods the space with light so bright it hurts my eyes. "Isabella? Isabella?" I gently shake her shoulders.

Her eyelids flutter. She cringes away from the light then seems to remember where she is. A whimper breaks from between her cracked lips and she scrambles away.

"It's okay, it's okay." I point at the initials on my vest. "We're FBI." I hold out my hand.

She looks from my face to my vest and then all around the room at the other officers. Relief flashes in her eyes and she bursts into tears. Someone passes me a blanket and I draw it around her shoulders, covering her naked chest. I undo the rope around her wrists and she clings to the edges of the blanket.

"Can you walk?" I ask.

She nods and I help her to her feet. I guide her over to Oz. He's the gentlest of the guys. It's in his eyes, in the way he uses his hands. He's who Isabella needs right now. I'd go with her myself, but my mind is still stuck in this basement, on what I saw on the wall behind her.

"This is Oz," I say, softly. "He's going to take you outside to an ambulance. Is that okay?"

Isabella nods.

I smile at her, trying to keep the inner panic off my face.

Oz shoots me a questioning look but I give a subtle shake of my head. I pass Isabella over to him and when she's safely up the steps I turn back to the wall.

Jude's the first one to notice what I'm looking at. He catches River and Eli's attention and nods to the wall then he comes to stand by my side.

"What does it say?" he asks.

I decode the scribbles on the wall, my voice flat as I read the message out loud. "'She looks like Eli's mother don't you think? What a shame you couldn't save her too'".

I hear Eli stop breathing from across the room. He doesn't say anything, just climbs back upstairs. A crash sounds in the distance and I flinch.

"They've been watching us. How is he getting so close without anyone noticing?" Jude's question is directed at River, but River doesn't answer. He's too busy watching me, his eyes narrowed.

"Freya, what is it?"

I still haven't looked away from the wall. My body's gone numb and even if my dad swanned back into the room right this second, I'm not sure I could do anything other than stare.

"Freya," River snaps and it breaks me out of it a little. My heart kicks into overdrive. The panic rises inside of me and I look away from the wall to face River.

"He knew," I choke out. "All this time he knew."

River strides towards me. He grips me by the elbows, one hand coming up to guide my face back to his when I look towards the wall again. "Knew what?"

"The code. It was the one thing we had. The one thing that was just ours and not his. Something he couldn't touch." A sob wrenches from my chest. "But he knew, all this time, he knew exactly what we were saying to each other. Every word. Every message. He knew." The words tumble from my mouth. They mix with my sobs and stop making sense, just garbled sounds of suppressed pain. Even six years after I escaped, my father can still hurt me. I've spent so long trying to heal myself, but I'm still broken.

And now he's gone. Again.

Free to keep on killing and killing. And every single death will be on my hands because I failed.

Again.

I failed to tell anyone when I was a child.

I failed to hunt him down after I was free.

And now, even with a whole team of FBI agents on my side, I've failed again.

My legs give out beneath me.

River catches me under my arms and picks me up. He shifts till he's holding me against his chest, one arm underneath my legs, the other at my back. He murmurs soft words in my ear and carries me out of the basement.

I bury my face in the crook of his arm.

"We'll get him, Freya, I promise you," River swears.

I don't say anything. I can't. For the first time, I'm not sure I believe him.

58

ELI

"Go away, Eli."

That's the first thing Freya says to me when I open the door to River's room. The lights are off, with just a single bedside lamp lending a soft glow to the room. His usually neatly made bed is a little creased, like it's been slept in all day. Freya's sitting on the window seat, staring out into the street.

I ignore her edict and take a step inside.

"I said, leave."

She did, but she's been saying that to all of us for the past two weeks and I'm done with it. She slept for a long time after we got back from Maxwell's house. When she woke up, she tried to go hide away in her room, but River wasn't having that, so she's hiding in here instead.

"No," I say.

She's got her legs pulled up to her chest, her feet pressing into the navy seat cushion and her arms hugging her knees. She seems so small and fragile like this but when she looks over at me, a storm brews in her eyes. "I'm resting," she says.

"You're hurting," I counter.

She lifts her shoulders and turns back to face the window and the darkening sky outside. "Maybe I deserve to hurt."

Oh no, she doesn't get to do that. She does not get to give up. We may not have found Maxwell, but we saved a woman's life. And we got Freya's sister out.

We will catch Maxwell, I will allow nothing less. And Freya is going to be by our side when we do, not wallowing in her own misery.

"Get up," I say.

She doesn't listen.

I cross the room and pull her up from under her arms, dragging her off the window seat.

"Hey!" she scrambles in my arms like a little kitten. She's barely eaten the last couple of weeks and she's light as a feather. Whatever's going on inside her head, it needs to stop.

"Put me down, Eli."

I do as she says but spin her to face me and grab her wrists the second she tries to pull away.

Her face crumples. "Just leave me alone."

"No."

"Why are you even here? Jude or Oz I'd understand, even River, but you? You hate me."

"I don't hate you."

Her green eyes are ice cold as she stares up at me. "I cut your mother."

My hands squeeze her wrists, tightening of their own accord. "Don't do that." I was wrong before. Freya is guilty of nothing. After seeing her break down in Maxwell's basement all I can picture is a seven-year-old her being put through the same horrors over and over again.

"You were a child."

"I was a monster."

I see in her eyes that she means it. That she believes it. I swallow against the emotions clogging my throat. I shouldn't have let it go this long without talking to her. I may not blame Freya anymore, but she still blames herself.

"I carved into her chest as she screamed, Eli." She steps closer into me. "And then I watched as my dad slit her throat. She begged him not to. Begged him to let her go. She said she had a son at home, waiting for her."

I breathe through my nose. "This isn't going to work," I say, even as her words claw at me. I spent years imagining what happened to my mother, but I pictured Maxwell's smirk, not a little girl. It breaks my heart all over again to relive the worst time of my life through Freya's eyes.

"You hate me, remember? I could have saved your mother, but I didn't, I killed her. Her and countless others." Freya keeps pushing but I'm a skilled enough profiler to know that's all this is. She's in a dark place right now and she thinks if she pushes me far enough, I'll snap.

"I'm not going to hurt you Freya, not like you want."

"Argh!" she screams at me and lashes out, pounding at my chest with weak fists. I gather her in my arms and spin her around till her back is against my front and her arms are pinned to her sides.

She doesn't stop struggling.

I cringe. I don't want to cause Freya anymore pain, but maybe that's what she needs.

Fuck it. If we're doing this, then we're doing it my

way. I release Freya and push her away from me. "Get on the bed."

She raises a petulant eyebrow. "Seriously?" Her voice is raw. "You're going to fuck the woman who tortured your mother?"

Her false attitude is making her bratty, but her goading finally pays off.

I collar her throat and pull her towards me. "You're drowning, I get that, but I am trying to help. If you don't do as you're told I'll call River up here and trust me, you can't handle both of us right now." A glimpse of vulnerability flickers in her eyes. "Now. Get. On. The. Bed."

She holds my stare for a while longer than pushes my hand off her neck and walks to the bed.

I fish a couple of River's ties out of his wardrobe and secure Freya's wrists to the corners of the headboard.

"What, no crop?" she asks.

I finish my last knot, the silk tie soft and erotic against her skin. I run the back of my fingers down the inside of her arm and lean over her. "There's more than one form of torture, Kitten" I whisper against her lips.

I move to the end of the bed and hook my fingers into the waistband of her pants, making sure to catch her panties too. With one sharp yank she's bare to me, and I groan at the sight of her. So soft and pretty.

Freya squirms but I hook my arms around her thighs and hold her still. "Eli..." unease threads her voice. She doesn't like being exposed to me but that's all right. This isn't about what she likes. It's about what she needs. And maybe a small part of me needs it too. I've wanted to have her like this since the first day we met after all.

I breathe her in, her sweet, musky scent going straight to my cock. I nuzzle her clit with my nose and draw my tongue through her folds. She's dripping for me, and I lap her up like a man starved, holding her down as she writhes.

Freya arches her back, her arms pulled taut against the restraints. "This isn't what I want," she bites out through gritted teeth.

I know it's not. I'm being too gentle. She wants me to hurt her. She thinks she deserves it.

"I know what you␣what," I say, "but you're not getting it."

"For fuck's sake, Eli."

I carry on with my ministrations, pushing my tongue inside of her and flicking at her clit.

Freya pants. "She cried, you know, as I made the first cut. She tried not to, but she did."

I still. I pull myself up the bed and nip at her jaw. "Enough. That's enough," I growl. "I know what you need, now *I* need *you* to trust me. Do you understand or do I need to gag you too?" I wait till she gives me the slightest nod then make my way back down her body.

I play with her, switching it up between sucking at her clit and licking the perfect pink folds of her pussy. I keep going till she starts to come then I stop abruptly, killing her orgasm before it can properly take her. I wait. This is the worst form of edging and from Freya's frustrated cry I'd say she's just realized that a ruined orgasm is worse than no orgasm at all.

"What the fuck?" she pants.

I smirk into her thigh then dive back in, winding her up again with my tongue. I bring her back to the edge, let her fall, then stop.

I repeat the process over and over until my jaw aches and Freya is a trembling mess beneath me. Tears streak her face, and her hands grip the ties keeping her trapped. The thing about this method is that it's similar to forced orgasms – you keep going and it starts to get painful.

"Stop, please stop," Freya sobs.

I sit back on my heels and look down at her. "You are not responsible for my mother's murder or any of the others," I tell her. "Say it."

She shakes her head.

"Say it, or I carry on." I'm met with stubborn silence. "Your choice, Kitten."

I lean back down. Freya jerks when my tongue touches her oversensitive clit. She struggles, trying to pull away from me but I pin down her hips and get back to work.

My teeth nip at her folds, my tongue licking a trail of fire over her slit. I thrust two fingers into her pussy, and she screams. She tastes like heaven and the sounds she's making shudder over my skin. I'm so hard it's starting to hurt but I force three more ruined orgasms on Freya before stopping again. I cup her burning mound with my palm and look down at her. "Tell me what I want to hear," I order.

Tears fall from her eyes. She's collapsed into the mattress, her body limp. Her hair is fanned out around her in a tangled mess of orange curls. But still, she shakes her head.

I squeeze her pussy hard. "Stubborn woman." She doesn't fight me this time, I don't think she has the energy. My plan was to keep this up till she gave in but when her cunt starts fluttering with the need for release, I can't hold back anymore. I reach down and free myself from my pants. In one, brutal thrust, I'm buried inside of her.

Freya's eyes widen then roll back in her head as she moans.

I pound into her. I have no doubt she's hurting but her hips thrust upwards, seeking me out as my cock fills her greedy little pussy. I feel her tighten around me and I bury my face in her neck. I suck and bite at her skin, marking her up.

"Eli, please." Her voice is tortured, desperate.

Being inside her is fucking intoxicating and I'm starting to lose my control. I need to end this, quick.

I use her juices to lube up my fingers then press the tip of my index finger against the rim of her asshole. I threatened her with this before and she tenses at my touch. She cries out as I push inside to my first, then second knuckle and the darker part of me gets off on her pain. On pushing her. Bending her. Forcing her to submit.

I bring my free hand to her throat and tilt her chin up with my thumb. "Tell me what I want to hear, and I'll let you come."

Her eyes flicker open.

"It wasn't your fault, Freya, none of it was your fault."

She swallows. Her tongue darts out, wetting her lips. "It wasn't my fault," she whispers.

I thrust into her. "Again," I say as I push my finger deeper.

"It's not my fault," she gasps.

"Good girl."

I drop my hand, squeeze her clit, and press my lips to hers as she comes apart. The orgasm tears through her and her pussy clamps down on me, milking my cock. I groan as I spill inside of her, filling her so completely with me.

My hips slow. I stay inside her as I catch my breath.

Freya gazes up at me.

I brush her curls away from her face and she leans into my palm.

"I think I hate you," she says.

I laugh and kiss her forehead. "Sure you do, Kitten."

I pull out of her slowly, the sensation shooting up my spine.

Freya winces and I smirk down at her. "Don't go anywhere," I say.

"Fucker," she murmurs, her eyes closed.

I chuckle then go into River's ensuite, clean myself up and come back with a warm cloth.

"Jesus fucking Christ, Eli," she curses when I stroke the cloth through her folds. Her cunt is red and puffy and so very well used. *Yeah, she'll be feeling that for a couple of days.* The sadist in me hums in satisfaction. Maybe I did want to hurt her, just a little.

Once I've finished cleaning her up, I untie Freya's wrists. I help her take her now sweaty t-shirt off and replace it with mine, then I lie down next to her on the bed. I'll need to get Oz in here later to redo her bandages but for now I draw her into me and trail my fingers up and down her back. She's all loose and floppy, the fight fucked out of her.

After a while she sits up, wincing again as she crosses her legs. "I want to tell you something."

"You don't have to-"

"I know, but I want to. Your mum talked about you," she says. She picks up my hand and I let her fiddle with it as she talks. "She said you were older than me, that you thought you were already a man but you'd always be her little boy."

My chest tightens but Freya isn't finished. She studies the chest of drawers opposite the bed as she talks.

"She told me to run. She said no matter how long it takes, never give up on being free, because there's a boy out there who'd do everything in his power to keep me safe."

My eyes blur. I blink and let the tears fall.

Freya looks down at me. "She loved you so much, Eli."

I nod. "I know," I say. "I always knew." I pull Freya back down beside me and hold her to my chest. I will never fully heal from losing my mother but in this moment, with Freya in my arms, I know she would be proud of me.

59

JUDE

The elevator button lights up under my finger as I press it.

Freya leans into me.

"Why am I scared?" she whispers as we ride up in the elevator to the top of Quantico.

I chuckle. Today is a good day. If you take into account all factors then logically the meeting we're heading to could go very badly. But for once in my life I feel calm. Everything's going to be alright. "You don't need to be scared."

Freya rolls her eyes at the silver doors. "Says the man who didn't commit identity fraud and run from the FBI not once but three times."

Eli snorts.

Oz takes Freya's hand and gives it a squeeze.

Freya watches the numbers on the panel light up as we rise. River's already up there, speaking to our boss. I'd try to reassure Freya more but the head of the SCU division is a formidable woman. The only one of us not at least a little bit wary of her is River and well, he's a robot.

We got a call this morning summoning us all to a meeting, our 'new asset' included. No further details were given so I don't blame Freya for being anxious. I take one of my stones out of my pocket and hand it to her.

She smiles at me and turns it over in her fingers. "What if she sends me to prison?" she asks.

Eli shrugs. "Then we'll break you out."

Freya looks over her shoulder at him. "Seriously?"

Eli raises his eyebrows. "You're not going to prison, Kitten." His gaze softens. "But yeah, I have a feeling we'd do a lot of stupid shit for you."

I nudge Freya's shoulder and grin. "What do you think? Wanna rob a bank with me?"

She laughs but the sound cuts short when the elevator stops, and the doors slide open.

River waits for us outside. He looks Freya up and down. "You ready?"

She nods.

"Farrah is strict but fair. Listen to her, tell the truth, and don't sass, understand?"

Freya salutes him. "Yes, sir."

River scowls. "Freya," he warns.

"What? I was being good!" There's a twinkle in her eye that I'm still getting used to seeing. Whatever Eli said to her last week worked wonders. She still has moments where she withdraws and gets lost in her past but she's no longer hiding away. The house feels happier with her in it. More alive.

We walk down the hall together towards Farrah's office. Her PA, Zach, makes a call then waves us through. "She's ready for you." His eyes linger on Freya as we walk past, and I move myself to block his line of sight. Turns out I'm possessive as hell when it comes to my woman.

I open the door for Freya and step back to let her pass. "Woah," Freya murmurs under her breath as she takes in the office. Large glass windows span the wall in front of us. Farrah's desk is off to the right but before it, two leather couches and an armchair surround a sharp glass coffee table.

Heels click against the wooden floor as Farrah crosses the room. She holds a posh black coffee mug in one hand and gestures to the couches with her other. "Take a seat."

We sit on the couches and Farrah settles in the armchair, crossing one slender leg over the other. She's wearing a pant suit so deep a purple it's almost black. Her nails are painted to the same purple, the color a perfect match for her brown skin.

River clears his throat and nods at Farrah. "Freya, this is SCU Unit Chief Farrah Syed."

"It's a pleasure to meet you, Ma'am," Freya says.

Farrah analyses Freya before eventually dipping her head in response. "I'd like to offer you a job."

I have to bite my cheeks to stop from grinning. I knew today was going to be a good day.

Freya sits up straighter and blinks. "What?"

"I've spent the morning going through your files. You're a very impressive young woman." Farrah places her coffee on a side table and clasps her hands together. "Finished top of your class at the Police Academy, promoted to detective in just four years. The only other person I know to have done that is sitting right next to you."

Freya glances at River then back at Farrah. "I don't understand."

"I'm offering you a job as a profiler for the Serial Crimes Unit. You'll be on Agent Park's team, your primary case will be to catch Maxwell, but the contract is permanent."

"But I broke the law."

I kick Freya's foot.

Farrah smirks. "You're not the first criminal the FBI has hired, and I very much doubt you'll be the last. I believe you'll do more good on our side than behind bars. Now, I need an answer."

"Uh, yes," Freya stutters, "I mean yes please. I'd like the job."

Farrah nods and stands up. "Good. I have some forms for you to fill out. We'll need to legally change your name of course, assuming you don't want to be known as Angelica?"

Freya shakes her head. "I don't."

Farrah strides over to her desk. Freya gets up to follow but not before turning back to us with wide eyes and a dropped jaw. All four of us grin up at her. *Welcome to the team, baby girl.*

We go out to Mozzy's bar to celebrate. Freya calls Luke and he meets us there.

"Do you think he's going to be upset I'm leaving?" Freya asks as we walk into the bar.

"I really don't care," River says.

Oz hooks his arm around Freya's shoulder. "Ignore him. Luke will miss you, but he'll understand."

I drop back to walk with River. "Careful, your jealousy is showing."

His face stays blank. "Nothing to be jealous of. She's mine."

I raise a brow. "Ours."

"Ours," he reluctantly concedes.

I shake my head. "Possessive bastard."

He smirks at me. "Don't worry, I'll share."

I feel myself start to harden at that. The idea of all of us taking Freya together. "Fuck, yes."

We join Freya, Eli, and Oz at the table. Luke is already here, sitting across from Freya. She introduces us all and I settle back in my seat, happy to just watch as Freya catches Luke up on everything. She tells him the whole story, her voice only cracking when she gets to her sister.

"River found her a place in a secure psychiatric unit. It's good there. She's safe. She'll have a trial, but the doctors are pretty sure she'll qualify for the insanity plea."

Luke lets out a low whistle when she's done. "I knew you were keeping secrets, Freya, but geez."

"There's one more thing." Her hand finds mine under the table and I give her fingers a squeeze. "I've been offered a job with the FBI."

A smile breaks out across Luke's face. "You did it," he says.

Freya smiles back. "Yeah, I did it."

"I'm going to miss you."

"Me too."

"Drinks?"

"Hell yes."

Luke waves over the bartender. He brushes his hand across the back of the bartender's leg as he places our order. The guy's cheeks blush deeply and the second he's gone Freya squeals.

"Oh my god, you totally slept with Josh!"

"Shh." Luke chuckles.

Freya sobers. "Please tell me this isn't a one-night stand or a fling to you?"

"It's not." Luke's face softens as he watches Josh behind the bar. "We're... taking things slow. He's different. *It's* different with him."

Freya smiles. "I'm happy for you."

"Yeah," Luke says, "me too."

The drinks arrive and the subjects turn to less serious stuff. We exchange our craziest case stories and Luke's actually pretty good company. Even River stops sulking eventually.

We're two rounds in and Freya's freckled cheeks are flushed pink from the alcohol when her phone rings. We gave it back to her after we'd been to Maxwell's place. She slips it out of her pocket and glances at the screen.

"I need to take this."

I slide out of the booth to let her pass and River nods at me to follow. Freya's no longer wearing the tracker but we're all too aware her father is still out there. She's not going anywhere without our protection.

Freya heads to the corridor with the toilets and I stop a few meters away, making sure she knows I'm here.

She brings the phone to her ear. "Hi," she says. "Yeah, I'm good."

There's a pause as whoever she's talking to speaks then Freya's eyebrows shoot up. "News travels fast I see." She looks over at me then turns her back and lowers her voice.

I have a feeling she's talking to the woman who helped her when she escaped from her dad. We're pretty sure she's also the person who gave Freya the means to take off her anklet. The piece of tech she used was beyond impressive and Oz is having a field day studying it. He tried using it, along with Freya's burner phone, to track Freya's contact down but hit a brick wall. We have a hunch about who this mystery woman is, but we've not told Farrah. If we're right then she's doing more good than bad, despite her illegal methods.

Freya finishes on the phone and strolls back over to me. "You're nosy, you know that?"

I hold up my hands. "If she helps keep you safe, in my books, she's golden."

Freya's eyes shine then she throws her arms around me.

I hug her back, brushing my fingers over her hair.

"Thank you," she says into my chest. "For everything."

I press a kiss to the top of her head. "Anytime, Angel. Anytime."

60

FREYA

I use my shiny new key to open the front door. My lips curl upwards as the lock disengages. This newfound freedom feels good.

The guys are still hovering a lot, but I managed to convince them to let me go out for a ride. I've finally fully healed from my sister's handiwork, and I reveled in the feeling of speeding down the roads, the vibrations rolling through my body, the force of the wind pressing against me. And now, instead of returning to an empty house, I get to come home to the guys.

I tuck my helmet under my arm and push the door open. I love how the hallway opens out straight into the living room. All I have to do is kick off my boots and take a few steps and I'm in the heart of the house.

River, Eli, Oz, and Jude are sitting on the couches. They go quiet when I come in and for a second I panic, until I see the smile on Jude's face.

I put my helmet on the side and join them in the living area. I'm about to ask what's going on when I see the FBI badge sitting on the coffee table. I grin. "Is that mine?"

River nods.

I go to reach for it, but Eli leans forward and hooks an arm around my waist, pulling me back.

"Nuh uh," he mutters, "not so fast."

I pout. "I want my badge."

"And you'll have it," River says. "But we need to get a few things straight first."

Eli tugs against my waist and I fall back onto his lap. He keeps his arm secured around me as I narrow my eyes at River.

He turns the tumbler he's been drinking from around on the side table like some sort of mafia don. He's got that look too, his eyes dark as he watches me. "This team works because we trust each other, and we work together. You are now officially one of us which means... there will be no more lies, no more secrets and most importantly no more running."

I nod, that's fair enough. They know all my secrets now anyway and the last thing I want to do is run from them. "Okay," I say.

River quirks a brow. "Try again."

Oh. I glance at the others and squirm a little in Eli's lap before giving River what he wants. "Yes, Sir."

Eli groans, his chest vibrating behind me.

"Better," River says.

I squeeze my thighs together, trying to ignore the flush of heat running through me. "Can I have my badge now?"

Eli brings his lips to my neck, and I can feel his smirk.

"Not quite," River says.

Eli's breath tickles my skin as he chuckles. "You're due a punishment, Kitten."

"Excuse me?" Indignation surges through me, competing with the fire his threat sparked. I try to push off Eli's lap, but his arm tightens like steel around my waist.

"You lied to us. You took off your tracker and you put yourself in danger," River states. "Did you really think there would be no consequences?"

I shrink into Eli's hold. At the time, I knew they'd be mad but when weeks passed by, and no-one said anything I figured I was in the clear. Apparently, River was just biding his time. I look over at Jude. "And you're all on board with this?"

Jude shrugs. "Sorry, Angel. Rules are rules."

I don't bother pointing out I seem to have a different set of rules to them, I just turn to Oz. "I saved your life."

"And I'd rather die than watch you sacrifice yourself for me again." Oz's eyes swirl with a pain I've not seen in him before. Some of my fight slips away. I hadn't thought about what it must have been like for him when I arrived at the warehouse. I was too focused on stopping my sister, but I can barely imagine the terror I'd feel if one of the guys traded their place for mine. It's the firm set of Oz's jaw and the way his hand clenches the arm of the couch that makes me realize I'm not getting out of this.

River stands up and walks over to me. He cups my cheek and draws my gaze to his face. "I think it's best we start with a clean slate, don't you?"

I scowl up at him. "If that translates as 'let me whip you with a crop before I give you your badge' then no, I don't."

Eli laughs and presses a kiss to my collarbone. "Too

bad it's not your choice." Before I can even think to do anything about it, he stands up and throws me over his shoulder.

I shriek but all that does is get me a smack on the ass. They take me upstairs to Oz's bedroom. I'm confused until all four of them walk inside. I guess this is going to be a team effort. My core tightens.

Eli places me down on the ground and my eyes dart between them. I'm equal parts scared and turned on right now and the effect it's having on my body is catching me off guard.

Oz closes the door behind him and takes a seat in an armchair to the side of the room. The chair's positioned to face the bed and it makes me wonder whether it was put there just for this. He likes to watch, after all.

River nods at Jude and Eli. "Get her ready," he orders before heading to the wardrobe.

"Woah." I hold up my hands as Jude and Eli turn to me but that just makes their lives easier as they each grab one of my arms and drag me over to the foot of the bed. Eli passes my wrists to Jude who promptly cuffs them behind my back. The familiar click resonates in my bones. "Are the cuffs really necessary?" I ask.

Eli reaches into his pocket and the flick of a pen knife cuts through the air. I freeze. The light glints off the silver blade and I can't take my eyes off it.

Eli curls his hand around the back of my neck, his thumb settling over my fluttering pulse. "Do you trust me?" he asks.

I nod. My heart thunders as he brings the blade closer towards me. I know he's not going to cut me, but the fear comes anyway.

"Hold still," he says as he slides the knife under my

shirt and slices through the material. My bra goes next, and Jude pulls the remaining scraps of clothing off of my body.

I sink against him, my heart still playing havoc in my chest.

Eli catches my eye as he puts the knife away. He presses his lips to mine. "You did good."

I let out a shaky breath as his words wash over me. I've never not been terrified of knives, but the way Eli just used his blade mixed that fear with arousal and my already damp panties are now soaked.

Eli grabs a pillow from the top of the bed and brings it down to the bottom.

I'm spun around and Jude uses his grip on my wrists to guide my upper body onto the bed. The pillow is beneath my hips, raising my ass up in the air. I swallow. It doesn't take a detective to figure out what's about to happen.

River rattles about in the wardrobe. I try to turn to see him but Jude places his hand on my head, keeping my cheek pressed against the bed.

Eli smirks again then disappears behind me. Fingers reach under me to undo my pants and with Jude holding me down all I can do is look at Oz as he sits across from me. He stares right back, his eyes dilated.

Cool air hits my skin as my pants are tugged down. Eli doesn't pull them off all the way, leaving them tangled around my ankles. A soft hand caresses my ass.

"So pretty," Eli whispers. "Such a shame it's about to be ruined."

"Not ruined," River growls, his voice low with arousal. "Marked."

A hiss whips through the air. The first hit makes me

scream. He has to have got the crop, nothing else would feel so sharp. A thin stinging line throbs against my ass. I'm still gasping from the pain when a second line of fire lights my cheeks.

I push against the bed with my shoulders trying to roll away.

"Hold her," River says.

Jude undoes the cuffs and I think for a second that might be it but then he and Eli grab my arms and sit on the bed either side of me. They keep me spread out across the mattress, their hands holding me down at the shoulders and wrists.

The next hit lands partially on top of the last one and the pain doubles. I try to kick out with my legs, but they're too caught up in my pants to do any damage.

River's fingers touch the base of my spine. "Seven more and you're done."

Seven. I close my eyes and sob into the bed but Oz snaps his fingers. "Eyes on me, Freya."

"Screw you."

River tuts. "Make that eight more."

"No, no." I twist my neck to look back at River, but he just raises a brow.

"That's not your safe word. Where are you supposed to be looking?"

I bite my tongue and turn back to face Oz.

"Good girl." The praise sends a shiver running through me and this time when the crop hits the pain merges with desire. I moan, feeling my pussy flutter.

River must notice the shift in me because he pauses to draw the flat tip of the crop through my swollen core. "Very nice. Maybe we should do this more often."

My jaw tightens. "I'd like to see you try."

River stills. He breathes in, then lays the crop on the bed, right in front of my face. The black leather tip glistens with my arousal.

River's breath tickles my neck as he leans over me. "I won't have to try, you'll let me do as I please. Just like you're letting me right now because you know you need this." His teeth catch my earlobe. "That you like this." He picks up the crop. Goosebumps prick my skin as he draws the tip of it down my back. "You have no idea what it felt like for us to find you missing. To learn that you'd run right into danger when we'd been doing everything in our power to keep you out of it.

You could have come to us, told us who had Oz and where he was, and we could have gone and got him together. You wouldn't have ended up in your sister's grasp. But instead, you played right into her hands."

My eyes start to sting. He's right. I didn't think when I ran. I needed to save Oz and trading him for myself seemed like the only option.

I wince as River presses the crop against my sore ass.

"Your life is no longer yours to risk," he says, his words a declaration. "You belong to us and if you ever put yourself in danger like that again we will be right back here until you learn your lesson. Until you understand that your life is worth something. Is worth *everything*."

I try to keep looking at Oz but tears well in my eyes. I've longed to have people who care for me, people who will protect me, all my life. It's just not an easy thing to accept when you're so used to it being you against the world. River is right though. I need to start thinking about my life as something worth saving. If I'm going to be a part of this team, I need to think beyond just myself. Because I'm not alone anymore.

"So, let's try this again."

The next eight whips come in quick succession. I scream with each one and my throat is raw by the time River's finished. My whole ass burns but it's nothing compared to the need building inside of me. I want them. I *need* them.

River's hand curls around my neck and he presses a kiss to my damp cheek. "You did well, darling." He nods at Jude and Eli to let go of my arms, but I don't move until he picks me up and turns me to face him. I'm unsteady on my feet, and I grip onto his shirt to stay standing. "Please, River."

"Shh, I've got you." River cups my pussy and draws his fingers through my folds. Everything is so much more sensitive after the crop and my eyes roll back in my head. River thrusts two fingers inside of me and I practically choke on the pleasure as he curls those fingers towards him, hitting just the right spot. I'm about to fall apart when Oz speaks up.

"Stop."

River pulls back his hand.

"What?" I cling on to him, needing him to carry on but he just smirks and says, "Sorry, darling. It's Oz's turn to call the shots."

"Put her on the bed," Oz says.

My fogged brain is still trying to figure out what's happening as River picks me up and lays me on the bed.

"I want her cuffed again, Jude."

"On it."

My gaze snaps to Oz but he meets my glare with no mercy and Jude's already moving. He cuffs one wrist then threads the chain through a bar in the headboard before snapping the bracelet round my other wrist.

"I thought my punishment was over," I say.

"Oh, this isn't punishment," Oz replies, "this is pleasure." He nods at River and then River's mouth is on my core, feasting on me. My back arches and Eli and Jude join in, clever hands molding my breasts, tugging and rolling my nipples.

"Oh, God."

River grabs my legs and spreads me wide open for him. I've never had so many hands on me at once. Oz is the only one not touching me, but his heated gaze is so tangible he may as well be.

"Make her come," Oz orders.

"Yes, please," I breath.

I feel River smile against my core. "With pleasure."

I cry out as Eli and Jude pinch my nipples hard while River seals his lips around my clit and sucks. The tension coils tight in my stomach. My hips push up towards River's face as my climax shatters through my body.

River flattens his tongue and draws it over my pussy. He sits back on his heels, his face glistening with my juices.

"How does she taste?" Oz asks.

River licks his lips and hums. "Like heaven. I want more." He doesn't wait for Oz's permission, he just dives right in and brings me to another orgasm.

I'm panting as I come down. My clit throbs like it has its own heartbeat and sweat clings to my skin. Every nerve is on fire.

"Again."

I whip my head to look at Oz. "No, no more. I can't."

Oz holds my gaze. "Again."

I try to squeeze my legs together, but Eli and Jude take hold of my thighs and keep me open.

"Son of a–"

Eli collars my throat. He squeezes till my air thins. "What do you say?" he asks, an edge of the darker Eli to his voice.

I swallow. With my arms cuffed to the bed and three powerful men above me I'm not exactly in a position to argue. I grit my teeth. "Yes, Oz."

"Good choice." Eli stops squeezing but he keeps his hand on my neck as River thrusts two fingers inside of me. He lowers his head again and flicks my clit with his tongue. I'm so sensitive and it's too much. I try to squirm away from him but I've nowhere to go and when Jude and Eli take my nipples between their teeth all I can do is lie there and take it.

Oz's groan has me twisting to face him. My eyes widen hungrily. He's got his cock out, his hand stroking his thick length as he watches me. "You look so beautiful like this," he says, "tied up and helpless."

I moan, tingles cascading over me.

"I want you to come for me again. Can you do that?" Oz asks.

I'm oversensitive and overwhelmed but the desire to please him fills my chest. I lick my lips and nod.

He flashes a cocky smile. "That's my good little slut. Come for me."

River adds a third finger and presses the pad of his thumb down on my clit.

I stop breathing, my mouth open in a silent scream as I do exactly what Oz ordered.

I'm still recovering as my wrists are released from the cuffs and Jude gathers me up in his arms. "God, you're gorgeous." He kisses me, fierce and seductive. "We need to have you, babygirl. All of us. You think you can do that?"

Images of them all inside of me flash through my mind. I kiss him back. "Yes. Please. I want that."

Jude grins smugly and looks over my shoulder at Eli and River. "I told you she was the one."

"Yeah, yeah." Eli rolls his eyes and lies back on the bed. At some point he's shucked off his clothes and I'm caught admiring his naked body. The scattering of blond hair on his chest. The hard planes of his abs. The long, hard, slightly curved cock, standing to attention against his stomach. "Come here, Kitten. Ride me."

Yes please. The orgasms were shattering. Too much but not enough all at once. I untangle myself from Jude's arms and scramble over to Eli, crazed by the need to be filled. I straddle him and take his cock in my hand. He's hot and heavy, silky smooth yet hard. I guide the head to my entrance. Any ounce of control I have is torn away when Eli grabs my hips and slams me down on his cock.

I rock forward, bracing my hands on his shoulders. He buries himself so deep I know I'll be feeling it tomorrow.

Jude brushes my hair back from my face and holds it in a ponytail as I grind against Eli, gyrating my hips and clenching down on him.

Eli's hands flex on my waist. He tilts his head back against the pillow and groans.

"River, you better hurry the hell up man or I'm not going to last," Eli calls out.

"I'm here." River's hand settles on my shoulder, his thumb spreads out to trail up the back of my neck. "Lean forward," he says, guiding me down with his hand.

The snick of a lid opening comes from behind me, and then cool gel runs down between my cheeks. River's fingers dip low as he works the lube against my tightest hole.

I tense up.

Two knuckles tap the small of my back. "Relax."

"Easy for you to say, no one's trying to stick their finger up your ass," I bite out.

"Brat." River smacks my sore butt and I shriek, burying my face in Eli's neck. River is relentless. He pushes one finger inside me, then two.

My stomach flips, the sensations traveling all the way up my spine. He scissors his fingers, opening me up.

"How does it feel?" Jude asks.

"Weird. Good." The feelings are so intense I keep needing to remind myself to breathe.

"She's ready." River withdraws his fingers and I get a brief reprieve before the blunt head of his cock presses into me.

I grip the sheets. He's so much bigger than just his fingers. Instinct has me pulling away, but Eli's cock anchors me in place. His hold on my waist tightens.

"It's too much," I gasp.

Jude strokes my back. "Shh, it's okay babygirl, you've got this. Let me help." He dips his hand to my pussy and plays with my clit.

"Jesus fucking Christ," River curses. "Push back, Freya. Let me in."

Jude's ministrations distract me from the pain, and I do what River says. A little of the resistance gives and he thrusts forward till his hips meet my bruised ass.

"Good girl."

My reply is a breathless moan. I've never felt so full before. Pinned between Eli and River all I can do is take it as they find a rhythm and move, pumping in and out of me.

"You're not done yet, Freya." Arousal thickens Oz's voice and I look over to him before Jude cups my face and guides me back. He's kneeling on the bed by Eli's shoulder, his pierced cock bobbing in front of my face. Pre-cum beads at the tip.

Jude's thumb drags at my bottom lip. "Open."

Hungry to taste him, I stretch my jaw wide and let him feed me his cock. The metal piercing drags against the roof of my mouth. I gag a little when he hits the back off my throat, but he keeps me in place with his hands on my head.

"Breathe through your nose. That's it. Good girl. Look at you, taking my cock so well," Jude croons and pleasure ripples through me.

River's thrusts get quicker.

Eli's hand drops to my pussy his fingers circling where we join but when he moves up to my clit River smacks his hand away.

"No. This is a punishment. She comes from our cocks inside of her or she doesn't come at all."

I don't bother complaining because I can already feel myself at the edge.

River and Eli find the perfect rhythm, hitting that spot deep inside of me and I scream around Jude's cock as I climax. He follows me over the edge and I choke on his cum, swallowing him down as best I can while his dick is still lodged inside of me.

He pulls out and my arms give way. I collapse onto Eli's chest as he and River bury themselves deep and grind against me, their groans filling the room as they come.

I'm so thoroughly fucked I can't do anything but lie there as the guys draw out of me. Aftershocks pulse through my core, fluttering around their lengths as they leave. I'm rolled onto my back.

Jude and Eli lean back against the headboard either side of me, their hands trailing up and down my arms and chest.

River disappears into the bathroom as Oz stands up and rounds the bed to look at me. My cheeks heat. I can feel the guys' release leaking out of me. Oz climbs onto the bed and dips his fingers into my pussy, gathering their cum. "You're a mess, Mo Leannan." He paints my stomach with their cum, his eyes dark and sinful. "A beautiful fucking mess." He lips crash onto mine, devouring my mouth. Feasting on me.

Without pulling back he undoes his pants and slides into me. It feels different being fucked with Eli's cum still inside of me. I'm so wet Oz glides right in. He takes it slow, drawing out to the very tip before plunging back in again.

My body is limp and satisfied and I don't think there's any chance I can come again but with Jude and Eli's hands on my tits and Oz's slow love making, I feel myself start to rise. My breathing picks up and Oz changes pace, pounding into me until we're both crying out.

I lose track of reality a little. My eyes flutter closed and I'm vaguely aware of the guys whispering words of adoration as I'm lifted off the bed. Moments later I'm lowered into a bath. A hiss escapes my lips as the welts on my ass hit the hot water but then it starts to soothe. I let the guys wash me as I drift, only coming to as I'm laid upon what smells like a fresh set of sheets.

Eli, River, Jude, and Oz climb into the bed,

surrounding me like a cocoon. River props up on his elbow and looks down at me. "Welcome back, darling. How are you feeling?"

I nod. "I'm good," I say, my voice croaky. My lips curve up. "A little sore, but I feel lighter somehow." *Who knew getting your ass whipped and being fucked so thoroughly was kind of therapeutic?*

"You were incredible," River says. He presses a kiss to my forehead. "Get some rest. We'll be here."

I nod and close my eyes.

My life may not be perfect but it's the best it's ever been. I trust the guys to be here when I wake up. The rest can wait.

61

FREYA

Life is good. It's been two weeks since I officially became an FBI agent and, in some sort of unspoken agreement, moved in with the guys.

Jude helped me pack up the rest of my things, and I'm toying with the idea of renting out my house. Everything feels pretty much perfect until Oz picks up the box. "No, no, don't you dare!" I launch myself across the couh, leaning over Jude's legs as I reach to grab the last apple fritter.

Oz raises his eyebrows but gives in and hands the box over to me. "You're addicted to sugar."

I sit back in the couch, my new prized possession in my grasp. "And the problem with that is...?"

Everyone just shakes their head, indulging me as I happily bite into the crisp, caramelized fritter. I shouldn't be hungry still. I've eaten at last three portions of the Chinese we ordered for dinner. Once I've finished the fritter, I lick my fingers and relax back into the couch.

The last time I sat in this room eating Chinese was the day I told the guys who I really was. It's fair to say things have changed since then. Eli, for example, no longer wants to strangle me. And it feels good to not have secrets from the guys anymore. This might be the first time in my life, aside from Carmen, that I've been around people who know my story. Who know me.

We eventually get too full to eat anymore and put on a movie. We're halfway through when River's phone rings. He heads into the hall to take the call and when he returns a few minutes later I know our evening of bliss has come to an end.

Oz pauses the movie.

"That was Zach, Agent Syed's PA," River adds for my sake. "We need to go. Arthur Maxwell's killed again. He's gone back to his original victim type. A mother in her thirties named Adelaide Janson."

I wait, knowing there's something else. Another victim is bad but, to be honest, we all knew it was coming. River looks too shaken by the news.

Jude must pick up on it too because he sits forward. "What is it?"

River looks at Oz. He grimaces like he doesn't want to tell him, but knows he has to. "The victim lives in Danville, San Francisco."

Oz's already pale skin whitens.

Eli curses and Jude draws me closer to him.

"What?" I ask, looking between River and Oz. "Why is that bad?"

Oz takes a swig of his beer. "My parents live in Danville. It's where I grew up."

Well, shit. I want to believe that it doesn't mean anything but it's too big of a coincidence for my father to travel across states to kill in the exact town Oz's parents live in.

Based on everything Angelica knew about me and the guys it's clear she and my father were watching us.

He knows who I'm with and who the guys are.

This is a game to him, and if we're going to catch him, we have to play.

The End

Ready for more of Freya and her guys?

Read on for Chapter One of Secrets of Mine, Of Mine Book 2 Coming 2025

Chapter One / Freya

I stare at the sleek white jet in front of me. "You know if you'd told me you had a private plane I might not have kept running away."

Jude snorts but River just glowers at me, his face all serious and official.

I hold up my hands. "Joking."

Jude slides my rucksack off my shoulder and follows Oz and Eli up the steps to the aircraft leaving me to fend for myself with Mr. All-Business-No-Play.

Now no one's watching, River rakes his eyes over me. His gaze caresses my body, and my new, FBI approved, black slacks and silk shirt may as well be lingerie. "Think of it as a warning," he says, closing in on me until I have to crane my neck to look at him. "If you ever run again, I've got the entire FBI at my disposal, and I will chase you to the ends of the earth."

I place my palm to his chest and rub my thumb back and forth until his jaw loses its tension. "I'm not going to run again. I promise."

River buries his hand in my hair and pulls me in for a demanding kiss. "Damn right you're not," he grumbles when we come apart.

"No more secrets, no more running. We do this

together." I'm no longer a criminal asset, I'm a fully-fledged FBI profiler and what better declaration of love than teaming up to catch a serial killer who also happens to be my father? Talk about meeting the parents...

I haven't told River that I love him yet. I haven't told any of them but I'm pretty sure that's what's happening here and I'm only slightly terrified. I've gone from having a grand total of one healthy relationship in my entire life to dating four guys at once. It's...a lot and if I think about it too much breathing becomes challenging. Before I can start panicking River takes my hand and leads me up the steps to the plane.

It's like I took a detour and walked into the life of a billionaire. The plane is open plan with four seating areas. Oz is already setting up his laptop on one of the shiny wooden tables and Eli is kicked back across the longer row of seats running along the right side of the plane. He picks his Stetson up off his face and winks at me before replacing the hat presumably to go back to his nap because I'm discovering Eli, when not full of hatred for me, is pretty much just a cat. He's flirty and playful and he thinks he has nine lives. River calls him reckless, but I get it. Sometimes the only way to dull the pain is to chase the adrenaline high.

River ushers me further down the aisle. I don't want to get in Oz's way, so I sit down at the table near the back of the plane.

River stows his bag overhead and presses a kiss to my head before heading up front to talk to the captain.

Jude ducks round the curtains at the end of the aisle, a couple of mini-coke cans in his hands. He sits down opposite me and hands me one of the cans.

"Thanks," I say. The can hisses as I open it.

"No problem. You want to join the mile high club?"

I splutter, choking on the sip of coke I just took. "Seriously?" I ask, wiping my face.

Jude shrugs. "It would be fun."

I glare at him. "It would be unprofessional."

"It's official, you've been spending too much time with River. I'm kidnapping you for the whole flight."

"So you've got, what, five hours to corrupt me?"

Jude smirks. "Closer to six but if you come sit over here, I can have you squirming in minutes."

I shove his shin under the table and smile at him from behind my coke can. "Stop it." Across from us, Oz taps away at his computer. My smile falls. "We should be working." My father has reverted back to his old victim type. Not only has he killed another young mother, he's killed her in Oz's home town.

Jude takes my free hand and turns it over, linking our fingers together. "Before we see the crime scene and talk to the local police there's only so much we can do."

I don't take my eyes off Oz. He's fully focused on his screen, information whizzing past him at an indecipherable rate. "Is he okay?" I ask, lowering my voice. It can't be easy knowing Maxwell deliberately chose a victim in the same small town his parents live in. When my dad was killing twins, it felt like I was somehow guilty, because the only reason they were dead was to send a message to me. Now my own twin is in a secure psychiatric facility and my dad is still at large.

Jude gives my hand a squeeze. "We've got agents stationed outside his parents' house but he'll feel better once he's there himself."

"He's not staying at the hotel with us?"

Jude's smile is rueful. "I think his mum might disown

him if he dared stay anywhere but home. She'd take us all in if she had the space."

"You like her," I say.

Jude nods. "So will you and she'll adore you. Oz is one of the lucky ones. His parents are golden."

I realize then that there's still so much I don't know about the guys. "What about yours?"

"They're good." Jude lets go of my hand and fiddles with his drink. "They live in LA, so I don't see them much."

"Maybe we could stop by before we go back home."

"Yeah. Maybe."

Hurt blooms in my chest and I stare out the window as we begin to taxi along the runway. Jude just lied to me, and I know I have no right to be upset after all the secrets I kept from them, but I can't help feeling rejected. Joining the team was supposed to be a fresh start but apparently 'no more secrets' is a one-way street. I might have expected it from Eli or River but never from Jude.

He clears his throat and changes the subject. I let him distract me while we take off then when River joins us, I rest my head against his shoulder.

I wake with a start, sweat coating my skin. Images slip from the edges of my mind. Long blonde hair. Gentle fingers. A face I can't quite make out.

Strong hands hold my arms. "Hey, are you alright?" River asks.

I swallow. "Sorry, yeah."

He brushes my hair back from my face. "Bad dream?"

"What?" I shake my head. "No. Just a little disorientated. How long till we land?"

River narrows his eyes at me. "Just under three hours."

"Cool. I'm just going to freshen up." I slip from his grasp and head to the restroom. I run the taps and splash cool water on my face. I don't remember what I dreamt about but my heart beats erratically and a crawling sensation lingers on the back of my neck.

I brace my hands against the sink and stare into the mirror. I try to picture the face from my dream but the more I think about it the further it drifts away, like a ghost disappearing into limbo. I squeeze my eyes shut and shake off the feeling that I'm forgetting something important. My father is still out there, killing innocent women, I need to focus on catching him. I don't have time to fall apart.

When I leave the restroom, River's eyes find me. He tracks me as I walk down the aisle but I'm not ready for his questions, so I carry on past him and sit down opposite Oz.

He doesn't notice me sitting down. I have to wave my hand in front of his screen to break his attention. "Earth to Oz. Your eyes are going square."

He jolts before relaxing back in his seat. He takes off his glasses and rubs the bridge of his nose. "My mom used to say that to me." He smiles sheepishly at me.

"You should take a break."

He sighs. "I know, it's just…" he trails off.

I nudge his foot with mine under the table. "I get it."

He puts his glasses back on, the rectangular frames giving him highland Scot meets Clark Kent vibes. "My parents knew her. Adelaide. Mom said she was a regular at her bookshop."

"Shit. That's awful."

Oz nods. "She's strong, she'll be okay, but I just want to be there for them. She'll mother me like her life depends on it but I know she'll be happier with me there."

It's been less than twenty-four hours since River got the call about Adelaide Janson, but Oz already looks overtired. Dark bags hide behind his glasses and his hand taps at the table, anxious to get back to his research. I'm glad he's close with his parents but it feels wrong to be apart from him right now.

I wring my hands under the table and just say it. "Can I stay with you? At your parents?"

Oz stops fidgeting. "Yes. I'd like that." He looks over at the guys and smirks. "I'm not sure the others will, but I will."

I tangle my legs with his and grin when River's suspicious eyes land on me. "They'll get over it." I turn back to Oz. "Also, can we loop back round to your mom owning a book shop because I think I might love her."

Oz laughs. "She'll be pleased to hear it."

We talk about his family for the rest of the flight and by the time we land I've pretty much forgotten about my dream and the mystery face. Then, after we land, I turn my phone off airplane mode and a text message comes through.

Unknown: Do you remember our mother?

ACKNOWLEDGMENTS

Okay, first and foremost thank you to you. For picking up this book. For reading it to the end. It means the world to me.

Thank you to my parents for supporting me through the process, essentially learning how to publish a book with me and not freaking out when your daughter told you she wrote a smutty novel.

Thank you to my editor, for being so on my wavelength and making this book shine.

Thank you to Ali for the absolutely gorgeous cover. It's perfect.

To my ARC readers, I didn't know how I was going to find you but I'm glad I did. Your kind words and your love and investment in Freya and her story is more than I could ever have asked for.

To my very first readers over on Wattpad, you are truly the best audience a girl could ask for. Your comments and votes have brought me so much joy over the last year and a half and I cannot thank you enough.

To my friends, for keeping this book a secret until I was ready to share it and for being my people.

And once again, thank you to you, the reader. I hope you loved Freya and her guys as much as I do.

ABOUT THE AUTHOR

Alexis Grace is a British girl living amongst books. She is a hopeless romantic and an obsessive reader. When she's not writing she spends her days working, baking, and wishing the TV world would catch on and make a reverse harem show. You can stay up to date with Alexis' future projects on social media and for exclusive previews and bonus content join The Lair, her Facebook reader group.

Instagram: @alexisgrace_author
Tiktok: @alexisgraceauthor
Facebook: The Lair - Alexis Grace's Reader Group

Printed in Great Britain
by Amazon